LONGARM SMILED DOWN AT THE BUXOM LITTLE BLONDE . . .

The dimple in her chin was looking more delightful by the minute. Perhaps, he thought, the moon was having its effect on him. And he should not forget why he was sleeping out here alone like this, away from the main camp—or why he had constructed that dummy figure and left it by the fire. Now was no time to drop his guard.

But she was still leaning her eager body against his—even as he pondered his dilemma . . .

*Also in the LONGARM series
from Jove*

LONGARM
LONGARM ON THE BORDER
LONGARM AND THE AVENGING ANGELS
LONGARM AND THE WENDIGO
LONGARM IN THE INDIAN NATION
LONGARM AND THE LOGGERS
LONGARM AND THE HIGHGRADERS
LONGARM AND THE NESTERS
LONGARM AND THE HATCHET MEN
LONGARM AND THE MOLLY MAGUIRES
LONGARM AND THE TEXAS RANGERS
LONGARM IN LINCOLN COUNTY
LONGARM IN THE SAND HILLS
LONGARM IN LEADVILLE
LONGARM ON THE DEVIL'S TRAIL
LONGARM AND THE MOUNTIES
LONGARM AND THE BANDIT QUEEN

TABOR EVANS

LONGARM ON THE YELLOWSTONE

A JOVE BOOK

Copyright © 1980 by Jove Publications, Inc.

All rights reserved. No part of this publication
may be reproduced or transmitted in any form or
by any means, electronic or mechanical, including
photocopy, recording, or any information storage
and retrieval system, without permission in
writing from the publisher.

Requests for permission to make copies of any part
of the work should be mailed to: Permissions,
Jove Publications, Inc., 200 Madison Avenue,
New York, NY 10016

First Jove edition published March 1980

10 9 8 7 6 5 4 3 2

Printed in the United States of America

Jove books are published by Jove Publications, Inc.,
200 Madison Avenue, New York, NY 10016

Chapter 1

It was a Tuesday morning and Longarm stood fully dressed before the open window of his room, looking down at the streets of Denver. The air was reasonably fresh and perhaps even invigorating, if one discounted the pungent fragrance of coal smoke and horse manure —and that persistent, mysterious smell of burning leaves.

Longarm turned away from the window. He had not slept alone the previous night, but in the predawn hours had returned to his room to freshen up and get ready for this day. His chief, Marshal Billy Vail, had been quite insistent the night before, when he had found Longarm at the hotel, in reminding him to show up on time this morning. As Longarm walked across the room to pick his hat up off the dresser, he was an impressive sight.

He was a big man, lean and muscular, with a body any athlete would have been proud to inhabit. There was nothing young about his face, however. It was seamed and cured to a saddle-leather brown by the persistent suns and cutting winds he had experienced since leaving his native West-by-God-Virginia, where he had fought in the late unpleasantness between the states. His eyes were gunmetal blue, his close-cropped hair the color of aged tobacco leaf, and he wore proudly his well-trimmed longhorn mustache. It gave his appearance a certain unpredictable ferocity he needed at times in his line of work.

Taking his snuff-brown Stetson off the wall peg by his door, he positioned it carefully on his head—dead center, tilted slightly forward, cavalry-style. He was wearing a brown tweed suit and vest, and a blue-gray shirt, with a string tie knotted at his neck. His cordovan leather boots were low-heeled army issue.

Longarm squared his shoulders in readiness for the new day and strode toward the door, he moved with a swift, catlike tread, his tall figure seeming to loom in the semidarkness of the corner room. He was aware that his swift movements, combined with his height, tended to spook livestock and make most men thoughtful, but there was little he could do about that except continue to go where he was going by the most direct route, and not apologize.

He was just reaching his hand out for the doorknob when he heard a soft, insistent rapping on his door. He was instantly alert, and his eyes narrowed warily.

"Mr. Long!" he heard. "Are you in there?"

It was a woman, and Longarm just managed to remember her voice. It sounded as if she had her face pressed against the door. "Rose?" he asked, pulling his hand away from the doorknob. "That you?"

"Yes! Thank God I caught you before you left!"

"What's wrong, Rose?" Longarm stood away from the doorway now, his right hand reaching across his vest front and clasping firmly the grips of his double-action .44-40 Colt in its cross-draw holster.

"Nothin's the matter, Longarm," she whispered through the door. "You all wore out this early? I can't talk through the door! Open up!"

Longarm was not usually this reluctant to let a young lady into his room. But his memory of Rose O'Brien was disconcerting, and he did not remove his hand from the Colt under his tweed coat. She had been annoyingly persistent the evening before as she pressed her charms upon him at the hotel bar while he tried to watch a most interesting poker game. Oddly suspicious of the woman—a stranger to him until that night—he had deliberately escorted another woman from the bar and left without allowing Rose to catch even a glimpse of his departure.

Now here she was, outside his door in the wee hours of a Denver morning. He thought that either he should congratulate himself on his awesome attractiveness to nubile females, or this woman was up to no good. Besides, he had introduced himself to her as Custis Long, not Longarm. There were only one or two favored acquaintances of his in that bar who knew him by his nickname, and they would not have told it to *this* young lady.

"Are you alone?" he asked.

"Of course! What do you think? Please, Longarm! I must speak to you! I need your help!"

"All right," he said, pressing himself against the door and resting his left ear against the paneling. He thought he could hear a low, whispered instruction from someone standing beside the girl.

Removing his Colt from its holster, he stepped swiftly to one side of the door and yanked it open with his left hand, flattening himself against the wall as the door swung wide. The ugly snout of a nickel-plated Smith & Wesson pocket .38 was thrust past the doorframe and bucked twice as its muzzle belched flame, its sharp detonations filling the tiny room.

Before its owner realized the Smith & Wesson had no target, Longarm brought the barrel of his sixgun down on the gunhand of the intruder. There was a scream of pain and the gun clattered to the floor. Reaching over with his left hand, Longarm grabbed the man's shirt and yanked him into the room.

Rose's accomplice was a ferret-faced, slant-browed sneak Longarm had noticed prowling the back alleys and sleazier saloons around the hotel. Longarm kicked his gun into a corner, then hauled the scrawny accomplice closer to him.

"My hand!" the little man bleated. "My hand! You broke it!"

With a grunt of disgust, Longarm flung the man past him onto the bed. He saw the fellow fly across the coverlet and heard him land with a crash on the floor beyond, but paid no heed as he darted out of the room after the girl.

He still held his Colt in his right hand, and was in time to catch a clear glimpse of the woman's head and shoulders as she started down the stairs. He stopped and aimed, then swore and holstered the gun. He couldn't see shooting a woman—not even this one— unless it was in self-defense. And even then he might find it impossible.

He raced down the dim hall, took the stairs in giant strides, and burst out through the front door and down the porch steps. The woman was nowhere in sight. Longarm's rooming house was in the no-longer-fashionable quarter on the wrong side of Cherry Creek, a rabbit warren of dirt lanes and sidestreets, back alleys and festering ditches. He looked up and down the damp cinder path that led to the Colfax Avenue Bridge, then gave it up as a bad job and hurried back inside the building and up the stairs.

He heard doors opening as he mounted the stairs, and saw his landlady's frightened face peering up at him through the bannister. "It's all right," he called down to her. "Stay in your room until I nail this jasper upstairs!"

Her face vanished and, as Longarm started swiftly down the corridor toward his open door, he heard a door below him slam shut, followed by the sound of a bolt being pushed home. He would have some explaining to do to his landlady and the other roomers before this day was out, he realized.

The fellow was on his feet behind the bed, holding the Smith & Wesson in his trembling left hand.

Longarm halted in the doorway and smiled. "Go

ahead, you punk. Raise that gun and fire it again. Try it. I'd like to see that."

The menace in Longarm's tone sent a shudder up the man's spine. Longarm saw him tremble visibly and let his hand drop. The Smith & Wesson struck the floor a second time.

"You broke my hand," the man whimpered, his face screwing itself up into the semblance of a prune as he prepared himself to cry.

"Stow that," Longarm told him, striding into the room and picking up the weapon.

The fellow's narrow, pasty face lost its grimace as the man straightened and looked Longarm squarely in the eye. He was going to try to be a true Western Hero now, Longarm realized as the fellow's mouth twisted into a snarl and his pale, lustreless eyes grew defiant.

"You ain't going to turn me in! What's the charge? I was just helping a lady, that's all."

Longarm's big hand reached out, wrapped itself around the fellow's face, and pushed. The man went stumbling back onto the bed. "What's your name, punk?" he demanded.

"Sammy. Sammy Wentworth."

"Well, Sammy, looks like your pal left you with your pants hanging down. Just helping a lady, is it?"

"That's right. That's all it was. You stole her money!"

"How do you know that?"

"She told me."

"And you would be the kind of man who believes everything a woman tells you."

Sammy lifted his right hand onto his lap with his left hand, and held it tenderly. His face was pale from the excruciating pain. "Jesus, she was so convincing," Sammy told Longarm, gazing up at him with a pathetic, woebegone look.

"What's her name?"

"Rose."

"What's her *name,* Sammy!"

The man appeared to shrink noticeably under the weight of Longarm's heavy voice. "Theresa Mirelda," he replied meekly, as he began to rock back and forth on the bed while holding onto his hand.

At once Longarm understood. This was the wife of a murderer he had brought back not too long before from San Francisco. The man had been a docile prisoner until he hit the city, at which point he broke from the train station. In the ensuing gun battle, Longarm had had to shoot him. He did not recover from his wounds. Someone on the train or on the platform had slipped Mirelda a gun—his wife, undoubtedly. And now she was after the tall lawman for killing her husband.

"Where does she live, Sammy?"

"I don't know."

"How did you meet her?"

"She met *me.* Last week. She had all this money and all she wanted, she said, was to throw a scare into you."

"Sure. What was the plan, Sammy?"

"She was going to come here with you last night, and as soon as you two were in the sack, I was going to break in—and scare you."

"Sure."

"Honest to God! She said she knew you from way back, and you'd laugh when we pulled this little joke."

"I never laid eyes on the woman before, Sammy. And you know damn well this wasn't any practical joke. Let's go!"

Like a whipped dog, and still clutching at his broken hand, Sammy slipped off the bed and proceeded ahead of Longarm out of the room and down the hall to the stairs. Longarm followed close behind Sammy as they descended. He was about to pull open the downstairs door for the wounded man when he heard the living room's sliding door creak back on its rail. He turned to see his landlady poking her head out.

"Mr. Long," she said, her voice quavering, "could you please come in here?"

"Later," Longarm told her, not unkindly. "I'll explain about this commotion later."

"Please," the landlady persisted. "I would like you to come in here for a cup of tea."

And then an incredible thing happened. The little old woman *winked* broadly.

Swiftly Longarm pulled Sammy around in front of him and said loudly, "Of course, a cup of tea would be a pure pleasure right now, after what I've just been through. That's right thoughtful of you."

The landlady stepped back and opened the sliding door wider. Longarm pushed Sammy ahead of him through the opening. He saw Theresa Mirelda standing in front of the coffee table, a pearl-handled .32 in her right fist. *Christ,* Longarm thought swiftly, *what the hell did she need Sammy Wentworth for?* Even as he thought this he ducked and, in the same motion, hurled Wentworth at Theresa. Her .32 went off just as Sammy went crashing into her.

Both of them went back over the coffee table in a tangle, and when they came to rest, it was with an ominously quiet Sammy Wentworth sprawled on top of the Mirelda woman. Longarm unholstered his Colt wearily and looked at his wide-eyed landlady.

"How about sending one of the boarders after a copper—and an ambulance too, it looks like. Then maybe we can see about that cup of tea. Unless you've got something stronger."

The landlady whisked swiftly from the room, and Longarm looked down into the weeping face of Theresa Mirelda. She was weeping, he knew, out of frustration at not having been able to finish off the man who had killed her husband. She wasn't even thinking of the possibly dead Sammy Wentworth collapsed on top of her. Longarm was now thinking, a bit incongruously, of how late all this was going to make him. Billy Vail was going to be purple in the face when Longarm finally strode into the chief's office.

Sammy Wentworth groaned and rolled off Theresa Mirelda's well-endowed figure. She still had the .32 in her hand. Longarm wrested it from her grasp, and bent to examine Sammy's wound.

It was well into the morning by the time Longarm left the police station and started up Colfax Avenue. The recently gilded dome of the Colorado State House gleamed proudly on Capitol Hill ahead of him. When he reached the U.S. Mint at Cherokee and Colfax, he turned the corner and headed for the federal courthouse. Inside, he elbowed his way through the lawyers with their briefcases, and climbed the marble staircase. He paused only momentarily in front of the big oak door whose gold-leaf lettering read, UNITED STATES MARSHAL, FIRST DISTRICT COURT OF COLORADO, then pushed his way inside.

The pale young clerk with his plastered-down, center-parted hair looked up from his typewriter and grinned. "Boy, Longarm, Marshal Vail is fit to be tied. He's been sending me all over looking for you."

"You ain't very good at finding people, are you?"

The clerk looked back down at his infernal machine. "Nope. Don't look like I am. Finding people is *your* job, Longarm."

"*Mister Long,* to you," Longarm snapped.

Just then the door to Marshal Vail's office was flung open, and a very unhappy Billy Vail was standing in the doorway. "I thought I heard that growl of yours, Longarm! Where in tarnation have you been? I told you last night I wanted you here on *time* for a change. Get in here!"

"Only if you say please, Chief."

"Please! Now get the hell in here!"

With an aggrieved sigh, Longarm walked past Billy Vail into his office. As the heavyset man closed the door and hustled around behind his desk, Longarm slumped into the chief's red leather armchair. A glance at the banjo clock on the wall told Longarm it was close to eleven-thirty.

One bushy eyebrow cocked angrily, the pink-cheeked, balding official planted his elbows on his desk blotter and leaned closer to Longarm, his eyes fixed with irate intensity on his subordinate. "You have an explanation, I assume."

"I do at that, Chief."

"That filly you squired out of the hotel so sneaky last night, eh? She wore you out. That it?"

"Not quite. It was that other filly, the one hanging onto me when you first got there. You remember her, don't you?"

"Sort of. Look, Longarm, let's just quit this fancy footwork! You've got a long ways to go and one hell of a lot of details to swallow and you don't have all that much time. I'm going to have to brief you through dinner hour, it looks like, and *that* makes me *angry*. I told you to get here early!"

"Do you want my explanation?"

"You just gave it. A woman wore you out."

"Well, that ain't it exactly." Longarm was smiling broadly at the marshal by this time. "But if you don't want to hear it, that's all right with me."

"All right, all right, let's have it," Vail said as he began pawing through the blizzard of paperwork that covered his desk. He was going to listen, but not too closely, it appeared.

Longarm told Vail what had happened to him that morning following the soft knock on his door, and when he had finished with his story, including the part about the shooting of Sammy Wentworth and the ensuing events, Billy Vail was no longer poking through his paperwork. In fact, his mouth was hanging open just a little.

"You mean Sammy just up and vanished?"

"Looks like it. He's a pretty good actor. Slippery as an eel, besides. His hand wasn't really broken, I found out, and that bullet wound was an ugly-looking thing, but, like the doctor told me afterward, it was only a flesh wound."

"We'll pick him up, don't worry."

"I ain't worrying, Chief. Besides, we got the Mirelda woman. I hope you can put her away for a good long time. She's dangerous. Sammy was just a fool."

"I'm sorry, Longarm," Vail said, shaking his head unhappily.

"Sorry?" The note of contrition in Vail's voice surprised Longarm.

"Yeah, sorry. Wallace told me last week there was a woman in town looking for you, asking around at bars and such. He thought I ought to tell you, but it slipped my mind. I just figured it was your notorious charm."

Longarm laughed. "I guess I ought to be flattered."

"Just don't tell Wallace," the chief said, sighing.

"Now what's this big assignment, Chief?"

Vail leaned back in his chair and eyed Longarm appraisingly. "You ever heard of the Yellowstone Act?"

"The one that turned Colter's Hell into a national park?"

"That's the one," Vail replied, nodding solemnly. "That means, since 1872, more than two million acres of untouched wilderness surrounding all those devilish geysers and springs have been set aside, protected from what the act calls 'commercial exploitation'—if you get my meaning. No prospecting, no cutting the timber. The land is set aside—" he glanced quickly at a government folder open on his desk—"'as a public pleasuring ground, for the preservation from injury or spoilation of all timber, mineral deposits, natural curiosities, or wonders within this area and their retention in their natural condition.'"

Vail glanced up, and Longarm shrugged.

"I knew all that," he said. "What's the matter? Someone trying to cut that timber?"

"It's not as simple as that. We've got some very important people who want to do some of that 'pleasuring' the act set the Yellowstone Park aside for. But it might be the beginning of the end for this park."

"You better explain that."

"We got a passel of congressmen and their women who want to explore this new park. They want to see if this isn't maybe a waste of good natural resources. All that timber and mineral wealth being allowed to sit there just riles the hell out of these men, it seems. So here they come, Longarm, and you're the one who has to take them there and back."

Vail stopped abruptly and rocked back in his chair to let that sink in. His eyes were lit with interest. He expected his deputy to protest the assignment, Longarm realized. On the other hand, Vail was anxious for Longarm to take it because the old lawman was interested in the fate of the Yellowstone Park.

"Which side are you on, Chief?" Longarm inquired.

"You mean do I think we should go in there and rip up that park? Hell, Longarm, you've seen enough ghost towns, ripped-up land, and washed-away slopes, haven't you? Remember that bunch of loggers up in Diggerland and what they did to that valley? Christ, the way you told it, the whole side of a mountain came down on those bastards when they got through slashing off that covering timber. Hell, you know where I stand."

Longarm laughed, nodding. "I just wanted to hear you spell it out. So I'm to take those bigwigs from Washington up there and maybe lose them, is that it?"

"No, damn it! Now you know better than that, Longarm. That would only cause worse trouble—" Marshal Vail stopped in mid-sentence when he saw the look on Longarm's face and realized the younger lawman was pulling his leg.

"How many did you say?" Longarm asked, no longer smiling.

"A party of fourteen, all told. Five congressmen and their ladies and maids. A federal deputy has been assigned to meet you in Billings with a scout familiar with the territory."

"Who's in charge of the park?"

"There's a park superintendent; Norris is his name. A strange cuss, as I understand it from a letter I got here from Tyson, the deputy. The fellow is supposed to be hoping for hordes of tourists, and has already constructed a 'road of glass' on the way to Firehole Basin."

Longarm's eyebrows rose. "How the hell did he do that?"

"He wore a ledge of exposed black obsidian into shape by building fires on it, and when it was well heated, he poured water on it. That's the way it sounds to me, but I'm no expert. You sound interested, Longarm," Vail said abruptly. "That so? You'll take this assignment?"

"Do I have a choice?"

"No, damn it, you don't. But I'd like for you to *want* to go. These people need the right handling, and if anything was to happen to any of them, the park would be blamed. That means a right nice idea would be down the drain. There's lots of other places out here that need protection from those Eastern moneylenders, but if this Yellowstone Park goes, there won't be much hope for any other parks like it."

Longarm nodded. He knew just what Marshal Vail meant. But shepherding a passel of congressional fat cats and their women into the wilderness west of the Big Horn Mountains was not going to be easy. And Vail was right; if any one of them got hurt or lost, the idea of a national park kept wild for visitors would be out the window. And in would swarm the nesters and lumbermen and gold-and-silver seekers. Longarm shuddered at the thought. He knew that Yellowstone country, and loved it.

"Fine, Chief," he said. "I'll go. And willingly."

"Good." Marshal Vail got to his feet and hurried around his desk. "I'm going out to tell my clerk I'm not to be disturbed. There's a lot I've got to tell you about this here expedition, and we don't have all that much time. You'll be leaving tonight, Longarm."

As Vail pulled the door shut behind him and started issuing orders to his clerk, Longarm took out a cheroot and lit it. He had been trying to cut out his smoking habit, and had been having moderate success this past week, but he needed something to get his brain cells to percolating. Vail had a lot to tell him, and there was a lot he needed to know.

For one thing, who was this Deputy Tyson? Longarm would have preferred Wallace, or at least someone he knew well enough to know he could be counted upon in an emergency. The way this assignment looked, there were sure as hell going to be enough emergencies to go around, what with him playing Mother Superior to five pasty-faced dudes and their hysterical womenfolk on a trip to the Yellowstone Park and back. The thought of it set his worry bells to clanging.

Longarm shook his head and inhaled deeply on his cheroot. He resembled a smoldering volcano when Vail returned.

Chapter 2

Longarm leaned back in his chair and studied Frank Tyson. The deputy had just introduced himself and sat down at his table. Longarm had arrived in Billings the night before, and had left word with the desk clerk at the hotel that anyone calling himself Frank Tyson could find him in the bar. Longarm had waited most of the morning. In a few minutes it would be noon, and his ass was sore from all this sitting.

But he kept his irritation in check as he looked over the man who was going to be his sidekick for the coming expedition up the Yellowstone. The fellow was lean. His eyes were a washed-out blue, his hair and eyebrows sandy, his face gaunt and drawn, with lines about his eyes and mouth that spoke of something painful that had worked itself down deep inside the man. He had spoken softly when he introduced himself, and had sat down carefully, as silently as a wet leaf settling on the ground after an autumn rain. Yet, despite the man's gentle, almost deferential manner, Longarm detected a latent wildness just below the surface—a fierce, bottled fury that the man kept under control only by dint of enormous effort.

The man's pale blue eyes met Longarm's, and he smiled. "Sorry to keep you waiting, Long. I was out looking for a guide, and seeing to our gear."

"You got my telegram, then."

"It got here day before yesterday. I just didn't think it would do any of us any good if I sat around on my duff to wait for the steamer to get in. Especially with those big shots due this afternoon."

"I thought I might wait and ride up the river with them on the *Far West*. Then I thought better of it," Longarm said, appraising the man coolly. "You've got some idea, then, what this is all about. That telegram didn't give me much room."

"Visitors. Sightseers. The West is filling up with them, now that the Indian problem has been solved." He put a sardonic emphasis on the word *solved*.

"You don't think it has been?"

"To *our* satisfaction it has, I'm sure." The man's drawn face seemed to grow even sharper and leaner as he reached for his beer. "Nobody's bothered to ask the Indians, though."

"That's not very healthy talk in Billings, Tyson. You got any special reasons for feeling like you do?"

The man looked at Longarm sharply. "You mean beyond a wish for simple human justice?"

Longarm smiled. "Yes, beyond that, if you could maybe spell it out for me, though I ain't never seen human justice that was very simple or very just. It sure as hell was human, though."

The man frowned in concentration as he lifted his beer mug to his mouth. He cocked an eye warily at Longarm. "You seem like an honorable man. What I'm going to tell you is something I don't want generally known."

"If you mean do I blab, the answer is no, I don't. Let's have this big secret, Tyson."

The man put his mug down heavily on the table and looked coldly at Longarm. "I was married seven years ago to a Crow woman. I had two children by her. The three of them were killed by drunken cavalrymen who found them washing clothes on the bank of a stream. The two cavalrymen made themselves a little entertainment before they killed my wife and drowned the children. An old Crow woman crouching in the bushes by the stream saw it all."

"That don't make much sense. The Crow were allies of the cavalry. They've sided with the whites against the Sioux since way back."

Tyson smiled thinly. "You know those damn fool young punks that rode in the Seventh couldn't tell a Crow from a Sioux if their lives depended on it."

"Did you report it?"

"All the way to the top. They let the cavalrymen escape. About that time, things began heating up around here, and they lost themselves in the area. Hell, half of this population is made up of army deserters, I'm thinking."

"If it was seven years ago, Tyson," Longarm said gently, "maybe you should think about forgetting it."

"Maybe. But I ran onto them a couple of years back. I'd nearly finished scalping one of them alive when the other came on us. I lost that skirmish, but I'll find them again."

Longarm studied Tyson carefully. He knew now the source of the man's deep anguish. But he had to figure out now whether or not he could afford such a man at his side on this upcoming trip into the Yellowstone country. A man bent on his own private vendetta could make very bad decisions at times.

As if he were reading Longarm's thoughts, the man smiled. "I know what you're thinking, Long. A man like me might go off at any moment on his own. You think I'm obsessed, that I lie awake at nights plotting ways to get those two. And if that's the kind of man I am, you don't think you can afford the luxury of having me with you on this trip with all those fancy congressmen and their women."

Longarm leaned back and sipped his Maryland rye. "Yep, Tyson. That's just about what I was thinking."

Tyson shrugged. "So what's so all-fired important about these congressmen coming to visit Yellowstone?

Since when are a couple of deputy U.S. marshals needed to wet-nurse tourists? I should think we've both got better things to do with our time."

"Ordinarily we have. But this here's a different bunch of tourists, and I think maybe you'll agree that we got to do it right or this country hereabouts is liable to suffer."

"You'd better explain that."

Longarm told him the purpose of the congressional party's visit and the significance it could have in the future development of the area. When he had finished, Tyson was thoughtful.

"You think they might decide it's foolish to keep Colter's Hell a park. You mean there's a chance they might go back to Washington and tell their buddies to open up this area to prospectors and the like?"

"Maybe, if something bad happens to one of them. They're coming out here to see what the hell we got that's so damn important we want to set it aside and keep it untouched," Longarm said. "I admit, it's a new idea to me. But I've been thinking on it since I left Denver, and damned if it don't seem to me like a very good notion at that."

Tyson nodded thoughtfully. "It's a good idea, all right. It's just a damn shame we couldn't feel the same about the Sioux and the Arapahoe and the Bannocks and the Crow as we feel about the land we've taken from them."

Longarm took a deep breath and decided not to reply. He knew the pain inside the man was what made him go on like that, and he didn't necessarily disagree with him. But Longarm had seen all kinds of Indians, just like he had seen all manner of white folks, Mexicans, Chinese, and all the rest. There were good and bad to be found in every mix. These Indian wars now winding down had seen that mix on both sides. Not every raw recruit in the cavalry was a punk, and not every cavalryman took advantage of an Indian female when he found her alone. On the other hand, not every Indian woman who found herself in a recruit's arms wanted it any other way. He had seen at one time how eagerly some drunken Indian fathers had been willing to sell their daughters to a soldier for another bottle of hooch.

It just wasn't all one way or the other; the right and the wrong of it got terribly mixed up at times, and the law of the land that Longarm was hired to enforce didn't seem to be able to do much about pain and confusion and folks' needs.

Tyson finished his beer. "If you want to get someone else for this job, Long, you can. I won't complain. No sense in riding alongside a man whose prejudices you can't stomach."

"Don't talk like a damn fool," Longarm said softly. "I reckon there ain't one of us who don't carry a passel of false notions and angry judgments bottled up inside him everywhere he goes. The thing is, Tyson, I'd like your undivided attention during this trip into the Yellowstone. If you think you can manage that, I'll be proud to have you with me. Is that too much to ask?"

The man smiled suddenly, relieved. "Hell, no, Long," he said, the tension easing at once in his face.

"Good," Longarm said, extending his hand across the table. "Call me Longarm. That's what my friends call me."

Tyson was about to respond when a shot rang out in the street just beyond the batwing doors of the hotel bar. Longarm and Tyson hurriedly left their table and dashed out of the bar. On the boardwalk, they saw a crowd gathered around a lone Indian. Even as they arrived, one of the men encircling the Indian loosed another shot at the Indian's feet. Terrified, the Indian jumped and tried to break through the grinning circle of men. With a roar of laughter, he was flung back into the center of the circle and someone else aimed a shot at the poor fellow's feet. In his anxiety to jump away from the glancing bullet, the Indian lost his footing and went sprawling on his back.

"Just an afternoon's funning is all this is," said Tyson bitterly.

"He don't look like a Sioux," Longarm observed.

"He's a Bannock. He isn't any more welcome around here than a Sioux, and that's for damn sure."

The Bannock was on his feet now, crouching warily, watching the faces about him with a terror matched only by his seething fury. He was dressed oddly, in a buckskin shirt and pants, with a battered cavalry campaign hat sporting a single feather on his head and a pair of battered cavalry stovepipes on his feet. Bigger than most Indians, he startled Longarm by glancing suddenly into the lawman's face. It was then that Longarm saw the bright blue eyes.

"He's a breed," said Longarm.

"Does that make a whole hell of a lot of difference?" Tyson remarked, stepping off the walk.

Before Longarm could hold Tyson, he had pushed his way angrily through the crowd. The last man he encountered tried to stop him. A swift backhand slap sent the man reeling into the arms of his friends. Tyson's sixgun was in his hand now as he turned swiftly to the Indian. Tyson smiled at the Bannock then, to reassure him—but the smile came too late. The Indian hurled himself at the gun in Tyson's hand and, with a powerful wrench, snatched it from him.

Brandishing the weapon wildly, the Indian shot into the crowd, then, with a shriek, he had dashed past Tyson and through the crowd that fell back in a panic before the Bannock's fury.

Down an alley toward the river the Indian raced. After a momentary confusion, the two men the Bannock had wounded were left to writhe in the dust as the rest of the crowd of enraged citizens, sixguns out and waving, took off down the alley after the fleeing Indian. Tyson was with them also, but his mission was obviously counter to that of the rest of the crowd, and Longarm realized, as he started down the alley after the mob, that Tyson was just liable to get himself killed. His interference had already caused bloodshed.

Since escape up river was impossible, Longarm noted, the Indian was not trying to run in that direction, but was leaping into the greenery along the shore, stumbling, falling, sliding in marshy ooze as he neared the bank. Shots cracked. Longarm saw the Indian pause to return the fire, then struggle through the ooze toward the open water.

Longarm was gaining only slightly on the mob howling on the Indian's heels. As he ran past the Yellowstone Dining Hall, a cook threw a pail of slops into a tributary of the river that wound under his establishment, narrowly missing Longarm as the lawman jumped over the narrow ditch and kept after the mob. The cook yelled after him, asking what all the fuss was about. Longarm did not pause to tell him.

Downstream now, closer to the Indian than the others since the fellow had backtracked to find more solid ground in his battle to reach the river. Longarm felt the sun thrusting its way through the willows bordering the river. He paused and, placing one hand on a willow trunk for support, yelled out to the Bannock and tried to tell the fellow he would be all right if he gave himself up.

Longarm did not really expect any response other than the one he got. The Indian paused in his flight and flung a shot at Longarm, who heard the round slam into the tree over his head. Then the Indian turned away and raced across a solid shoulder of land ending in a sandbar that reached out into the brilliant water. Longarm ran through the reeds after him. The mob spilled furiously closer as Longarm's path converged with its foremost citizen, a massive fellow with a gray beard and wild eyes. He was brandishing a huge Walker

Colt, and he almost knocked Longarm down in his haste to reach the sandbar ahead of him.

"Longarm!"

He turned. It was Tyson, out of breath and with his face beet-red from the exertion of the chase, who had called to him. He was obviously in an agony to reach the Bannock before the enraged crowd did.

"What do you want?" Longarm flung back over his shoulder. "Stay out of this now, Tyson! You've done enough damage!"

At that moment, someone coming up beside Tyson clubbed him with the barrel of his sixgun. Longarm glimpsed the deputy's sudden topple forward and got himself a good look at the man responsible, then turned his attention back to the Indian.

Wading through the glutinous mud, the Bannock was waist deep in the Yellowstone. As Longarm left the center of the sandbar and found his own boots being seized by the mud, the Indian dove forward into the water and began stroking swiftly out into the channel. The men pulled up around Longarm and began firing at the swimming figure. Spouts of water roiled the surface around his thrashing body.

Longarm shouted at the men and made an effort to knock the weapons from the hands of some of them. He saw Tyson flinging himself at one man who held a rifle. But it was just the two of them, and the firing, a regular volley by this time, poured after the swimmer.

"Hold it! Look!" someone cried.

The Bannock was swimming directly into the path of a steamer charging around the bend and heading upstream to dock. The firing ceased then. Everyone watched, transfixed, as the struggling figure neared the steamboat's prow. It was the *Far West,* and Longarm thought he could make out the figures of resplendent men and women crowding the rail in front of the pilot's house. They too were watching the figure struggling in the water.

The *Far West*'s whistle sounded shrilly. The bow began to swing away from the Indian. The Bannock had evidently been so anxious to put distance between himself and the shore he had recently fled that he had failed to notice the oncoming steamboat. Now, however, he was aware of his danger, and Longarm watched tensely as he saw the Indian strike out downstream in an effort to swim parallel with the steamboat without being sucked under.

His dark hair was now barely visible as the wake snatched at his head and began toying with it. Again the *Far West*'s whistle shrilled in warning, and with the whistle's scream, the bow swung swiftly around in an effort to miss the Indian. But the bow swung too far, and Longarm saw the stern wheel's splashing uproar appear just in front of the Bannock.

The crowd was as silent as death as each man in it watched. The Indian's head disappeared in the turbulence. Then a hand appeared. Longarm saw the engineer standing on the walking deck, peering over, the frame of the walking beam dipping just behind him. Then the Bannock's body was being lifted out of the water by the paddle wheel. A distant woman's scream echoed over the water as the already-dead body was pulled up through the remorseless wheel, an enormous, still fish that reached the top and then was plunged down again into the broiling water.

Longarm looked around at the crowd. Each pair of eyes that met his looked away sheepishly. He took out his wallet and flashed his badge. Then he explained that Indians were wards of the state, that their well-being was a federal responsibility. His words cut sharply, bitterly, at the men. Now that the Bannock was dead, their bloodlust was no longer upon them, and they finally had time for proper remorse. Not a voice was raised in defense of their action. Beside him, a grim Tyson was also facing the crowd.

Longarm turned to him. "You know any of these men? Reckon we should press charges, do you?"

Tyson shook his head wearily. And as Longarm looked around at the sullen crowd, one of them shouted from the rear of the crowd, "That feller beside you was responsible! He gave that Indian a gun! It went all to hell after that! Why, we was just having a little fun, is all!"

Longarm saw Tyson wince.

"Go on!" Longarm told them. "Get out of here. The day is young. Maybe if you really work at it, you can find yourself another poor Indian to haze! Now git!"

As the crowd straggled unhappily toward the shore, Tyson fell in beside Longarm.

"That was my fault, wasn't it?"

"Not necessarily, though you did add your two cent's worth, and that's a fact."

"What you said back there, that I should stay out of it, that I'd done enough damage. You feel that way, do you?"

"I spoke in haste. And I was thinking of the mood of that crowd if the Indian got away."

"Did you see who hit me?"

"Yep."

"I wish you'd point him out to me."

"Later, maybe I will. But right now we got to meet that steamboat. There's going to be some mighty unhappy women on it. You heard that scream, didn't you?"

"I heard it."

"Most likely it came from one of the congressmen's women. I'd appreciate it if you'd meet them as they come off the boat and give them my apologies. I'm going to have to see about those wounded men back there. If that Indian killed either of them, I'll have to wire a full report to the Bureau of Indian Affairs and to my office in Denver."

"I can handle it, Longarm," the deputy said.

As the two men regained the willows along the bank of the river, Longarm squinted through the noon sunshine at the steamboat while it resumed its passage up the river to the dock. Then he glanced at Tyson. "You say you got us a guide and have seen to our gear already?"

Tyson nodded. "The guide's name is Jim Travers, and we've got a full-sized camp already pitched among the hills back of town. With all those people, I figured we'd never be able to get enough hotel rooms."

Longarm nodded. "And they might as well start now learning what it will be like sleeping under canvas. I suspicion they've been pampered plenty in that riverboat." He nodded decisively. "Take them out to the camp. If anyone in their party gives you any noise about continuing on up the Yellowstone, you just make it clear it's my intention that we go overland from this point on."

Tyson smiled. "That's just about what that guide told me," he said. "This is no time to trust that sneaky Yellowstone."

"All right, then. See to it, Tyson."

As the man nodded and hurried off upstream toward the dockyard, Longarm stood for a moment to watch him. The fellow had been hit a pretty mean blow on the side of his head, and a bloody, coagulating scab had formed already. But not once had the man complained of it or lifted his hand to inspect the extent of the damage. He was a man who acted on his principles, it seemed, no matter what it might cost him.

Trouble was, he acted first and thought later.

It was just after sundown when Longarm rode into the camp the guide had set up outside Billings, and he was not out of his saddle before he was being approached by one of the congressmen, a look of fiery displeasure flashing in his eyes, and a silver whiskey flask in his right hand.

"Are you Custis Long?" this worthy demanded, spreading his legs and planting himself firmly in Longarm's path. "The man who is in charge of this expedition?"

Longarm pulled his horse up sharply, then pushed his Stetson back on his forehead and contemplated the fellow standing before him. In the rapidly fading light, the most prominent features Longarm could discern were the man's broad shoulders and ruddy complexion. A shock of unruly gray hair had fallen over his impressive brow, and his eyes were bright with the alcohol he had already consumed. He maintained his stance in front of Longarm's large claybank gelding with an impertinent, if cheerful, disregard for his safety.

"Yes," Longarm replied laconically, as he carefully guided his mount around the big, bluff figure and then rode on past him toward the fire.

Longarm saw Tyson and the man who was undoubtedly the guide, Travers, coming toward him from the fire. He dismounted and handed the reins of his horse to a small, narrow-faced fellow undoubtedly serving as the wrangler.

"That's Tim," said Tyson, indicating the retreating wrangler with a nod of his head. "And this here is Jim Travers, our guide."

Longarm shook the elderly guide's hand and found it firm and calloused. "Pleased to meet you, Jim. You can call me Longarm, if you've a mind to."

"Longarm, is it?" the man asked shrewdly. "Seems to me I've heard tell of a lawman using that name." He smiled then, showing ragged yellow teeth. "But it's only a whisper in the back of my mind, nothing to worry about a-tall, I'm sure."

"Not unless you're a horse thief or a murderer," agreed Longarm, smiling at the old man.

Travers's face was covered with a curly salt-and-pepper crop of wiry hair, so that only his bronzed brow and cheekbones protruded. From behind all this foliage, two coal-black agates peered out somberly at Longarm. "In my time," the oldtimer allowed, "I might have had a hand in both of them desperate undertakings. But that was a long time afore you was abroad, Longarm."

"What about those two men the Indian wounded?" Tyson asked Longarm. It was obvious the deputy was still anxious about the incident that noon in Billings.

"No need to bother yourself about that anymore," Longarm replied with a smile. "Their wounds weren't serious. One of those hellers will have to eat standing up for a while and the other will go around with his left arm in a sling for some time, but they'll both live. I wired a full report to my office in Denver and to the BIA in Washington, though, just in case. That's what took me so long."

"Now just a moment there, Long!" boomed a heavy voice from behind Longarm.

Longarm caught Tyson's weary wince as he turned to greet again the burly fellow who had tried to get himself ridden over earlier. The man was still brandishing his whiskey flask, and it looked as if he must have taken a few more swallows from it since Longarm had ridden deliberately around him. He seemed just a mite unsteady on his feet. Behind him, hurrying through the dusk to catch up with him, Longarm saw a tall, slim, red-haired beauty. She was wrapped tightly in a long, frilly dress of pale lavender. Despite the tight wrapping, there was no way her dress could conceal the voluptuous lines of her marvelously full figure.

"Paul!" she called, as she caught up to the fellow. "I thought you were asleep in your tent!"

"Well, I'm not, Jean, as you can see," the fellow retorted, a devilish grin on his broad face, "and I want to speak to Custis Long here. If you'll just leave things to me, I'm sure we'll all be back on that steamboat."

"Do you want me to take that flask back to the tent?" the girl inquired carefully.

The man beamed at her and swiftly tipped the flask

up. In two enormous gulps he had swallowed its contents. He handed the empty flask to her. "Yes," he said, "take it back. And refill it."

She took the whiskey flask from him, smiled thinly, hopelessly, then turned swiftly on her heel and hurried across the dark ground to a tent on the far side of the encampment. Paul—as the girl had called him—watched her go for a minute, obviously deriving enormous pleasure from the mere sight of her, then turned back to Longarm. He smiled broadly and stuck out a powerful, meaty hand. Longarm took it and shook it warmly. It was impossible not to respond to the big fellow's vast good nature.

"You must excuse me," the man said. "I have the advantage on you, Long. I am Congressman Paul Laxalte, representing the great state of Massachusetts as well as the Congress of the United States." He smiled proudly before going on. "And I have just recently been chosen as the spokesman for this intrepid band of travelers who are about to explore your fabulous country."

"Congratulations," Longarm said. "It's a pleasure to meet you, Congressman."

"I am afraid we might have gotten off on the wrong foot back there. Is that it? Did I do or say anything to offend you? You westerners, I find, are deucedly difficult to get along with at times."

"I was able to stop my horse in plenty of time," Longarm told him, "or we might have gotten off on the wrong foot, as you say. No harm done. Congratulations on your election to the post of Chief Spokesman." There was a small smile on Longarm's face to take the bite out of his sarcasm, but in the dim light from the campfire, Longarm could see that Paul Laxalte was catching it all.

Jim Travers spoke up then, his voice betraying his exasperation: "They all want to go back on that river steamboat. That's what he's been elected to tell you, Longarm."

Longarm glanced back at Laxalte. "Is that it, Congressman?"

"Call me Paul," the man said, taking a deep breath. "And yes, that's it. I and the rest of my party see no sense in traipsing over this wilderness when we can take the *Far West* all the way up to the Big Horn River, as far as the mouth of the Little Big Horn."

"In normal times, maybe. But the Yellowstone is too shallow this time of year. We'd most likely lose our bottom somewhere between here and the Big Horn, and that would be the end of this expedition. I prefer a more direct route overland to the Yellowstone Park."

"And so do I," seconded Jim Travers emphatically.

Laxalte pulled himself up to his full height. "Are you aware, Long, that Captain Marsh of the *Far West* took his ship from the mouth of the Big Horn twelve miles upstream to the mouth of the Little Big Horn, fifteen miles from the site of the Custer Massacre, loaded the wounded on board, and then traveled down the Big Horn into the Yellowstone and down the Yellowstone into the Missouri, and on to Bismarck, a total of seven hundred and ten miles in fifty-four hours—an average speed of better than *thirteen miles* per hour? We, sir, are in the midst of an Industrial Revolution, a remarkable age in which machines now serve man! The steamboat is one of those marvelous machines. And I say we would be fools not to use it!"

"I know all about that trip," drawled Travers. "I was one of them troopers that got took downriver on the *Far West*. But that was a few years back, Congressman, and this year the river ain't near so high. Deputy Marshal Long is right, the overland road is safer. Since the three of us is responsible for the safety of you and your womenfolk, I advise you to listen to the marshal."

Laxalte looked from Travers to Longarm. "Are you going to let this old man speak for you, Long?"

"I thought he did a right nice job of it," Longarm responded.

The man seemed astonished at this reply. He looked from Longarm to the others, then shook his head. The steam seemed to have gone out of him. At that moment, hurrying through the darkness, the girl whom Laxalte had sent to refill his flask called out to the man. He turned, staggering slightly. The girl caught up to him and lent her weight to his as she handed him the silver flask.

Steadying himself with the aid of the girl, Laxalte turned back to the three men. "Let me introduce my secretary, Jean McPhee, gentlemen. A most lovely and intelligent aide, I can assure you."

The three men nodded to the woman, who bowed slightly, just the hint of a blush on her lovely face. Of course it could have been the campfire, Longarm realized. Still, he thought not. She was certainly aware of the implications of her traveling alone with the congressman on this expedition.

Jean looked at them. "Have you gentlemen finished with the congressman? I think he should turn in now." She smiled slightly. "I can guess that we are not about to go back to that lovely steamboat and that we will have to break camp quite early tomorrow morning."

Longarm smiled back at her. "You've figured right, ma'am. Maybe you can help the congressman break the news to the rest of his party."

She nodded and started to help Laxalte turn around. He was busy sampling the refilled flask. He took the neck of the flask from his mouth and glanced back at Longarm. "Until tomorrow morning, Long! I expect to see us on the trail at sunup!"

Frank Tyson chuckled.

Laxalte blinked blearily as sudden exhaustion overtook him. He staggered and almost collapsed, but Jean seemed more than able. She caught the big man under his arms, steadied him, then led him off across the dark ground. Longarm, watching, shook his head in admiration. That was some fine woman. It must be nice, he mused, to be able to afford that kind of secretary—or aide, as Laxalte put it.

He turned then to the others. "Well, then. That's settled. What can you tell me about the rest of our crew?"

"You've already met our wrangler," said Tyson. "We got ourselves a cook. His name is Amos."

"What's his last name?"

"He don't have none," said Travers with a chuckle. "But take my word for it, he's one damn fine cook."

"That's all that matters, I guess," Longarm agreed. "Anything else?"

"Only that it took them dudes most of the afternoon to get settled in," said Travers. "I never seen so many contraptions. They even got themselves portable privies and bathtubs that fold up. It's a sight to see, I tell you."

"Do we have enough packhorses?"

"Yes, we do, I reckon. But they sure figure to get a workout. Some of the ponies is pretty green and ain't been broke to picket yet. But I'll see to that at the next camp."

Longarm nodded. "Then let's get some shut-eye. Like Laxalte says, we're going to have to be on the trail at sunup!"

Both Tyson and Travers chuckled at that as they walked over to their bedrolls on the far side of the fire. Longarm was about to go find the wrangler who'd taken his horse when the boy approached through the gloom, carrying Longarm's saddle and the rest of his gear on his shoulders. The lad was walking slowly but steadily.

"Where do you want this, mister?" he asked, his voice tight from the exertion.

"Right down here, close to the fire. I hear it gets chilly up here at night."

"It sure does," the fellow said, dropping Longarm's

gear as gently as he could to the ground. As Longarm bent to untie his soogan, Tim cleared his throat. "Mr. Long?"

Longarm glanced up. "Yes?"

"That Miss Jean, the one with Mr. Laxalte, she says she needs your help, something about the congressman, I think. I told her I'd tell you as soon as I got here."

"Thanks, Tim," Longarm said, getting to his feet. "You go on now and get your sleep. We got ourselves a big day tomorrow."

The boy nodded, turned, and walked off into the darkness. Longarm watched him go for a moment or two, then hurried across the encampment toward the congressman's tent without a word to Jim Tyson or Travers.

A lantern was lit on a small fold-up table inside Laxalte's tent when Longarm lifted the flap and stepped inside. As he had thought, Laxalte was out cold on the ground beside his cot while Jean McPhee was sitting on a chair beside him, looking wearily down at the still form.

"I can't budge him," she told Longarm, looking up at him with exasperation. "He's quite heavy. And once he's out like this, there's no waking him."

"Here, let me give you a hand," Longarm offered.

He straddled the heavy torso, grabbed the man under his armpits, and heaved. His upper torso landed on the bunk. His lower body and legs were still on the ground. He lay in a kind of kneeling position, still sleeping like a baby, his head to one side, his arms folded under his head.

"Maybe we should leave him like that," Jean said. "He looks so angelic."

Longarm chuckled, grabbed the man under the armpits a second time, and dragged him all the way up onto the cot. With a sigh, Jean got up from her chair and began to undress the congressman.

Longarm turned to go.

"Don't leave yet, Mr. Long," she said. "Please."

Longarm turned.

"Sit down," she said, "in that chair, why don't you? You can see how a secretary takes care of her boss in the wild country."

Astonished but intrigued, Longarm did as Jean suggested. He sat down in the canvas folding chair and watched with some amusement as the deft fingers of the young lady peeled Laxalte's clothing from him. It was amazing how swiftly the operation was accomplished. When Jean got to the part of pulling off the man's long underwear, Longarm felt his face burn slightly. But she might just as easily have been preparing a side of beef for a barbecue, the way she handled the man's pale, naked torso. Without bothering to put his nightgown on, she covered him with sheets and a blanket, then straightened and turned to look at Longarm.

Brushing a lock of scarlet hair off her moist brow, she said, "How was that?"

"Too bad he was too drunk to notice it."

"Yes, isn't it? Are you drunk, Mr. Long?"

"No, ma'am, I'm as sober as a judge." He added with a grin, "Other elected officials can do as they please."

"Then come to my tent. I want to explain to you my position on this expedition."

Longarm got to his feet almost meekly. Jean blew out the lantern, then led the way from the congressman's tent across the moonlit ground and into her own tent. She lit her lantern and then sat down on her cot. She indicated the chair beside the cot with a nod of her head, and Longarm obediently sat in it.

"I know how it must look," she said to Longarm. "A pretty girl traveling alone with her employer. How cozy. I assure you, Mr. Long, it is nothing of the sort. You saw how he was just now. This is typical behavior. I did not realize a man could consume so much alcohol and still stay on his feet. The man drinks continually, hour after hour, and it only seems to sharpen his mind."

"His mind?"

She caught the note on Longarm's voice and nodded swiftly, the hint of a smile on her face. "Yes, his mind. I see you understand perfectly. His performance as a man—suffers, you might say. I think it was Shakespeare, wasn't it, who said that drink makes a man anxious to perform—but incapable of it at the same time?"

If Longarm did not know it was impossible, he would have thought he had just blushed. Jean McPhee was sitting on a cot in front of him complaining that Congressman Laxalte was unable to satisfy her womanly needs. "I'm not much of an authority on Shakespeare, Miss McPhee," Longarm said.

"You take my meaning, however, I am sure."

"Yes, indeed."

She smiled. "Good. I just wanted you to know, Mr. Long, that the congressman and I are not lovers. I am here to help the man. He needs help. I am his 'girl Friday,' as he calls it."

"If I might ask, where is his wife, Miss McPhee?"

"She died three years ago. Tuberculosis. She had been ill for years. The man has been drinking heavily since her death. I believe he still grieves for her. He has told me that he will do the best he can for his remaining time on this earth, but that he will not be sad when it comes time to rejoin his wife. He is convinced he will meet her again—and this time she will be healthy, the woman he married so many years ago."

"I see."

"Do you?" She got up and walked over to Longarm. She took both of his hands in hers and pulled him gently out of his seat. As soon as he was standing before her, she put her arms around him and leaned her head gently on his chest. "You are so tall and so quiet. There is so much strength in you, Mr. Long. I saw it when you rode in, and when you stood up to Paul. I see so many weak men. Do you understand? So many. It is nice to feel someone like you standing so close to me."

She lifted her face to his. In the dim light from the lantern, her face was ruddy, her eyes flecked with color. He kissed her.

It was a long kiss, one that revealed to him the depth of her hunger and need. When she pulled back, her face was aflame, her eyes aglow. She had made up her mind, it seemed.

"These damned clothes!" she muttered fiercely. "Help me, Longarm!"

It was a job. It did not help that Longarm's own need rendered his ten fingers almost helpless. First it was her bodice that had to be unlaced. Next came the dress, and after that a chemise, followed by a seemingly impregnable corset. Jean was almost weeping with frustration as Longarm untied the laces. She flung the corset from her finally, stepped out of the last chemise, and flung herself back upon her cot.

"Quick! Oh, quick, Mr. Long!"

And then she realized that Longarm had remained fully dressed through all this. With a tiny shriek, she sat up and clawed at his pants, unbuttoning his fly and peeling down his trousers with a frightening speed that had Longarm momentarily afraid she might lose all his buttons. Taking off his gunbelt and boots, and stepping out of his trousers and longjohns, but still wearing his shirt and vest, he let her pull him onto her hungrily. She let out a startled cry.

"What is it, Mr. Long? What have you *got* there?"

Chuckling nervously, Longarm peeled off his vest and shirt. "I'll explain later," he told her.

"Yes, later," she murmured, spreading her legs wide for him.

He entered her almost without effort, probing so deeply that he nearly stopped breathing with the sheer delight of her tight, embracing warmth. He began to stroke slowly, carefully, not wanting to climax too quickly.

"Kiss me!" Jean hissed through clenched teeth. "Otherwise I'll cry out and wake the whole camp!"

His mouth enclosed hers at once, and as he continued his steady thrusting, he heard the muffled cries that gurgled up from her throat while her tongue reached deep into his mouth. Once or twice she almost broke away from his kiss to let out a scream, but he devoured her mouth with his and stifled the scream.

By that time he could hold himself back no longer. She sensed this and her thrusting grew tumultuous as she too neared her climax. He exploded within her, clinging to her tightly, then he sank slowly off her and came to rest on the narrow cot beside her. It was a tight fit for the two of them.

She kissed him lightly on the forehead and laughed softly, her voice deep and melodious, sounding not at all like the nervous, brittle woman of a few minutes before.

"Kiss my breasts," she told him softly. "They still ache for your mouth."

As his mouth toyed with her nipples, she purred, uttering small cries of delight, allowing him to know what each flourish of his tongue or nip of his teeth was accomplishing. She seemed insatiable, and when at last she whispered a request in his ear, he was not surprised.

His mouth left her breasts and moved down her warm stomach, past her navel, and farther. Her cries of delight were barely audible. Her fingers caught in his thick hair as she pressed him closer. He felt her heaving then, and heard her tiny cry. She wanted him to mount her again.

Longarm complied, again drowning her cries of delight with his kisses, and when it was over a second time, he found that Jean had still more requests. And more.

Standing almost fully dressed before her, he slipped his vest back on and took from the right-hand pocket the double-barreled .44 derringer. "This was what you felt, Jean," he told her, smiling. "It's a little something extra I sometimes find a need for—when I find myself between a rock and a hard place, that is."

"How clever." She was sitting up on the bed, her naked form glowing in the lantern's light. She made no effort to hide her nudity, and that caused Longarm's breath to catch whenever his eyes found her.

"It's attached by a clip to this watch chain," he explained as matter-of-factly as he could under the circumstances, "and the chain is attached to my watch. It's a kind of double-duty watch fob."

"Clever—and deadly," Jean acknowledged, as Longarm dropped the watch and derringer into his vest pockets and reached for his coat and hat.

"Good night, Jean," he said.

She smiled. "I would have thought it was almost morning by now."

"It might well be. If I fall off my horse tomorrow, you'll know why."

"You say I should call you Longarm, is that right?"

"My friends do."

"I think I had better not, Longarm," she said, getting to her feet and moving close to him, a devilish gleam in her eye. "You see, I don't think we should let anyone know that . . . we know each other, if you see what I mean. It would hurt the congressman if he knew. We must, after all, be *more* than discreet. Do you understand why?"

"Politics?"

"Something like that. We'll still have each other, whenever we can. But no glance must pass between us, no blush. We must make no attempt at all to be close.

We must act as perfect strangers—polite and civil, of course, at all times—but strangers. It will be difficult, Longarm, but we must do it."

He smiled at her. "I was about to suggest the same thing. It's a sensible notion but, like you say, it won't exactly be easy."

"I'm so glad you understand. I knew you would. I knew I could count on you—in so *many* ways!" She flung her arms impulsively about his neck, and kissed him.

He turned and left the tent, her kiss still burning on his lips. She was right, he realized, as he moved as silently as he could across the dark ground to the campfire. It would be a good idea not to give the impression that the two of them were anything more than casual acquaintances, and he was pleased that she had been the one to suggest this course. But Longarm realized just how difficult it was going to be to stay cool, with a woman like that nearby.

He went through the weary process of undressing for the second time that night, and slipped gratefully into his bedroll. Before he closed his eyes, however, he took a telegram from his trousers pocket. The telegram was from Vail, and Longarm would not have seen it had he not gone into the Western Union office to wire his reports to Washington and Denver.

It read:

TO DEPUTY LONG BILLINGS MONTANA STOP SAMMY WENTWORTH RELATED TO KILLER YOU BROUGHT IN STOP WENTWORTH LAST SEEN BOARDING SAME TRAIN YOU TOOK FROM DENVER STOP THERESA MIRELDA SWEARS SAMMY WILL GET YOU STOP SHE IS STILL IN CUSTODY STOP KEEP YOUR BACKSIDE COVERED STOP VAIL U S MARSHAL DENVER

Longarm smiled once again at that last advice from his chief, refolded the telegram, and placed it back in his pocket. Yes, it would be a good idea for him to keep his ass covered with that sneak, Sammy Wentworth, on his tail. It was the sneaky fellows, those who felt they had to prove their manhood with a pistol, that always turned out to be the most treacherous and the most difficult to defend against. Wild Bill's demise in Deadwood City certainly proved that.

And if Wentworth *had* followed Longarm to Billings, there was no doubt in Longarm's mind that the man knew precisely where Longarm could be found at that moment. There was not a citizen in Billings who had not heard by this time of that party of fat-cat congressmen and their womenfolk who had piled off the *Far West* and set up camp in the hills behind the town. Nor was there a citizen who did not know of their eventual destination.

Somewhere on the trail into Yellowstone, then, Longarm could expect to find Sammy Wentworth, trembling like a dog with fleas, perched behind a boulder or windfall, waiting to prove he was a man—if not to himself, then to Theresa Mirelda.

Longarm took the derringer from his vest pocket and placed it under the folded blanket that served as his pillow. He pulled the soogan's flaps about him, thrust his hands in under the folded blanket, and closed his eyes. He felt the cool breeze from off the Big Horn Mountains, thought again of the whispered urgencies of Jean McPhee, and with her last kiss still fresh upon his lips, he slept.

Far above the camp, shivering miserably with the cold, his teeth chattering uncontrollably, Sammy Wentworth led his mount through the treacherous darkness. He tripped often, and swore bitterly each time. His nose was running. But he kept going, determined to find a spot well ahead of this camp on the other side of the trail that led from the Big Horn Mountains to the Yellowstone Park.

He'd get that big, mean son of a bitch. He'd promised Theresa. And she had told him she loved him. The thought of that warmed him even as he shivered violently from the increasing chill of this night.

Chapter 3

To Longarm's surprise, Laxalte was as good as his word, up and busy packing at sunup. As a matter of fact, Tyson and Jim Travers had things pretty well organized. The young wrangler was good with the horses and obviously knew how to pack, and the cook, Amos, had prepared a splendid breakfast that had the women astonished and the congressmen pleased, despite the simple fare of fresh eggs and venison, coffee and tea, and thick slices of light, sweet bread, baked in frying pans braced on the edges of the two fires.

Before they set out, Longarm gathered the party around him and let Jim Travers explain to the lot of them what Longarm had told Laxalte the night before. Following the river, Jim Travers emphasized, would take them on a wide loop north. By striking out on a southwesterly course, keeping to the watershed ridges between the valleys, it should take them no more than a week to reach the park, assuming they were able to cover roughly twenty miles a day.

There was considerable discussion at that, but Jim Travers's answers were blunt and authoritative. Soon Longarm could see that Jim was impressing the congressmen and their women with his intimate knowledge of the country, and the guide perked them all up considerably when he told the men he would need their help in shooting fresh game for their needs. There was not a single congressman who did not immediately make known his eagerness to join Travers in such an endeavor. Travers then went on to warn the congressmen not to shoot at game indiscriminately, and certainly not without warning to the others, while they were on the trail. This injunction brought an almost immediate storm, and Longarm had to smile as he saw how decisively the crusty old guide dealt with it.

During this extensive palavering, Longarm took the opportunity to look over his charges. He had already met Laxalte and his lovely secretary. True to her whispered precautions of the night before, she hardly looked at him as he stood beside Frank Tyson. And when her eyes did happen to meet his, it seemed as if she were looking clear through him, that no one could possibly have appeared more unappealing to her. Longarm felt somewhat unsettled as he looked away at the other congressmen standing about in the early-morning mist.

The youngest was a tall, handsome fellow, who sported a thick, dark mustache. He had a full crop of curly hair swept back off a high, almost lofty forehead. He was smoking a meerschaum pipe as he watched Jim Travers with alert, intelligent eyes. Longarm knew all their names by now, and this one was Charles Evans Clinton, a New Yorker who opposed setting aside the park's resources for the public. This, it seemed, he had made quite clear in his brief chats with Frank Tyson the day before. Melinda Clinton, his wife—a frail, bemused creature—stood beside him, and beside her hovered her maid, Cindy Lou Ryan, a robust, dark-haired beauty who seemed fiercely protective of her frail mistress.

Congressman Peter Eliot and his wife Mary were newlyweds, and stood to one side of Clinton. Like Clinton, Peter Eliot was an exuberantly handsome fellow. He was clean-shaven, with snapping, clear blue eyes. He seemed to laugh readily, as did his young wife—a stunning, auburn-haired girl with skin so pale it made her dark eyes seem to jump out at Longarm whenever she glanced his way. She was a thin, wiry girl, but despite this, she did not appear at all frail. Her maid, Daisy Foster, looked like a heller. She was blonde and blue-eyed, and had an impudent, dimpled smile that she flashed about her with devastating effect. Even the dour Jim Travers, Longarm had noted earlier that morning, was not immune to its dazzle.

Standing beside Peter Eliot were two men of an entirely different stamp. One of them was Big Jim McAllister, as he had informed Frank Tyson the day before, and the other was David Baxter. Big Jim was indeed large. In a booming mining town a few years earlier, Longarm had seen a traveling Shakespearean troupe put on one of the Bard's histories. In it, a character called Falstaff dominated the action. Big Jim McAllister reminded him of Falstaff. His stomach was as prodigious, his complexion as ruddy, and his outlook as jovial. A huge cigar was stuck in one corner of his mouth as he listened to Jim Travers, and more than once his laughter at one of Jim's more salty expressions rumbled out with such vigor and infectious mirth that everyone around him joined in.

His companion, David Baxter, was, by comparison, a miracle of compactness. Lean, wiry, his eyes like gimlets, he too smoked a cigar. But it was a small, blunt stogie the man kept chewing on as he squinted through its smoke. Where Big Jim rose close to six feet, Baxter could have been no taller than five feet five, or just a bit less. He was bald. He seemed quick and nervous in his movements, and it was his sharp voice, more than anyone else's, that seemed to cut through the babble of voices about him. Also, it was his questions that Jim Travers seemed to consider more worthy of a detailed response, since they were sharp and incisive and always made an excellent point.

McAllister's wife and Baxter's daughter stood together, their maids also standing side by side. Olivia, Baxter's daughter, was a shy, stringy young lady who blushed with maddening regularity. At the moment she seemed to be clinging to her maid with one hand, and to the tall, commanding Irene McAllister with the other. Hilda Guernsback, the McAllisters' maid, seemed to stand apart, a very prim, very proper young lady who was dressed to the teeth, as if she were determined to hide every square inch of pink skin from view. She had even wrapped a blue scarf about her large hat and then down under her chin; whether it was to keep her hat on or to hide most of her face, Longarm couldn't tell. At the moment there was little wind.

". . . Mr. Long?"

Longarm glanced over at the guide. The man had evidently addressed a comment to him. Longarm smiled. "I'm sorry, Jim. I didn't get that."

Jim Travers grinned at Longarm's discomfiture. "I asked if there was something you might want to add to what I told them."

"I think you covered it nicely," said Longarm, smiling back at the guide. "There is one thing, though. We had better warn the women not to raise a fuss if any Indians appear hereabouts . . ."

"Indians!" Daisy Foster cried. "Ain't they all penned in their reservations?"

"I'm sure, Miss Foster," Longarm replied, "that you've seen Indians during your trip up the Missouri and the Yellowstone. They weren't penned up, were they?"

"Yes," boomed Paul Laxalte, "but those were peaceful Indians, not the ones that massacred General Custer not so long ago, not the Sioux!"

"Indians," Frank Tyson spoke up, his voice tight, "are allowed off their reservations as long as they tell the agent where they are going and about how long they intend to be out. They are not permanently 'penned,' Miss Foster. The United States Government is not in the business of running zoos for fellow humans, though I am sure there are some in Washington who would like nothing better!"

"Hold it there, Frank," Longarm said soothingly. "I don't reckon Miss Foster meant anything by her use of the word 'penned.' Did you, Miss Foster?" Longarm smiled at Daisy.

She blushed and shook her head. "I . . . I guess I used the wrong word. I thought they just had to stay in their reservations—because of all them massacres."

"And maybe these aborigines *ought* to be kept in pens—and well away from here!" boomed Laxalte, eyeing Frank Tyson angrily. Laxalte was obviously spoiling for a confrontation with Tyson, having sensed immediately that the deputy was prone to take the Indian's side.

Longarm turned to Frank. "Easy now, Frank. Reckon this filibuster is all my own fault. I maybe shouldn't have mentioned the possibility of us meeting up with any Indian hunting parties."

"Hunting parties!" cried Mary Eliot, her eyes wide.

"They ain't huntin' scalps, ma'am," Jim Travers said with a chuckle. "Food. They can still hunt for fresh meat if they're of a mind to. Saves the government, it does. It don't have to ship so large a beef ration to the reservation if the Indians can maybe scratch up a little meat of their own."

Laxalte was still smoldering, his gaze directed at Frank Tyson, so Longarm decided to end the discussion. "I suggest we get a move on," he said somewhat impatiently. "We've jawboned enough." Longarm glanced at Jim Travers and grinned. "Would you agree, Jim?"

The man nodded quickly.

By the middle of that morning, with the party well under way and every member of the congressional delegation beginning to appreciate the beauty of the countryside, Longarm spurred his claybank gelding ahead to overtake Tyson and Jim Travers, and had almost reached them when one of the women called his name.

He pulled up and found himself riding beside Melinda Clinton. At once, her frail wispiness touched Longarm. That she should be out here in this rugged wilderness, and riding through it sidesaddle, caused him to wonder how in the devil Clinton could let himself do this to his wife. "Yes, ma'am?" he asked, touching the brim of his hat to her. "Anything wrong?"

"I have been thinking," she told him, "about that incident yesterday. The poor man back in Billings, the one who . . . drowned."

"Oh yes. The Bannock."

"The Bannock?"

"He was a Bannock Indian, a half-breed, I reckon."

"It was most terrible, Mr. Long. I cannot get it out of my mind. Perhaps you could tell me what caused such a terrible thing."

"I wish I knew, ma'am. He was a town Indian, but I guess he rubbed someone the wrong way and a few whites took out their guns and tried to make him dance. It was too much for him, so he grabbed a gun, shot a few of his tormentors, and lit out. You saw the end of it, I'm afraid."

She spoke more softly now: "And it was Mr. Tyson's gun he stole. Is that correct, Mr. Long?"

Longarm nodded. "That's right. Frank was trying to break up the hazing, and the Indian grabbed his gun." Longarm smiled at the woman. "You seem to know quite a bit about it."

"It's the talk of the camp, Mr. Long. But I've been getting garbled accounts and I decided I'd rather find out the truth."

"Well, that's it, ma'am, as nearly as I can piece it together."

"Do you feel sorry for the Indians, Mr. Long?" She

asked this in a soft, confidential manner, as if she meant to keep his answer strictly between them.

Longarm smiled and nudged his hatbrim back a little. "I feel sorry for anyone who finds himself between a rock and a hard place, Indian *or* white man. I guess that's why I'm a lawman." He glanced at her shrewdly. "Does that answer your question, ma'am?"

"Yes it does, Mr. Long," she said with a smile. "It surely does."

Once again, he touched his hatbrim to her and spurred on past her.

Frank Tyson turned in his saddle as Longarm neared him. Longarm pulled his horse close to Frank, then leaned forward in his saddle so that he could see the old guide's bearded face as he rode on the other side of Tyson.

"How's it look so far?" Longarm asked the guide.

"Now that we're movin' and not talkin', we're doin' just fine, Longarm. But I don't look for it to last. Not with all them females underfoot." He shook his head in disgust.

"They seem to be doing all right," Frank said. "Most of them can ride pretty well."

"Sure," said Jim, snorting. "Over this country here, they'll do fine ridin' sidesaddle. But you wait till we get a mite higher, where there ain't no trails and grassy meadows like this."

Longarm nodded gloomily. Jim had a point. The meadow they were now crossing was carpeted with wildflowers and was reasonably easy on their mounts. They could not expect such easy going to continue. Nevertheless, he was pleased that the party was seeing, this early on, how kind to the eye this country could be; it might help to make up for any hardships they were liable to encounter when the going got tougher.

As Longarm looked about him, he realized that the Rockies were still in "the Shining Times," as the Indians and Mountain Men called that period before the white man had swept in to change it all. Abruptly, Longarm topped a gentle rise and caught sight of an entire hillside covered with columbine, a pale lavender, lilylike flower. Longarm was not a demonstrative man, and he had come across many such valleys on his various assignments, but he could not help reflecting on how rare such a sight was getting to be, what with the white settlers' insistence on overgrazing the foothills or plowing under any and all arable land.

"Frank," Longarm said, "maybe you better read this." Longarm fished out of his pocket the telegram he had received from Vail the day before, and handed it across to the deputy.

Frank took it, read it quickly, then handed it back to Longarm. The wind tugged at the flimsy yellow paper, and Longarm had a little difficulty in folding it again and tucking it away. When he did so and looked again at Tyson, he saw that Frank was watching him with concern.

"What do you think you should do, Longarm?" he asked.

"I been thinking on that. First thing to consider is the congressmen and their women. Wouldn't be proper to get them in a crossfire between me and this fellow. And I figure he's mean and sneaky enough not to care one way or the other. So what I'll do is ride point and keep myself some distance from the rest of the party."

"You're setting yourself up that way."

"Maybe. But this is one silly jasper. He misses a lot. The farther away I stay from the rest of you, the less likely you'll be to catch a stray shot."

"You goin' to tell me what this is all about?" snapped the guide.

Longarm laughed. "Frank will fill you in. For now, I'll be riding ahead."

"Jest don't get lost, then," the old codger growled.

Longarm spurred his horse, waved, and cut toward a ridge off to his left.

The shot Longarm had been waiting for all afternoon came not from Sammy Wentworth, but from far below him in the narrow valley through which the party was now threading its way. Glancing back and down the long slope, he saw Peter Eliot, still astride his mount, with his rifle out, charging through the thick grass after a grizzly.

Cursing aloud, Longarm spun his horse about and charged down the slope toward the party. As he rode, he saw the grizzly rear to his full height, turn, and snarl furiously at his fast-approaching assailant. The effect on Peter Eliot was immediate. He reined in his horse abruptly, so abruptly that it reared for a moment on its hind legs. Seeing this, the grizzly charged. Peter brought his horse under control and spurred away from the charging animal, leading him back to the party less than a hundred yards away on the other side of the valley, all of whom had halted by this time to watch the excitement.

Longarm pushed his mount savagely in a desperate attempt to overtake and turn the grizzly. He was gaining a bit when he saw Eliot suddenly, belatedly realize his mistake and turn away from the others. This took him on a course parallel to the trail, and the furious grizzly bounded swiftly through the tall grass after him, still cutting dangerously near the rest of the party.

Longarm saw one of the women's horses rear in terror as the bear swept close by her. Dimly he heard her shriek, and recognized Melinda Clinton's voice. Her mount was out of control. He swerved toward her just as her horse came down and swept off the trail, heading at full gallop toward a boulder-filled gully. Abandoning the foolish Eliot to his own devices, Longarm put his heels to his horse in an effort to overtake Melinda Clinton.

She was having a devil of a time staying on the panicked beast, and twice Longarm thought she was going to lose her precarious perch. Her horse was wild-eyed and still straining when Longarm finally pulled alongside, reached over, and snatched the nearly exhausted woman from her sidesaddle. Her thin arms went around his neck like hoops of steel, and as he reined his mount in and steadied her, he could feel her heart thudding against his chest. Her face was pale, her eyes wide.

"You all right, ma'am?" Longarm asked her gently as he let her down.

"Yes . . . I'm fine, I think!" She was confused and out of breath. "Where . . . where did you *come* from, Mr. Long?"

Longarm dismounted and smiled at her. "I was on the ridge back there when all the excitement began."

At that moment, Charles Clinton pounded up. His face a mask of concern, he flung himself from his horse and caught up his wife in a shuddering embrace, almost knocking her over.

"My God, Melly! Are you all right?" he cried.

When all she could manage was a quick nod to his passionate query, he turned to Longarm and began wringing his hand fervently.

"That was magnificent riding, Long! Magnificent! You came out of nowhere, it seemed! I couldn't believe it!"

"Settle down, now," Longarm counseled, smiling, "and go look for that horse. It's liable to hurt itself in among those rocks. And what about that grizzly? Has it caught up with Eliot yet?"

"That fool!" Clinton cried, glancing suddenly back up the valley. "Last thing I knew, he'd finally turned the beast with a shot."

"I'll go take a look-see," said Longarm, swinging back up into his saddle. "You take care of your wife, and see if you can recover that mount."

"I'll do that, Long," said the young man, looking up at Longarm with something approaching hero-worship. "And thanks again for what you did."

"Yes," said his wife, shading her eyes as she looked up at Longarm. "Thank you very much, Mr. Long. Tell me—was I between a rock and a hard place then?"

Longarm laughed. "You were that, ma'am!"

He turned his gelding then, and drove it hard back up the valley. When he saw Travers cutting across to intercept him, he veered toward the guide. The two men met within sight of the still-huddled party.

"That damn fool Eliot has wounded the grizzly," Jim said. "The bear's in that brush at the head of the canyon. Eliot wants to go in and finish him. I told him he was loco, but he's insisting. Says it'll make a great rug to set in front of his fireplace."

"Go on back to the others and keep an eye out. Just our luck that grizzly'll have a family hereabouts. I'll go see to Mr. Eliot."

The old guide smiled, his bewhiskered face screwing up so that his eyes were hardly visible. "Young dudes like this'n really get to you, don't they?"

Longarm nodded wearily. "That they do, Jim. Go on back to the others now, and keep a sharp eye out."

The guide wheeled his horse about, and Longarm set off after the dim figure of Peter Eliot, no longer astride his horse, moving cautiously but foolishly closer to a pocket of brush close against the side of a steep slope. He raised his mount to a gallop and was about ready to call out, when the young congressman caught sight of him and halted.

There was a pleased smile on his face as he went to greet Longarm, who was off his horse before it came to a complete halt. "He's in there, Mr. Long! Biggest damn grizzly I ever did see, and that's a fact."

In that instant, Longarm realized that Peter Eliot had no idea what trouble his enthusiasm for bear rugs had caused Melly and Charles Clinton. He had been too busy fleeing before the shambling beast to notice. Now he was heady with the prospect of obtaining a magnificent trophy. Heady and foolish.

"Most grizzlies *are* a mite big, at that, Mr. Eliot. Have you wounded the animal for sure?"

"The first bullet caught him high on the right shoulder, I'm afraid, but my second tore into his thigh. It really knocked him for a loop." The man turned around to face the brush. Pointing to the far corner, he said, "It went in there. I'm sure it is still in there. If we hurry—"

"I suggest you leave it, Mr. Eliot."

"Leave it!"

A moment before, Longarm had been furious with Eliot. But now, standing before the man and noting his disarming eagerness, his youthful exuberance, Longarm felt his anger draining helplessly away. Choosing his words carefully, he said, "Yes, leave it. It is my opinion, Congressman Eliot, that it would be foolish to mess with a wounded grizzly in this unfamiliar terrain."

"Foolish, is it?"

"That's what I said," Longarm replied. "And dangerous."

"I would be a coward not to go in there and relieve that beast of his misery, or worse, to leave him in this condition, ready to fall upon unwary travelers passing through this valley. Are you aware that, wounded in this fashion, this bear might well become a rogue—a marauder preying upon nearby settlements?"

"It's more likely he'll stay away from settlements after this. The smell of a human would drive him away, I'm thinking." Even as Longarm spoke, however, he was aware of just how futile it was to try to change this young dude's mind. The fact that he should have thought it incumbent upon him to lecture Longarm in these matters should have raised the lawman's hackles, but Longarm kept his temper under tight control and remembered how a place like Washington could pump up a fellow.

"I've hunted tigers, sir, in Bengal," Eliot replied. "Man-eaters. More than once. And those tigers had been driven to that extremity because of old wounds festering in their carcasses, wounds left by natives too frightened to finish what they started."

"This here ain't Bengal, Eliot," Longarm snapped. "And the grizzly ain't a tiger."

"As you wish, sir. You may stay back here, out of danger. I shall go in after the beast alone."

As Eliot turned and headed for the thicket, Longarm drew his Winchester from its saddle scabbard and started after him. "Eliot!"

Impatiently, the congressman stopped and looked back.

"I understand you're on your honeymoon," Longarm said.

"And what of it?"

Longarm caught up to the man. "I'll go in there with you, Eliot. But it's not your foolish hide I'm thinking of, it's that new young wife of yours."

Eliot's face darkened, but before he could respond, Longarm had brushed through the tall grass past him on the way to the thicket.

Silently, the two men strode cautiously toward the heavy brush that now revealed itself as a tangle of berry bushes and junipers that reached higher than a man's head—or a grizzly's. Directly behind the thicket, the slope rose almost straight up. Somewhere between that slope and the thicket, or crouching deep within the bushes, was that wounded grizzly, and if Longarm did not exactly think much of Eliot's good sense, he could not fault the man for his courage.

Both men carried Winchesters, whose range exceeded two hundred yards. Longarm knew his .44-40 had sufficient stopping power, but the bullet would have to be well placed, as Eliot's two earlier shots had proved. As

Longarm moved closer to the brush, he wished he had himself a shotgun loaded with buckshot. At close range, it could practically cut a man in two; a grizzly it would surely stop.

But Longarm decided not to think about that as he skirted a muddy quagmire that surrounded a ground spring directly in their path. Eliot preferred to wade through it, however, and soon found himself sinking into mud, clear to the tops of his high-laced boots. Longarm said nothing to him as he turned back and helped the man struggle free of the glutinous mud.

There was a clump of willows screening the thicket. As they approached within a few yards of it, Longarm indicated with a brisk nod that Eliot might better skirt the willows on the far side, while Longarm took the side nearest him. Without protest, Eliot moved briskly off at an angle, and was soon out of sight on the far side of the willows.

Longarm half-expected the grizzly to spring up at them from out of the tall meadow grass once they reached the other side of the willows, but the two men rejoined and continued on toward the thicket without incident. Each man had already levered a fresh cartridge into the firing chamber of his Winchester, and as they walked, they presented their weapons toward the thicket. By this time, Longarm could see the trail of matted grass and the occasional footprints left in the marshy ground by the fleeing grizzly.

He had stopped to inspect one particularly clear print, when he heard a sullen growl from the thicket, which was now about twenty feet from them. Standing upright, he was just in time to see the bear, his enormous jaws gaping, his eyes bloodshot with rage, burst from cover and start for them.

Longarm heard Eliot's startled cry. The man fired quickly, too quickly, and a tuft of silver hair and flesh lifted off the bear's head. This only enraged the animal further. He reared now to his full height, and Longarm saw the biggest goddamned grizzly he had ever seen in his life. He had seen his share of them over the years, most of the time from a good distance. There now appeared to be no distance at all between him and this monster. Rearing still higher, to a full eight feet if he stood an inch, he let out a shattering roar. Longarm could see tiny flecks of blood on the bear's snout as a result of Eliot's last shot.

Eliot fired a second time, and this round missed entirely. Longarm sighted quickly, but before he could get off a shot, the bear turned swiftly, came down on his four feet, and charged Eliot. Heavy and cumbersome though he appeared, the animal covered the distance between them with startling swiftness.

Longarm saw Eliot turn and start to run at an angle for the protection of the willows. The bear veered after him. Longarm darted swiftly to his right, then turned and drew a bead on the bear as it lumbered close after the fleeing congressman. His first shot caught the animal in the shoulder and bowled him over. Roaring with rage, the grizzly turned then on Longarm, gathered his feet under him, and charged. Longarm levered swiftly, sighted on one of the enraged eyes, and fired. The bullet clipped away a portion of the beast's face, but it didn't stop him. He levered another cartridge into the chamber and fired, this time from the hip. He was sure he heard the sound of the slug as it pounded into the bear's solid hide, but it appeared to have no effect on the animal at all, apart from increasing his anger.

There was no time now for levering and firing. Longarm dropped his rifle and ran back past the willows. He glanced over his shoulder and saw that the animal had indeed been wounded severely by that last shot of his and, as a result, was slowing down. But it was not giving up.

He passed the willows and saw Jim Travers, a rifle in his hand, galloping across the narrow meadow toward him. And behind him rode the deputy. But they were still some distance away. Where the hell, he wondered furiously, was Peter Eliot, the author of this party?

He glanced back a second time. The grizzly was gaining. He was a fearsome sight, with his teeth and gums and red tongue visible as he snarled after Longarm. A great stain of thick blood had already darkened one side of the animal's face, causing him to look even more frightening. Longarm looked back around again, too late. Before he could stop himself, he found that he was well into the muddy wallow from which he had recently extricated Eliot. He made a desperate, herculean effort to pull himself through the bog, but each step only caused him to sink deeper.

With his last remaining strength, he flung himself around and backward so that he was lying on his back, facing the grizzly's charge. As he did so, he reached across his belly and drew his Colt. The grizzly was having no difficulty at all, it seemed, in wading toward him across the sucking mud. Longarm aimed calmly and fired. His first shot stitched a hole in the bear's chest just below the sternum, and his next round caught the fellow in the neck. A thick gout of blood spurted from the jugular. His third slug smashed into the grizzly's right shoulder.

But still the animal came on!

Out of the corner of his eye, Longarm saw Eliot racing toward him from the willows, brandishing his Winchester high, like a club. The weapon must have jammed! At the same time, Longarm felt the ground throbbing as Jim Travers's horse galloped closer. He had little time to take this in as the shaggy form darkened the sky over Longarm. Before he could fire again, the hoofbeats behind Longarm became a thunder, and a rifle cracked. He saw the side of the bear's skull explode into a gory sunburst of blood and brain and bone. The bear paused then, what was left of his head lowered and swaying. A bright red gout of arterial blood spouted from his mouth. He hung upright a moment, then toppled over.

Longarm managed to pull himself to one side as the bear came to earth. The hot smell of the bear's blood was heavy about him as he pushed himself away from the massive body sprawled in the quagmire beside him. The great silvery coat was matted with blood from his earlier wounds, and flies and gleaming lice were still crawling in among the thick hairs of the pelt. Jim rode into view and swung from his horse, his rifle in hand, and rushed to Longarm's side, the mud sucking loudly at his boots.

Longarm took the old guide's powerful hand and struggled up onto his feet, and then, together, the two men pulled themselves back onto solid ground as Eliot, panting and wild-eyed, raced up also. A moment later, Frank Tyson flung himself from his horse.

"My God, Longarm," the deputy said, looking over at the grizzly's massive hulk and shaking his head, "that's the biggest one I've ever seen."

Longarm smiled. "And it's the biggest one I hope to see." He glanced at the rifle in Jim Travers's hand. It looked like a Sharps buffalo gun. "You used a Sharps, Jim?"

"Yep."

"What were you shooting?"

"A .50 caliber," the man replied, smiling. "Enough to stop a buffalo—and sometimes almost enough to stop a grizzly."

"That's what I needed, all right," Longarm said, shaking his head wearily. "You'd a' thought I was using a willow switch, for all the good it did me."

The old guide grinned and moved carefully out onto the bog beside Eliot to examine the bear. After a moment, he looked back at Longarm. "This critter was already dead, from the looks of it. Trouble is, these fellers don't often let that stop them."

Returning with Congressman Eliot from his inspection of the carcass, the old guide looked at the tall young man. He was no longer as shaken as he had been a moment before, but his face was uncommonly pale. "Well," Travers drawled, "looks like you got yourself a bear rug to put before that fireplace."

"No I haven't," the man said, his voice registering deep disappointment and not a little scorn. "You ruined the head with that size bullet. It's all blown apart. It just disintegrated. Can you imagine how that would look?"

There was a dead silence. Jim Travers looked at the deputy. Then they both looked at Longarm.

Longarm cleared his throat. "Well, now," he said softly to the congressman, "ain't that just too goddamn bad."

Chapter 4

They camped that evening on the banks of a swift mountain stream. It offered icy, clean water filled with leaping trout, and after the meal, it was loud with the slapping of beaver tails. Relaxing around the campfire with the deputy and Jim Travers, Longarm was smoking a cheroot. The guide and Tyson were smoking pipes. The cook had taken advantage of the well-stocked stream and had done himself proud, and Longarm was pleased to be at rest finally. He would sleep apart, he had already decided; but for the moment he was enjoying both men's company.

Neither the deputy nor Travers seemed very anxious to bring up the events of that afternoon, and as Longarm smoked and listened to the two, he found himself quite interested in the conversation. Travers had trapped beaver in this region in the days when beaver hats were the fashion, and he had just pointed out to the deputy that the reason beavers never overpopulated a valley or stream was because the mothers practiced infanticide. Tyson tipped his head, a slight frown on his face.

"You say it's the mother that kills the kittens? How do you know it isn't the father? That's what I heard."

Jim scratched his thick beard and nodded. "Yep, that's what most people think, who don't know no better. But I had plenty of long summers up here with nothing much to do but watch. The female brings forth her young in April, and births from two to six offspring, but she only raises two of them, a male and a female. There ain't much discussion about that."

"No there isn't," admitted Frank. "But I can't see a dam killing her own young. It just doesn't seem natural."

"What's natural, mister?"

Tyson shrugged. "You know what I mean, Jim."

The old man took his pipe from his mouth and spat into the fire. "I know what you mean. If it's natural, it's got to be good." He chuckled and shook his head. "Well, shit is natural, and it *stinks*."

Both Longarm and Frank laughed at that, and the old man resumed his explanation of why he thought the dam killed her young and not the father. "First off," he began, "the male is seldom found around the lodge for ten or fifteen days after the female brings forth her litter. Second, there's always a male and a female saved alive. Third, I have seen the dead kittens floating in the ponds freshly killed, and at the same time, I've caught the male where he was living, more than a half-mile from the lodge."

He leaned back after that, puffing quietly on his pipe, and looked at Tyson, waiting for a rejoinder. But there was none. The man frowned thoughtfully and gazed into the fire. "Guess you're right," he said. "Seems strange, though."

"No, sir, it don't seem all that strange, oncet you get to thinking about it."

"Why not, Jim?" Longarm inquired.

"Why, hell, it's always the female who's got the gumption. She's always the deadlier of the species. Ain't you never heard that? If the male killed the young, you think he'd be bright enough to always be sure to leave a male and a female?" He chuckled and looked closely at Frank. "I'm surprised your Crow wife never told you about the beaver."

Tyson flinched at mention of his wife so abruptly.

But he only said, "We never did get to talk about beaver, and that's a fact."

"You say she was your wife. I heard the Crow don't let their women marry and leave the tribe."

"I lived with the Crows."

"A squaw man, hey?"

"They were decent, clean. I liked them a damn sight better than some whites I've lived with."

"I can feature that," the old man said, taking no offense at Frank's tone. "I lived with a Shoshone girl once for purty near two years. But that was a long time ago. They come on hard times since. Their principal chief died suddenly one winter, and the following year, his brother went too. They were good chiefs, and the tribe never did amount to much after that. They just scattered, with no chief left who could control them." He spat into the fire. "They sure went downhill fast."

Just then, Longarm looked up to see Charles Clinton and his wife approaching, with Melinda's robust maid following just behind. Longarm and the two men got to their feet at the approach of the women. Clinton nodded courteously to Jim and the deputy, then looked at Longarm.

"I'm sorry to disturb you, Longarm," Clinton said, "but my wife and I wanted to thank you once again for what you did this afternoon." He stuck out his hand, and Longarm shook it. But before Longarm could say anything, the man continued, "We also came over here to warn you."

His wife giggled.

"Stop it, Melly," Clinton said, without anger. "This is serious."

"I think it's priceless." Melly glanced at her maid. "Don't you think so, Cindy Lou?"

Cindy Lou nodded. She wore her dark hair loose. It was quite full and beautiful. Turning her sharp eyes on Longarm, she said, "The men are placing bets already."

"What's this all about?" Longarm asked, getting a bit impatient.

"It's Peter Eliot," said Clinton. "He's worked himself into a lather about this afternoon. He's convinced you mean to bully him from now on, and he's determined to settle matters here and now, before we get any farther."

"Settle matters?" Longarm was not sure he was hearing right.

Melly stepped closer to Longarm. "You see, Mr. Long, Peter Eliot's feelings are hurt, as I understand it. He thinks you spoke sharply to him earlier this afternoon, too sharply. You don't have the proper respect for a congressman."

"Well, now, he's not so far off, at that," Longarm drawled. "I would say his foolhardy, headstrong actions this afternoon endangered you, Mrs. Clinton—and added a few gray hairs to my own head in the bargain. I was meaning to have a word with him about that before we set out again tomorrow. Seems to me I remember Jim telling all of us, before we left this morning, that he didn't want anyone shooting at game while we were on the trail." Longarm glanced at Jim. "That right, Jim?"

The old man allowed himself a quiet chuckle. "I was thinkin' of remindin' them all of that again tomorrow. Figured maybe it might set better after this afternoon."

Longarm looked back at Clinton. "What does Peter Eliot have in mind? A duel?"

"Something like that."

"He wants to fight you. Now. With bare knuckles," Melly said, stepping back slightly, her voice suddenly hushed.

"And this is what they are betting on?"

Melly nodded solemnly. Cindy Lou was watching Longarm with big, dark eyes. Measuring him, Longarm was certain.

"And who will be in his corner?"

"Laxalte," Clinton replied quickly.

Longarm nodded. That was no surprise to him.

"Longarm," Clinton said quickly, "let me be in your corner. I would deem it an honor."

"You can be in his corner," said Frank Tyson, "but you ain't keeping Jim and me out of this. We're in Longarm's corner too."

"This is all plumb silly, the way I look at it," said Longarm. "I didn't think grown men still played these here games. Especially grown men who run the country."

"Will you meet his challenge?" Clinton asked.

"Bare knuckles, huh? He's about my age, and he's only an inch or so shorter than I am." Longarm shrugged. "If it don't take too long," he said, chuckling. "But if there's no hurry, I want to finish this cheroot."

Laughing softly and shaking his head at this arrant nonsense, Longarm sat back down in front of the campfire. Clinton and the two women turned quickly around and hurried across the camp to tell the others.

Jim looked down at Longarm. "You teach that fool newlywed a lesson now, might make it some easier on us the rest of this trip."

"Yep," replied Longarm. "That would do it, all right. Unless, of course, I happen to get beat!" He stuck the cheroot back into his mouth and inhaled deeply. As he exhaled, he began to chuckle again.

There was still plenty of light in the sky when Longarm, bare to the waist, stepped into the large circle Laxalte had scratched out on the ground. The men were outside the circle, but still crowding close upon it, while the women were a discreet distance away, but craning their necks eagerly, all the same.

Peter Eliot was also naked from the waist up, revealing an astonishingly well-developed physique. His shoulders were impressively wide, his pectorals robust. Muscles, like mole tunnels, rippled on his upper torso. As he stood before Longarm, his fists held comically high, he could not help glancing over at his young wife to see what impression his heroics were having on her.

Longarm had known a few club fighters in Denver. Their advice, he knew, would be for him to wrestle anybody lighter than he was, and box and outdistance anyone heavier. The trouble was, Clinton had already gone over the rules of this bout with him, and wrestling was not allowed.

"Here," said Clinton, "let me take that cheroot."

Longarm let him have it, then turned back to Peter Eliot. The handsome congressman moved toward him, his knuckles still held high, his back arched. Then, his fists performing a sudden milling movement, he closed on Longarm. Longarm danced back, suddenly feeling altogether ridiculous, just as Eliot took a vicious swipe at him. He missed, and Longarm smiled.

This infuriated the man. He faced him a second time and advanced resolutely, his fists now milling much slower, his head tucked down between his shoulders. Longarm heard one of the women laugh softly, delightedly. For some reason this irritated Longarm. He stopped backing up suddenly, and took Eliot's quick, hammering punches on his forearms and elbows, then managed to break past Eliot's guard to land a clumsy blow on the fellow's cheek.

It rocked him back slightly, but did little more than hurt his feelings. Longarm took a deep breath. It was almost impossible for him to take all this seriously. And then, suddenly, Eliot was upon him, pummeling him furiously with a lightning series of punches that caught him with stinging effectiveness about the head and shoulders. Longarm found himself losing his temper slightly, waded in closer, and swung a roundhouse right at Peter Eliot's weaving head. He missed and swore and caught a punch on the tip of his chin that sent him reeling backward, his eyes tearing from the force of the blow. He caught himself before he fell, and spread his legs wide to steady himself. Then he shook his head like a bull that has just been clubbed.

Dimly he heard the cheers of Laxalte and a few others lined up on the other side of the ring. There was no sound behind Longarm, from his side. Focusing his eyes as best he could, he straightened to meet Peter Eliot's next charge. It came hot and heavy; the man was confident now that he had Longarm in a bad way.

Longarm blocked most of the punches with his forearms, perfectly willing to wait out this fellow. He saw the look of pain that crossed the man's face occasionally as his bare fists caught Longarm's rock-solid arms and sharp elbows. After an enthusiastic flurry that netted him very little of consequence, he let up some and began to backpedal. Now Longarm followed him. Eliot probed at him tentatively.

At once, Longarm struck out. Knocking the man's weary guard down with an impatient swipe of his left hand, he rocketed in and plowed the man's face with a sledging right that came from as far back as he could reach. The sound of his bare knuckles striking the side of Eliot's jaw was loud in the sudden silence. Eliot spun completely around and then went down on his face. Longarm stepped back and watched as the fellow pushed himself slowly up off the ground, turned to blink up at him, and then got unsteadily to his feet.

The man shook his head blearily.

"You finished with this foolishness, Eliot?" Longarm inquired coldly.

The man shook his head doggedly. But even as he did so, his young wife's voice cried out, "Please, Peter! Stop it!"

But this cry only emboldened the man. His face red with indignation, he moved in swiftly, his punches coming with amazing speed, all of them landing with some effectiveness. Longarm saw what the man was doing, and began to jab and retreat carefully. He blocked an uppercut and managed to brush another aside, then lunged straight in to plant another right, this time catching Eliot on the side of the nose.

Eliot shook off its effects and continued to bear down on him, his nose now suddenly dripping blood down his handsome chest. Longarm blocked a punch that drove his arms back, then blocked another, after which he lashed out with his right again. This time he missed, and took a blow to the ribs that drove him back with a sudden gasp. His knees were weak, he realized in astonishment as he blocked another furious flurry from the aroused Eliot.

Circling backward before Eliot's relentless charge, Longarm waited for his legs to become steadier. He was no longer concerned with how foolish all this was. His only objective now was to end this thing as quickly and decisively as possible, his resolve hardening with each cheer he heard from the howling spectators. At last, with the ache in his chest fading and his legs solid under him once more, he pulled up suddenly and let his guard drop slightly.

With a grim smile, Eliot drove in. Longarm caught the first punch on his shoulder as he ducked low. Eliot's other blow glanced off the side of his head, but by this time, the man was in close and wide open. With all his hard-muscled weight, Longarm drove a punch to Eliot's chest, just under the man's heart. His guard came down with a grunt. Longarm waited just that split-second he needed to brace himself, and then looped a sledging right to the jaw, his follow-through pulling him so far around that his back was to Eliot as the congressman flew backward.

Turning around, Longarm saw Eliot sprawled on his back. The man groaned and rolled over on his side as if to get up, then rolled back and lay there breathing quietly.

Longarm strode from the ring, took his cheroot from Clinton, stuck it angrily into his mouth, and continued without a backward glance across the campsite to the spot where he had left his gear.

As dusk fell, Longarm, still anxious to keep himself apart from the rest of the party with Sammy Wentworth on the loose, was lugging his bedroll out of camp when Clinton overtook him.

"What is it, Clinton?" Longarm asked wearily, as the dark-haired fellow smiled apologetically at him.

"It's Peter Eliot. He wants to see you in his tent."

"He knows where I am."

"He's still a little groggy—and maybe a little more sensible too. I didn't want to ask you. I guess I know how you feel about that business, but Melly said she was sure you would come."

"She did, did she?" Longarm retorted with a smile.

The big man smiled back at Longarm. "Yes, Longarm, she did."

Longarm sighed. "Which tent is his?"

"The new one—at the end there."

As Clinton took out his meerschaum and began packing it from a pouch he took from the pocket of his hunting jacket, he joined Longarm in his trek across the campsite. "I suppose you think that fight was foolish," he said, sticking the pipe into his mouth.

Longarm glanced at the man. "I was a fool to take him up on his dare. I guess the reason was that I thought it might knock some sense into the man's head. But it was a fool thing to try to do it that way. Out here, Clinton, when a man fights, it is for his life, usually. It is not a game or a sport. I guess you might say we ain't that civilized. And after listening to those people cheering the two of us on, I'm glad we ain't."

Clinton paused a moment to light his pipe. Longarm stopped with him, and watched as the man cupped the flame over the pipe bowl. When the two resumed their walk, Clinton nodded emphatically. "I see your point, Longarm. This *is* a wild country, at that. As you know, perhaps, I am against this park business. This land must be developed, tamed. There are resources here that should be tapped by private interests for the good of all. There is no sense in romanticizing about this wilderness. It is a *wilderness*. Untamed. Savage. Useless, as it stands. Just as you turned from the savagery of that fight and those urging it on, we must turn from the savagery of this place and civilize it. Do you see my point, Longarm?"

"You don't think this land should be set aside for everyone?"

"I think it should be used, developed, for the *good* of everyone."

"I see. Well, we ain't reached the park yet. Maybe once you see it, you'll think different. Tell me, why did you bring your wife along, Clinton? This is rugged country, and your wife seems a mite frail."

The man nodded. "Yes. Melly is a very frail woman. But do not measure her spirit by the appearance of her body. She astounds me—and humbles me, Longarm. She insisted on coming. I could not prevail against her in this."

"She wanted to see the park."

"Yes. She'd heard about it, read about it. Hot springs seeping from the ground, leaping geysers. Some have even claimed to achieve cures by immersing themselves in the hot mineral springs that bubble to the surface. She heard all this, of course, and could not be dissuaded."

They were outside Peter Eliot's tent by this time. As the two men came to a stop, Melly stepped from the tent and smiled at Longarm. She brushed a wisp of blonde hair off her pale forehead. There were deep rings under her dark, luminous eyes. "I knew you'd come, Mr. Long."

"Call me Longarm, Melly," he told her gently.

She smiled, and in that instant, her fatigue seemed to lift miraculously. Longarm, too, was suddenly humbled by the strength of this woman's spirit. "I don't think Peter's jaw is broken, Longarm. We were afraid of that for a while. But he does want to talk to you."

"If you two will watch my bedroll, I'll go in."

"Let me have it," said Clinton.

Longarm handed it to the man, lifted the tent flap, and stepped into Peter Eliot's tent. His wife was sitting in one of the two camp chairs by Eliot's cot. He was lying on his back, his head and shoulders propped up. His nose was enlarged and red, the side of his face swollen, as if he were having trouble with a molar. The man smiled slightly, painfully, at Longarm's appearance, and raised his right hand in greeting.

Mary got up from her chair and looked almost shyly up at Longarm. He was surprised to find no hostility in her dark eyes. With a strong, wiry hand, she brushed back her thick auburn hair. "I'll leave you two, then," she said to Longarm. Glancing back at her husband, she told him she would be just outside, and left the tent.

Longarm sat down in the camp chair, feeling distinctly uncomfortable. A leather chest stood at the foot of the cot, with a coverlet over it. There was a field desk on the other side of the cot, standing on crossed legs, with a bottle of whiskey and two shotglasses sitting on top of it.

"Would you like a drink, Mr. Long?"

"Wouldn't mind."

Peter sat up straighter on the cot, reached over for the two glasses and the bottle, and handed Longarm one of the shotglasses. Longarm held it while the man poured. After they had tossed down their drinks, Eliot leaned back once more upon his pillows and looked with some nervousness at Longarm. "I suppose you wonder why I wanted to see you."

"Guess I did."

"I want to apologize, Mr. Long."

"For what? The fight? It was a fair fight, Mr. Eliot."

"Could you call me Peter?"

"Sure."

"I am apologizing, Mr. Long, for this afternoon as well. I almost got us killed, not to mention what could have happened to Melly Clinton if you hadn't taken her off that skittish horse when you did. I guess I am also responsible for the fact that the animal had to be shot."

Longarm nodded. Clinton and Laxalte had found the horse lying on its side, with its foreleg snapped, its neck and head wedged in between two boulders. It looked, according to Clinton, as if the deranged animal had tried to climb a sheer wall of rock in its panic. "I guess you might be, at that."

"I acted like a fool."

"Yes."

"And I tried to hide that fact from myself by challenging you to a fight. I think I felt that if I could thrash you good and proper, I would prove to myself that your anger was unjustified."

"Not very clear thinking," Longarm observed, smiling for the first time.

"No it wasn't," said Peter, smiling in return.

Longarm reached his hand out. Peter shook it warmly. "I accept your apology, Peter," Longarm said, getting to his feet.

"Fine!" the man said. "Shall we seal it with another drink?"

Longarm smiled. "That was plenty. You get some sleep now. We'll be on our way again, bright and early tomorrow morning."

"Yes. I'll . . . I'll do that. Would you send Mary back in?"

Longarm said he would and ducked out of the tent. Mary Eliot was standing with her maid off to one side, talking softly with her. Clinton beamed when he saw Longarm emerge and handed him his bedroll. Longarm thanked him, and as Clinton and his wife hurried through the gathering gloom toward their tent, Longarm walked over to Mary Eliot.

"Peter would like to see you now," he told her. Before she moved past him, he took her arm gently. "I think it's going to be all right, Mrs. Eliot. I don't think there'll be any more fisticuffs."

She blushed, her eyes flashing up at him. "Thank you for coming to see him. I'm sure you're right, Mr. Long. No more fisticuffs." She smiled then and hurried off to her husband.

Daisy Foster cleared her throat. Longarm looked down at her and smiled. "Good night, Miss Foster."

"Don't you want to be seen talking to a lady's maid, Mr. Long?"

"It ain't that. I'm tired."

"And so is Peter." She tipped her head as if she were sizing him up. "Would you consent to walk me to my tent, Mr. Long? It is getting quite dark, and I don't want to step on a snake."

"Of course."

As they walked the short distance, the continuous slapping of the beavers' tails on the water sounded like a dim fusillade. There were other sounds as well. Nighthawks and owls were moving in the trees, and coyotes were yapping off to the north, on a peak somewhere. Occasionally the sound of a heavy body moving through the pines would come to them. At one such instance, Daisy moved closer to Longarm.

"I never knew the nights could be so noisy out here," Daisy said. "The woods and the stream are filled with animals."

Longarm just nodded. A moment later they stopped in front of Daisy's small tent. "Thank you, Mr. Long," she said. "That was a pleasant walk." She looked at her tent and sighed. "Sleeping on the ground can be very hard on a person," she said. "I am not used to it."

"I am," Longarm said, shifting the bedroll to his other shoulder. "Once you get used to it, you'll like it fine."

"Well, that may be true, Mr. Long," she said, smiling impishly, darkening the dimple in her chin, "but there's one thing I'll never get used to."

"And what's that, Miss Foster?"

"Sleeping alone."

Longarm's eyebrows rose a notch.

"I'm a widow, Mr. Long. My husband of only one short year died in a steel mill accident."

"I'm sorry to hear that, Miss Foster."

She sighed. "There's nothing to be done about it, of course. But it does seem like such a waste—a fine young man like that. Reminded me some of Mr. Eliot, he did. All them fine muscles, and so full of vim and vinegar. Too bad he hasn't learned yet to please his wife the way my man could."

"Why are you telling me this, Miss Foster?"

"Because I'm impertinent, that's why." She smiled up at him. She was a blue-eyed heller, and that was for sure. "And besides that," she went on, "I think that's why the young man back there is so anxious to show off before his young wife. He can't show off in bed too well, so he has to do it some other way."

Longarm remembered the bottle of whiskey on the field desk beside Peter's cot. If the young congressman took too much of that firewater, there was no wonder he was disappointing his young wife.

"Maybe," said Longarm, "you'd be a big help to your mistress if you suggested to her that she keep the booze away from her new husband for a while."

"Yes," she said, smiling brilliantly. "I thought so myself. But I didn't want to say anything."

"That I do not believe," Longarm said, settling the

bedroll to a more comfortable position on his shoulder. "Now, if you'll excuse me, I'm going to look for a nice spot for the night. As I said before, I'm tired."

"Then why go traipsing off in the darkness when you are perfectly welcome right here?"

He smiled, then bent and kissed Daisy gently on her lips. "Thank you for the invitation, Daisy. But I have a reason for sleeping off by myself. It's right complicated, and I wish I had time to explain it to you, but I don't."

She had blushed when he kissed her. Now she smiled softly up at him. "That's all right, Mr. Long. You don't have to explain. Good night."

"Good night, Miss Foster."

Longarm turned and trudged off, heading upstream, looking for a secluded clearing, one that would be within sight of the main camp's night fire.

The snap of a twig awakened him. He closed his hand more tightly about the grips of his Colt and looked down the slope at the smoldering campfire he had lit before going to sleep. A dark figure was slowly approaching the blanket-covered dummy figure he had left by the fire. Flipping back his soogan's flap, he sat up and drew his Colt.

Something about the figure troubled him. He watched a moment longer before he slipped out of the soogan and catfooted it down the slope. The figure bending over his dummy uttered a tiny, startled cry, then drew back.

Longarm stopped short and took a deep breath. "What in tarnation you doing here, Daisy?" he demanded.

Daisy Foster spun about. "Oh my goodness!" she whispered. "What a fright! When I touched what I thought was you . . . ! It was like a nightmare . . ."

Longarm looked down at the maid. "I thought I told you I was tired."

She moved close to him and rested her head gently

on his chest. "I thought I told you," she replied softly, "that I would never get used to sleeping alone."

Longarm chuckled. "That you did."

"Why are you up there, away from the fire? It's chilly enough at night."

"I have reasons, like I said before."

"You like to be cold when you're sleeping?"

"I didn't say that."

"Then let me warm you."

Longarm looked down at the buxom little blonde. The dimple in her chin was looking more delightful by the minute. Perhaps, he thought, the moon was having its effect on him. And he should not forget why he was sleeping out here alone like this, away from the main camp—or why he had constructed that dummy figure and left it by the fire. Now was no time to drop his guard.

But she was still leaning her eager body against his, and even as he pondered his dilemma, he felt her pleasing warmth filling him. He was dressed only in his longjohns, and as she waited for his response to her suggestion, she wrapped her arms more tightly about his waist.

"We'll have to be discreet, Daisy. We don't want anybody to suspicion that—"

"I won't tell anyone. I promise. This will be our secret."

"It's only an ordinary-sized soogan."

"Stop protesting," she said, releasing him and taking his hand. "The smaller it is, the cozier."

Longarm shrugged and let her lead him back up the rise to his bedroll. "I'll get in first," he told her. Once he was comfortable, he held the soogan's flap open for her and was astonished at the speed with which she peeled out of her long dress. She had come prepared—that is, with nothing under the dress but herself.

"You're still wearing your underwear," she giggled,

as Longarm threw the soogan's flap over her and she cuddled close to him.

"You'll catch your death of cold," he chided her.

"Then warm me, Mr. Long."

"My friends call me Longarm."

"I'll call you something else, if you don't get busy."

With that, she slid on top of him, kissing him with a piercing urgency—her full, warm lips prying his apart, then playing with them with a maddening wantonness. His desire came alive suddenly, achingly. He swung her over and then pulled her swiftly in under him. He felt her silken loins under his, and the awesome, hungry parting of her legs to ease his entry. He thrust deep into the snug warmth of her, a fiery bolt riveting them flesh to flesh.

He heard her pleased grunt. "Later we will play," she told him urgently, scissoring her legs shut on his erection. "But now, just *go,* my love! *Go!*"

Longarm was on his knees astride her by this time, and needed no more urging. She was as tight as a fist, and met his every thrust with one of her own. Longarm felt himself mounting to a climax with breathtaking speed. He tried to hold off, but her bucking thrusts upward would not allow him, and then he was beyond the point where any control was possible. He heard her laughing then. She flung her arms about his neck, and a moment later he was exploding within her, his face buried in her thick blonde hair.

When finally the driving, emptying spasms died and he slid off her ample warmth, she leaned over and took a nip out of his right ear and said, "Now we can play." Suiting actions to words, she climbed on top of him and began fondling him with fingers that knew no boundaries and had a red-hot life of their own. Her lips, too, seemed made of fire as she swept her mouth across his chest and down across his stomach . . .

She was astride his new erection, triumphant, her back arched, when he saw Daisy's head stop its delirious tossing. She was staring down the slope at the campfire Longarm had lit.

"Oh my God!" she moaned. "Who is *that*?"

Longarm glanced down the slope—and immediately reached back under the blanket for his Colt. Someone —and it looked like Sammy Wentworth's scrawny figure —was standing over the dummy that Longarm had fashioned, his rifle raised like a club. Even as Longarm rolled out of the soogan and flung himself on bare feet down the slope, he heard Wentworth's hearty grunt as he brought his rifle's stock down on what he thought was the lawman's head.

And then, like Daisy earlier, the little man saw his mistake. At the same time, he heard Longarm's bare feet slipping through the grass toward him. Sammy spun. In the moonlight, he could see well enough to bring up his rifle. But Longarm was close enough by that time to throw himself through the air. He struck Sammy in the midsection, his head and shoulder cutting the man in half. With a startled cry, Sammy crumpled backward, the rifle flying up and out of his hand.

And then they were in the fire's embers, Longarm on top, Wentworth on the bottom. The man screamed, thrashed wildly, and flung himself away from Longarm. Longarm stepped through the coals and found himself running across the uneven meadow with a noticeable limp. He had burnt the soles of his feet. Wentworth disappeared into a dark clump of aspen. Longarm pulled up at the edge of the timber and listened. He could hear the man crashing frantically through the brush.

He started doggedly into the trees, then heard the sound of a horse's hooves pounding off into the night. Longarm swore softly and turned back to the campfire, limping now on painfully blistered feet. He found Wentworth's rifle and lugged it up the slope to where he had left Daisy Foster.

She was gone. He stood in the wet grass, letting it

soothe his feet, and smiled. Daisy was no fool. She knew that discretion was the better part of valor. And there would be—Longarm confidently expected—other nights for them to play.

Chapter 5

Three days later, well into the Absarokas, Longarm came upon tracks he had little difficulty in reading. They had been left by Sammy Wentworth's horse. Longarm had studied the tracks left by Wentworth the morning after their last meeting and knew them pretty well by now, since he had come across them twice in the past three days. Dismounting by the narrow stream, he went down on one knee and studied the hoofprints. As he had noticed the day before, the animal was favoring his right front leg and was close to being lame. But Sammy Wentworth was obviously paying little attention to such details.

Longarm mounted up, followed the tracks across the stream, and kept after them until he came to the remains of a camp. It was a sloppy affair, with tin cans lying about, the fire not properly doused, a bowel movement close to where the man had slept, and the camp itself in a poor location. If it had rained during the night, he would have drowned like a rat.

An hour or so later, Longarm lost Wentworth's sign in a rockstrewn gully that opened onto a stream. He searched both banks of the stream for close to a mile in either direction, then gave it up as a bad job and decided to ride back to meet the party. On his way, he cut through an impressive canyon.

It was a spectacular sight. So clean was the cleft and so steep its sides, that it looked to Longarm as if some gigantic Bunyan had sliced the gorge out of the mountain wall with an axe. The stream that cut through it, bare of timber on its banks, he found to be a beautiful mountain torrent of clear, sparkling water. Longarm had heard about this stream. It was called Stinking River, and the canyon was the Stinking River Canyon. Farther upstream, as he understood it, there was a small geyser that impregnated the water and the air about it with sulphurated hydrogen. Now, as Longarm rode into the canyon, he looked up at the towering rock walls looming above him and saw that they were composed of a beautiful granite veined with blue and rust and capped with limestone.

Longarm kept going, wondering if perhaps he should suggest that the party detour through this canyon. The sulphurous-smelling, swift, clear stream, the spectacular gorge with its towering marbled sides, were things these Easterners should see. Maybe then they would understand, as Longarm himself was beginning to, why some folks would want to set aside portions of this wilderness as a park.

Farther on, Longarm came upon two prospectors who had pitched their tent for the day near the water's edge. They were a strange pair. Neither of them seemed dressed for the adventure. They were wearing well-tailored trousers, and their shirts seemed to be of uncommonly fine quality. Neither man wore a collar, and both had their sleeves neatly rolled up past their pale elbows. One wore gold spectacles and peered up at Longarm with interest as he rode closer.

To preserve the amenities, Longarm dismounted when he got close enough, shook both men by the hand, and introduced himself. Each hand, he noted, was still surprisingly soft. They were both of average height, with flabby midsections and sloping shoulders, and looked to be in their late forties. One of them had an impressive thatch of sidewhiskers, which he now stroked casually as he regarded Longarm with his large, innocent, watery blue eyes.

They seemed to be grateful to be done for the moment with their panning.

"Any luck?" Longarm inquired amiably.

The fellow with the spectacles shook his head sagely. "No, sir, Marshal. And I did not really expect any—not in this region. It is useless to look for gold near a limestone ledge, or where there is a limestone cap. I consented to stop, however, to satisfy the curiosity of my partner Bob, here."

Bob was the fellow with the sidewhiskers. He shrugged good-naturedly. "Guess we'll keep going upstream," he said with an almost shy grin.

"Marshal, could you explain to us why there is this disagreeable odor in the air about this place?"

Longarm smiled and explained about the geyser farther on. This seemed to satisfy the two men, and Longarm mounted up. With a wave at the two greenhorns, he rode on up the canyon past them. He could not help but shake his head at the innocence of the two men. They were as fit for this wilderness as two hens would be at a fox party. He did not have the heart to contradict the professor with the spectacles, but Longarm himself had seen much gold mined from limestone in Nevada. Indeed, the vein had been unusually rich, not only in gold, but in copper as well.

Leaving the canyon at last, Longarm skirted the large, marshy, highland meadow from which the Stinking River issued. The sulphurous fumes were quite strong in the air. He was not yet at Colter's Hell, he realized, but he saw now why Colter's description of the hot springs and geysers had gained them that appellation. Fire and brimstone seemed to be lurking just beneath the surface. Longarm found himself looking forward to the park.

Breaking out of timber at the foot of a slope not long afterwards, Longarm surprised a small herd of buffalo bulls. There was not a cow in sight, and the menacing wall of humped forms seemed inordinately interested in Longarm's sudden appearance from the timber. As Longarm pulled up, the bulls formed a line in front of him, effectively barring his progress. Their leader, an impressive, shaggy creature with a truly formidable hump, moved slowly toward him, green tendrils of grass and saliva dripping from his now-still jaws. His small ears flicked nervously.

Longarm was in no mood for this sort of thing. He yanked his Winchester out of its scabbard, levered swiftly, and fired two quick shots into the air. The bulls hesitated in confusion. The lead bull lowered his massive head and seemed about to charge. Again Longarm fired, this time over the back of the buffalo, the bullet whining close to the big fellow.

With a surprisingly graceful dip and turn, the massive creature swung around and led the herd in a great, sweeping trot across the meadow. The ground shook under their passage, and a moment later they had disappeared into a broad gully. Longarm slipped the rifle back into its scabbard and urged his horse on across the meadow.

He was close upon a stream not long after, and he could see the white squares of tents blossoming on the far side about a mile farther on. He found a place to ford the stream and rode on down the bank, coming first to Tim, who was busy setting up a rope corral for the horses. The boy greeted him civilly as Longarm continued on past him. Amos had already set up the cook tent, and Longarm found Tyson and Travers helping start the campfire. The camp was a bustle of activity, most of it purposeful. The members of the congressional party were beginning to get the hang of it, Longarm noted.

No longer were packsaddles thrown carelessly down under trees, or blankets piled up, all in a mess, halters and packropes all tangled together. The camp was neat, the tents a discreet distance from each other. While he dismounted to unsaddle his horse, he savored the delicious smell of boiling stew coming from the cook tent.

As Longarm lifted the saddle from his gelding's steaming back, the deputy stopped beside him and inquired if he had had much luck. Longarm had told both men earlier of the event that had confirmed his fears concerning Wentworth, though he had been careful to say nothing of the activity that confirmation had disrupted.

"Lost his tracks northeast of here, this side of Stinking River Canyon. He's out there still, all right," Longarm commented, removing his horse's saddle blanket and feeling for any sores on the claybank's back.

He found none and stood back as Tim came over to take the horse.

The two men walked over to the fire and squatted beside it. Travers joined them and looked sideways at Longarm. "We're gettin' high now. It showered some this afternoon. We can expect more of that from now on. Trouble is, these dudes get all anxious and start runnin' around like chickens with their heads chopped off. I told them to keep ridin', that the dry air up here would dry them out, but they insisted on dismounting and huddlin' around a campfire."

"Better talk to them tomorrow morning before we set out," Longarm told the old guide. "I'll do it, if you want. They start doing that every time they get wet, we'll never reach the park. Besides, they're liable to catch a chill—or something worse—if they keep on acting like that."

Travers nodded at that, obviously pleased that Longarm thought it important enough for him to speak to the congressmen the next morning.

"How's Clinton's wife Melly?" Longarm asked. "I worry some about her. She's as frail as a spring flower."

"She's doin' all right," Travers said grudgingly, "even seems to be fillin' out some. She sure packs a lot away at mealtimes." He looked away from Longarm then, and stared into the fire. "I like her. I'll keep an eye out."

That pleased Longarm and he took out a cheroot. Perhaps he would stay a bit closer to the party tomorrow, at least within sight. They were better than halfway to the park and he was satisfied with the progress they had made so far, but this expedition's success depended, for the most part, on him.

"Any sound of mutiny?" Longarm asked the deputy, half-jokingly, "I mean while they were huddling around that fire to dry off?"

Frank nodded slightly, a dim smile lighting his lean, cynical face. "Just a little. Some of these congressmen don't think much of turning Colter's Hell into a park. And the tougher the going gets, the less they are going to like it, I'm thinking."

"I suspicion the deputy's right," said Jim. "If those men don't give out soon, their women will."

"I don't think so," Longarm mused. "In some ways, I think the women are tougher. Remember what you said the other night, Jim? The female is the one with the gumption, the deadlier of the species."

"Yep, I said that. And I meant it. But I don't see how women all wrapped up the way they is can do anything *but* complain."

"Well, I think we can count on Peter Eliot to keep on. He seems to have straightened out pretty well since that business with the grizzly."

"Yeah. You seen to that nice and proper." Jim spat emphatically into the fire.

Longarm stood up and looked beyond the fire toward the campsite. The guide had chosen a fine, high spot on the shore of the river, and from where he stood, he could see a broad, lush savanna reaching back from the river to a woodland of aspen and pine. It was a nice spot. This was beautiful country.

But there were serpents in the garden. Longarm wondered if he should mention the ticks. They were getting high enough now, and it would be better if they knew how to deal with them *before* they found them crawling on their clothing or bodies, rather than after. And it wasn't just the ticks he was worried about; it was the fever.

He was about to mention it to Frank when he heard the scream. It sounded like Jean McPhee, Laxalte's secretary. And then he saw the tall woman, her long, ruddy hair streaming luxuriantly out behind her as she raced across the grass toward her tent. She was wearing only a chemise. From the look of her, she had been bathing in the river upstream.

"Now, what in tarnation's wrong with that woman?" Jim drawled, getting to his feet.

The answer came the next instant. An Indian in full regalia, astride a magnificent paint, crested the ridge bordering the stream's bank and rode after the hysterical woman. Enjoying himself hugely, the Indian overtook Jean and then circled her as she ran, displaying superb horsemanship as he did so.

The Indian was just playing with this screaming woman, but it was obvious that Jean had no idea this was all in good, clean fun. By this time Longarm was racing across the ground toward Jean, with the deputy and Jim Travers right beside him. All Longarm could think of were those trigger-happy congressmen, each one of them more than willing to make an aborigine pay for molesting a white woman—and pay dearly.

Jean's screams were heartrending by this time. She had collapsed on the grass, and was hugging herself in terror as the foolish Indian pulled his pony to a halt, laughing. Longarm glanced to his right and saw what he most feared: the congressmen pouring from their tents, armed to the teeth.

"Oh Jesus," Tyson said softly, as he too saw the irate congressmen boiling across the meadow toward the spot where the Indian had brought the poor, sobbing Jean McPhee to bay.

Since the others were closer to Jean and the Indian, there was no doubt that they would reach them first. Longarm called out to them not to do anything rash, to put down their weapons, but his words had about as much influence as a fart in a windstorm. Paul Laxalte was in the lead, with Big Jim McAllister and David Baxter right behind.

Longarm shouted again as he saw Laxalte reach up and fling the savage from his horse. The Indian appeared stunned, but only for a moment. Then he was on his feet like a brightly painted bolt of lightning, and before Big Jim or Baxter could stop him, he had flung Laxalte to the ground. It was Big Jim who hauled the Indian off Laxalte, with Baxter coming between the two combatants as Laxalte jumped furiously to his feet. Luckily, the man had dropped his rifle earlier when he had reached up to pull the Indian from his horse.

He was scrambling for the weapon when Longarm reached it before him and snatched it away from the furious congressman. When the Indian saw this, he stopped struggling with the puffing Jim McAllister, threw his powerful shoulders back, and looked about him with proud insolence.

David Baxter, watching wide-eyed just behind Laxalte, said, "Goddamnit! I thought the army had collared all these damn Sioux!"

"He's not a Sioux," Longarm informed him. "He's a Crow."

As if to emphasize that point, the Indian grunted angrily, then fixed Longarm with a piercing stare. "And I speak English good!" he said. "I not hurt white squaw! She in deep water. Go down twice! I pull her out, and then she run like foolish chicken!"

Before Longarm could turn to the still-shuddering Jean McPhee, who was looking up at all this from the ground, he saw the rest of the Crow party topping the same ridge over which Jean and the Indian had come a moment before. A very impressive, colorful sight it was.

Their horses—nearly every man had an extra pony—were little beauties, and neighed shrilly as they pulled to a sudden halt on the crest. The halt was for only an instant, however, as they charged into the camp. In a moment, still astride their ponies, they began to encircle Longarm and the rest of the party, their faces impassive. But there was a light in their eyes that Longarm recognized at once. They were playing a game. They knew what manner of greenhorns they were dealing with. This was probably not the first band of tourists they had come across.

Each man wore a gaily colored mantle, handsome leggings, eagle feathers, and elaborately worked moccasins. In addition to their carbines and spears, they carried bows and arrows. Their hair was long, but gracefully tied up and gorgeously plumed. Many of them wore it in long braids, wrapped in what looked to Longarm like strips of otter skin. Most of the braids hung on either side of the head as far as the waist. Their hair was stiffened by white clay, giving it an upward curve over the forehead. Around their necks were hung brass ornaments and pink shells. They were, as Longarm knew and as this instance proved, the dandies of the Rocky Mountains.

Abruptly, one of the Indians flung himself from his pony and advanced on Longarm. He carried himself like a chief and had evidently noticed how everyone on the ground had looked to him the moment the Indians began their encirclement.

Longarm nodded cordially as the Indian pulled up before him. The chief spoke first.

"What do you want with Running Fox? He has done no harm. We have long been friends of the white man.

We fight the Sioux by their side! We lose many in the battles. But that is well. That is war. Now it is peace. Now we may hunt upon the mountains. We may fish in the streams. There are no longer any Sioux to steal our horses or murder our squaws, our children! Can we not ride across our land without trouble from the white man? Never has the scalp of a white man hung in our lodges. Our war was with the Sioux, and only them. Now it is over. Tell your man to release Running Fox."

Longarm looked past the chief. "Let that fellow go, McAllister."

"I'm damned if I will," Big Jim said truculently. Despite his oversized stomach, the man had the brute strength to continue to hold almost immobile the straining young Crow.

"You better let him go," Travers said softly. "This brave didn't do nothin'—'cept maybe save this silly girl's life."

Frowning in sudden indecision, Big Jim looked at Laxalte, who was still steaming, but who looked now as confused as Big Jim. It was David Baxter who spoke up then. "I suggest, McAllister," he said, his small eyes gleaming, his cigar working convulsively in the side of his mouth, "that you do what Longarm says. I don't want anything to happen to my daughter because you came down with a sudden attack of stubbornness. We are guests, you might say, in this chief's country. This looks like one place where he gets all the votes, if you see what I mean."

Longarm spoke then to the chief: "The brave was chasing this woman. Why was he doing this?"

The chief swung around and addressed the brave in their own language. It was a surprising melodious flow of words, and the exchange was sharp. When the Indian answered his chief, he got a quick rejoinder from the man and immediately sagged, his belligerence fading dramatically. The chief turned back to Longarm.

"Running Fox see white woman in water. The water

swift. She was carried from shore. She cry out. Running Fox save her. But woman not thank Running Fox. She scream and strike him, then run away. Running Fox say he follow her to show he is not bad Indian, but now one of your men has struck Running Fox. He is in disgrace and must kill that man to lift the shame from him. Hear me, brother. I speak the truth."

"You'd better let me handle this," said Frank.

Longarm nodded to the deputy and took a small step back, to signify to the chief that now Frank would act as spokesmen for the rest of them. The exchange between the two was lengthy; the Crow chief was obviously surprised and then impressed with Tyson's command of the Crow tongue. At the end of what seemed to Longarm an interminable palaver, the deputy turned about and faced Longarm, a relieved look on his face.

"I explained to the chief about the misunderstanding," he said. "And then I pointed out that these fellows were big medicine from Washington, where the Great White Father resides. This helped somewhat, and I think it is going to be all right. It would be nice, I think, if the girl could vouch for Running Fox's story."

They all turned then to Jean McPhee. Slowly she got to her feet. The chemise she was wearing was sopping wet, and though a lot of both her legs was visible, it managed to cover everything else up quite nicely. She looked very wet and very unhappy, her ruddy hair now dark and bedraggled. Even her green eyes were subdued.

"I was in deep water," she began softly. "The current was very strong. I am sure I could have swum back to shore. When that Indian grabbed me, I . . . I must have gotten hysterical. I didn't see him coming. It was all . . . so sudden."

"You weren't drowning, Jean?" Laxalte asked, his eyes narrowing. It was obvious that he was hoping Jean could shoot holes in the brave's story.

"Well, Paul," she admitted, "I guess I might have

looked like I was to the Indian. I . . . did cry out, now that I think of it. It was just that I was so surprised when the current caught me up."

"You were being carried along by it," said Longarm, encouraging Jean with a smile.

"Yes."

"If I had seen you, Jean, and you had seen me on the shore, would you have called out to me for help?"

Her sharp white teeth worried her upper lip. She nodded, and then turned and looked over at the Indian. "Thank you, Running Fox," she said to him, her voice subdued but clear and firm. "Thank you for saving me. I'm sorry I ran from you afterward."

The Indian drew himself up a few inches and shook himself free from Big Jim McAllister. Then he folded his arms and directed his gaze at Laxalte.

"Now, what's all this about Running Fox being in disgrace?" demanded David Baxter, taking his cigar out of his mouth. The tough little fellow seemed ready for a battle.

Frank answered, "Crows do not strike each other lightly. It is, for example, a high crime for a father or mother to strike their male children, and if a warrior is struck by a stranger, he is irretrievably disgraced unless he can kill the offender himself immediately."

"So Running Fox has to kill Laxalte," Baxter said dryly. "Is that it?"

Frank smiled slightly. "I'll see what I can do."

Frank turned around then, and resumed his palaver with the chief. It was not long before he smiled and turned to Laxalte. "If you have anything you think this brave might like as a peace offering, it would go far toward restoring his pride. An apology wouldn't hurt, either."

"An *apology?* To an *aborigine!*"

"To a Crow warrior who saved Jean's life," Longarm said quietly. "Jean just apologized a minute ago, and it didn't seem to do her any harm."

By that time the rest of the congressmen and the women had moved closer. The Crows on horseback offered no interference as they drifted through their ranks to stand beside Longarm and the others. Now, from all of them, came a general murmur of approval at Longarm's and Frank's suggestion. Jean looked at Paul.

"Go ahead," she said wearily. "Let's get this business over with. I don't like standing here like this."

Laxalte looked unhappily over at Longarm. "What kind of a present do you think he'd like?"

"Show him to your tent," Frank suggested. "He might see something he likes. But you better apologize now before you take him there."

"Damn it! I don't know how to apologize to an Indian! Tell him I'm sorry. Tell him I didn't know why he was chasing Jean. It was a mistake. Just tell him that."

Before Frank could do that, Running Fox stepped toward Laxalte. "I understand why you pull me from horse. Your woman make so much noise. You take me to tent and I see what you have. I think you fine man. You not understand good." Then he smiled broadly at Laxalte. "I will not kill you. Great White Father is your medicine. Brother, we go now to your tent."

Laxalte looked helplessly around him, and saw that there was nothing for it. He shrugged and, with Jean limping wetly along beside him, led Running Fox through the ranks of still-mounted Crow toward his tent, as Longarm and the rest of the congressional party trailed after.

The Indians were gone now. They had left in a whirl of brilliant color, and with cries wild enough to prickle all the party's scalps in apprehension. Running Fox's yell was the loudest and most triumphant of all as he carried off his prize, a magnificent hunting knife. Standing in the entrance to Paul Laxalte's tent, Longarm had seen the congressman flinch as Running Fox reached for it.

Dusk was coming on now, and the mountain chill was falling over the few who were still huddled around the crackling campfire. Longarm was sitting beside Tyson and Travers. Across from the three of them sat David Baxter and his daughter Olivia. Violet Fleur, Olivia's maid, and Hilda Guernsback, Irene McAllister's maid, were also sitting about the fire, hugging themselves against the chill, leaning as close to the dancing flames as they could get. Baxter and the women seemed reluctant to let this day's excitement pass. Baxter had been most interested in Frank's description of his life among the Crow. Olivia and the two maids seemed equally interested in the Crow woman Frank had married. He had not told any of them of the manner of her death.

". . . so what that means," said Frank, in answer to one of Baxter's queries, "is that they have no hereditary rulers. No office or station is hereditary, and neither does wealth constitute dignity or give an Indian power over his brothers. The greatest chief may fall below the meanest tribesman for any misconduct as chief, and the lowest tribesman may rise to the most exalted station by the performance of valiant deeds."

"You make it sound like a natural democracy," Baxter commented, looking at Frank shrewdly. As he spoke, he slapped at a mosquito that had landed on his bald head. The sound of the slap was sharp in the quiet night.

"I suppose you might call it that," Frank admitted.

"I thought Running Fox was very handsome," Olivia ventured boldly. "And so tall. I didn't know the Indians grow that tall. He was really quite impressive."

"That's right. The Crows, both male and female, are usually tall and well proportioned. And yes, they *are* handsome, especially with that light, copper-colored skin."

"Your Crow wife was pretty, I take it," said Baxter, peering closely at the deputy.

"Yes," Frank replied. "She was. Very pretty."

Something in Frank's voice gave all of them pause, and Baxter pulled back, took a puff on his cigar, and shook his head. "That was good work, deputy," he said, "talking that chief into letting Laxalte keep his scalp."

Frank chuckled.

"What did you tell the chief, really?" Baxter prodded.

The deputy looked at Longarm. "Think I should tell him?"

"Why not? It did the trick."

The deputy looked back at Baxter. "I told the chief that Laxalte was one of the Great White Father's children."

Hilda Guernsback was the only one who did not explode into laughter at that. She sniffed disapprovingly. "Seems to me that if them handsome heathen would believe that, they would believe anything. For all their manliness and love of show, they are really just children at heart, I'm afraid."

Her words dampened the spirits of all of them. It was as if Hilda had been sitting in their company all this time without hearing a word of which she had not disapproved. She was a most prim, thin-lipped woman, who cast a chill over all of them.

"We mustn't judge them so harshly," said Olivia, her voice still soft. She blushed as she spoke, as if she were alarmed at her own temerity in contradicting the prim Miss Guernsback. "We must not forget, Running Fox saved Jean McPhee's life."

This slight altercation seemed to disturb the easy familiarity of the group. Travers stirred restlessly, glancing sidelong at Longarm as he did so. Baxter took the cigar out of his mouth and exhaled a great cloud of blue smoke.

"Come, Olivia," he said, getting quickly to his feet. He reached down to take her hand. "It is getting late, and I fear we have another one of those days ahead of us." He glanced at Longarm as he spoke. "How many more days to the park?"

"Close to six." Longarm glanced at Jim. "Wouldn't you say, Jim?"

"Six is close enough," the old guide replied carefully, removing his pipe from his mouth. "If we don't run into any more Indians or grizzlies, and if everyone stays healthy and don't get themselves drowned. And we don't lose any more horses."

Longarm was on his feet by that time, as were all the rest. He said good night to Baxter and the three ladies, nodded to Tyson and Travers, and set out for a secluded spot he had already selected. He was halfway across the campsite when he saw Irene McAllister hurrying through the gathering dusk toward him. He stopped and was astonished to hear a sob escape the older woman as she neared him.

"Mr. Long!" she cried softly. "It's Big Jim! I . . . I think he's very sick. I think it's his heart! All that excitement this evening—and the exertion. Please, come quickly!"

When Longarm reached Big Jim McAllister's tent, he found Peter Eliot and Paul Laxalte in there also, along with Jean McPhee and Daisy Foster. Crowding in after Longarm was a grim Hilda Guernsback, obviously upset that she had been away from the tent when Big Jim had his attack.

Big Jim was lying on his cot, his back propped up by pillows. He was conscious, his face an unpleasant shade of gray. Despite his bulk, he appeared to have shrunk a little, and Longarm saw something approaching fear in the exuberant man's eyes. Irene had hurried in with Longarm, and now she turned to the others crowding anxiously around the cot, her face showing vividly the stark alarm she felt.

"Please," she said, "why don't you all leave for now?

I'm sure Jim is very grateful for your concern, but there are so many of you! I think he should rest."

Without a murmur of protest, Laxalte and Eliot left, Daisy and Jean following after them. Longarm waited until they were gone, then approached the cot and looked down at Big Jim.

"I guess it was wresting with that Crow Indian did me in, Long," Big Jim said softly. "It's my left arm. And I had some trouble breathing. But I'm getting better now. No need to get alarmed."

Longarm turned to Irene. She pushed a stray lock of white hair off her forehead as she met Longarm's gaze. "Has this happened before, Mrs. McAllister?"

She nodded. "I told Big Jim he shouldn't make this trip." She took a deep breath. "I *told* him."

"Now, Irene," McAllister said hoarsely, "there's no sense in getting all riled."

His wife put a hand on his arm, and then slumped in the canvas chair beside Big Jim's cot. "I know, I know," she told him wearily. "But this is such a cruel and difficult land." She glanced up at Longarm in a kind of panic. "It's such a . . . a wilderness, Mr. Long! And those wild savages! And grizzly bears!"

"Irene!" McAllister said, his voice stronger. "Now that's enough! I'm going to be all right. And this is great country. I have been reading about it for years, and now I'm seeing it with my own eyes. It's bigger than anything I could have imagined. If this park we're heading for is anything like this land, it'll be the finest present this generation can give all those who come after us. And that Indian! Running Fox! What a fine savage he was! Did you see, Mr. Long, how he handled that pony of his!"

"Now, don't get excited again," Irene protested nervously. "Just lie still!" She looked despairingly up at Longarm. "The doctor told him not to take this trip. The doctor warned him!"

"What's that pill-pusher know?" Big Jim demanded.

"If I'm going to die, I can't think of a better place than out here—away from those damn hospitals they're building everywhere! Charnel houses! That's all they are!"

"Jim!"

Longarm heard Hilda Guernsback gasp at Big Jim's statement concerning his possible death. She moved around to the other side of the man's cot, her hand over her mouth, a disapproving frown on her pinched face.

"Hilda," Irene said, "will you get Mr. McAllister some water?"

As Hilda hurried from the tent, Big Jim grunted derisively. "Water? Now *you* know what I need, Irene. It's not water. And you know where it is."

"It's all gone, Jim," Irene said. She smiled slightly at Longarm. "I didn't bring enough, Mr. Long, I'm afraid. Do you suppose you might ask one of the others? The doctor did say that a little medicinal whiskey would not harm him."

"I'll do that, Mrs. McAllister," Longarm said as he started from the tent. "And I think maybe it'd be best if we camped here for a couple of days until Big Jim's feeling some better."

"Oh, thank you, Mr. Long," the woman said, breathing easier at once. "That's what I hoped you'd say. I'm sure that's all Jim would need—just a few days."

"Yes," Big Jim said. "A couple of days and I'll be as good as new. But don't forget that whiskey, Long!"

Longarm grinned and waved to the big man as he left the tent. He passed Hilda in the darkness as she hurried toward the tent with a canteen of water. She was a grim-visaged attendant, and Longarm could not help wondering if perhaps Daisy Foster would not have been a more preferable attendant to a man in Big Jim's condition.

He saw Laxalte standing in his tent's entrance and headed for the man. He was certain Laxalte would have the whiskey Big Jim required. Then he would tell the bad news to Travers. The old guide had spoken more prophetically than he realized.

Everyone had not stayed healthy, which meant it would take considerably longer than six days before they reached that park.

Chapter 6

The next day, worried that Sammy Wentworth might still be out there waiting for another chance at him, Longarm decided to scout ahead and meet the party at Heart Butte, a landmark that Travers assured him he would have no difficulty in finding, since it was on the trail leading to the park.

Longarm visited with Big Jim before riding out. The man was moving about in the tent, trying to get his legs under him and protesting that his momentary shortness of breath was no reason for the entire party to come to a halt. But Longarm assured him that the others were more than willing to catch their own breaths at this spot. The man seemed somewhat grateful to hear this. He and his wife were standing in the entrance to his tent, waving, when Longarm rode out.

Later that morning, while riding through an aspen glade, he thought he heard shots far ahead of him. He pulled up and sat quietly, his ear cocked for more shots. But there was nothing except the sound of the wind in the leaves. He was willing to think it had been his imagination, or simply some hunters. Chiding himself for his jumpiness, he started up again, looking about him as he rode, enjoying the land through which he was riding. The sunlight, caught by the shimmering leaves, made the ground around him sparkle as tiny motes of reflected light flashed against the trees and grass and over the neck of his horse as he rode.

Leaving the glade, he rode on across an upland

savanna, the tall grass reaching at times up to his stirrups. The sun was warm on his back, but not oppressive, and there was always a fresh breeze. The savanna gave way to timber, and beyond the timber, he found himself in broken, boulder-filled country that lifted steadily under him.

Rounding a boulder as big as a house, which sat squarely on the trail he was following, he found himself staring into the twin bores of a shotgun. The weapon was being held by the bespectacled prospector Longarm had met earlier. When the little fellow saw that it was Longarm, he lowered the shotgun hurriedly, sweat beading his pale forehead. It was then that Longarm saw his partner Bob, propped on the trail behind him, his back against a boulder. His sidewhiskers were wilted, it appeared, his face a mask of pain. There was a bloodstained bandage wrapped around his right shoulder, and the glance he gave Longarm was fretful. He obviously had a fever.

"What happened?" Longarm inquired, dismounting swiftly and moving past the fellow with the shotgun to go down on one knee beside his companion.

"He was ambushed," the prospector said. He leaned his shotgun against the wall of rock beside Bob, and took out a handkerchief to mop his brow.

"Who ambushed you?" Longarm asked Bob.

"I don't know who he was," the wounded man whispered painfully. "He just stepped out of these rocks and began firing."

"Can you describe him?"

"A small, sneaky-looking fellow," the shotgun-toting prospector said, answering for Bob. He took off his spectacles and began polishing them with a filthy handkerchief. "He wore a derby and a gray suit. He looked like he was in terrible condition. I suppose he must have been, to have allowed himself such a desperate and dastardly action. He took Bob's horse and was rummaging through our supplies when I came upon him."

"Where were you when Bob was bushwhacked?"

"I was up there in the rocks, chasing a rabbit with this shotgun, when I heard the fellow open up on Bob. I scrambled back down as fast as I could, and when he saw me coming, he fired at me and rode off."

Longarm nodded and proceeded to examine Bob's wound. He did not like what he saw. The bullet had evidently smashed the man's collarbone; furthermore, the wound was not clean. The entire region was swollen and ugly, the bullet hole a neat but mean-looking pit in the purplish skin.

Longarm looked up at Thompson. "Where's the rest of your horses? I saw a packhorse and two saddle horses the last time I ran into you."

"I've hidden my horse and the packhorse back in there among the rocks." He smiled. "I did that when I heard you coming. I guess I assumed it was that other one coming back."

Longarm stood up. "You two better ride back the way I came. You'll come to a river by and by. There's a camp on this side of it. Tell the deputy in charge that I sent you. And tell him I said you'd better have Bob's wound cauterized."

"But how far is this camp?"

"You should get there a mite after dark if you get going now. And my advice is that you do just that."

"You mean I should ride that packhorse?" Bob asked.

"Unless you reckon you can make it on foot."

"But our supplies! We'll have to leave them."

"That's right. Stash them in here among the rocks somewhere. But I wouldn't be worrying about supplies, if I were you."

Bob took a deep breath and nodded somberly at Longarm's reminder of his condition. Longarm then proceeded to give Bob's partner more detailed directions on how to reach the camp, after which he wished them well and rode off, following fresh tracks this time, grimly pleased to find that he was now only a few hours behind Sammy Wentworth. As he rode, he wondered idly which one of the many killers he had brought in Sammy was related to, and how the Mirelda woman had managed to find him and ally herself with him. Longarm had recalled seeing Wentworth about the hotel and in the neighborhood for weeks before he had had that shootout with Theresa Mirelda's husband.

Longarm took a deep breath. Apparently, all that time, Sammy Wentworth had been stalking him. It had taken Theresa Mirelda to galvanize him into action.

Following Wentworth's tracks, he found himself swinging north, keeping to the side of a swift mountain stream to the point where it emerged from the mouth of a canyon. Here a trail wound upward through steep-faced bluffs bordering the streambed, which, over the countless centuries, had cut its path through the solid rock. Wentworth took this path and Longarm followed, regarding the trail ahead of him dubiously.

Just ahead of him amid the rocks or perched on the rim above, Wentworth might be waiting. Longarm could end up like that prospector—or worse. Still, he had little choice, if he wanted to rid himself of this dangerous flea. The man was obviously unstable enough to threaten the safety of the entire party.

Longarm climbed steadily. The skies remained clear, but that meant little at this altitude. A sudden, torrential thunderstorm could open up on him at any moment, and as the afternoon drew on, the more imminent a downpour became. The bright sun built up heat in the deep chasm. The shadows were sharp and hard. The air was humid. Longarm's shirt clung to his back, where the sweat ran freely. For a while the walls rose higher and steeper, closing in ominously, with the trail a little more than a slender track just above the rocky bed of the stream he was following. His horse's hoofs rang and clattered on the trail's rocky surface.

More and more troubled at his vulnerability, he kept going while he began to consider seriously the advisability of dismounting and climbing the rest of the way on foot. And then, to his relief, the walls of the canyon began to break up. More sky showed as the granite cliffs split into huge, irregular formations. Squinting up through the sunshine, Longarm saw the line that marked the head of the canyon.

At that moment, the first shot came. As it whined off the wall beside him, he swore bitterly. He had known it was coming and had bulled along regardless. Even as this taunting thought crossed his mind, he was digging in his heels, driving his horse toward a cleft in the rock just ahead of him. The animal leaped forward with a surge of power as another round ricocheted off the rock.

Horse and rider clawed their way up the talus-littered floor of the cleft, a passage so narrow that Longarm felt rock scraping his legs on either side. Then the cleft widened. Longarm glimpsed an opening ahead, and slid from his gelding's back, pulling his rifle from its scabbard at the same time.

Scrambling past the horse, Longarm flung himself down onto a flat rock at the rim overlooking the canyon. The shots had come not from the rim itself, but from a vantage point in among the rocks below the rim. He searched those rocks now, hoping for the glint of sunlight on metal. He caught the shine of sunlight on a long barrel at the same time that he saw the spurt of powder smoke.

The rock face in front of him exploded. He was pulling back even as the round cut into the ledge, and he managed to turn his face away in time to save his eyes. But the tiny shards of stone tore at the side of his face, and he flung himself back off the rock, dragging his Winchester behind him.

That little sneaking son of a bitch has the drop on me now, he thought, as he scrambled back down the steep cut. Another slug whined close, too close. Longarm ducked under a ledge. Looking up, he realized that he was safe for the moment. He could not be seen from above. His horse, he noted, had backed itself down the cleft and was out of sight somewhere on the trail below.

He would have to wait now for that little weasel to come after him. If he had the guts. The thought that he wouldn't, that he would ride off too chickenhearted to climb down here after him, caused Longarm to simmer. The lawman would be forced, then, to stay crouched under the ledge until dark.

He levered a cartridge into the chamber of his Winchester, then gingerly felt the side of his face where the rock fragments had stung him. As he brushed his right cheekbone off, he discovered it was not too bad. It sure could have been a whole hell of a lot worse.

A cold, chill wind brushed him. He heard the canyon walls mutter, and glanced skyward. The clear blue was gone. In its place, he caught a glimpse of roiling black cloud. A sudden, brilliant explosion of light fixed him, followed almost immediately by a crash of thunder so loud that he thought he was going to lose his back teeth. Another finger of lightning crackled, sizzled, snapped. His ears were ringing. Then came another titanic convulsion. The thunder rolled then, a continuous, furious, deranged, deafening sound that pushed down on him like something palpable, crushed him, rendered him tiny, insignificant—a mosquito caught in a cannon's blast.

He ducked in under the ledge and hung on, wincing uncontrollably from the battering thunder. Then came the rain. It was an awesome, drenching curtain of water that swept in sheets across his line of vision. The ledge offered only minimal protection. In less than a minute, his hatbrim had been pounded down about his ears, and his clothes were plastered icily to his frame.

For ten minutes the rain thundered down in an all-out cloudburst as Longarm clung to his perch just inside the narrow cleft. He could not help thinking of his horse. Caught up in this torrential rain and thunder, it had probably bolted. As soon as the rain had tapered off, he crept carefully out from under the ledge and picked his way down the sloppy talus to the narrow trail alongside the stream.

His horse was standing in the middle of the stream, his head down, his tail in the rushing, broiling water, his ears flattened, his eyes wild. The big claybank looked like a statue, except for an occasional twitching of his flank. The poor beast had been stunned into immobility by the hammering intensity of the cloudburst. Longarm no longer worried about Wentworth. The little rat was probably still running, or too wet or befuddled to think of Longarm.

That was the marshal's hope, anyway, as he picked his way back down the trail, stepped into the no-longer-shallow stream, and approached his mount. He called softly to him, gently. The beast's ears flicked. Longarm stepped through the swift water and called out again, just as softly. The gelding's nostrils flared then, and he turned to look warily at him. The critter would have whisked his tail if it hadn't been so heavy.

Longarm kept going and took the reins. Then he pulled the horse toward him, still speaking softly. He heard a distant rumbling. Glancing skyward, he saw not a cloud in the sky. The storm had passed over. Or had it? The rumbling grew louder. The walls about him seemed to be trembling. The building roar alarmed and confused him—until he realized suddenly what he was hearing.

He turned and dragged the horse, stumbling, back up onto the trail. Back toward the cleft Longarm raced frantically. A moment before the wall of water rushed down the canyon, he succeeded in pulling the horse into the narrow cleft. Both horse and man now struggled up the slippery draw until the water no longer sucked at their feet. Longarm looked back down at the brown, turgid water hurtling past the cleft. He looked in awe at the furious rush of water. Once before, he had been caught in a flash flood, but it had not been while he was trapped in a ravine as narrow and confining as this one. He had been out in the open, and although he had been swept along some thirty yards or more, he had survived. Nothing caught in the path of *this* torrent would have been that lucky.

His boots were underwater. The water was rising within the draw. The sound of its rushing flow seemed to fill the universe. He pulled the horse and himself higher and higher until he was once again close in under the ledge that had sheltered him before. He moved on past it, his feet slipping and sliding on the treacherous detritus.

He kept going past the flat rock he had thrown himself down upon earlier, and finally reached the rim of the canyon. He looked back down into the ravine. The flash flood had passed by this time, leaving behind a deeper stream that frothed white as it boiled over its rocky bed.

Longarm slammed his soaked Winchester into its dripping scabbard.

"Now that's a good idea, sonny."

Longarm whirled to face a towering fellow dressed in buckskins and a fur hat. His bearded face was a mess. An eyepatch covered his left eye, with two long, ridged scars leading from the socket down the full length of his face, disfiguring even the smoothness of his salt-and-pepper beard. What looked like an ancient Hawken was clasped in his big right fist as he stood there contemplating Longarm. The man had evidently just stepped out from behind a boulder on the crest, from which vantage point he had been watching Longarm struggle up the incline.

"Was that you firing at me before the cloudburst?" a furious Longarm demanded.

"If I was firing at you, sonny, I would've hit you. Each time."

"Did you see who it was?"

"I saw him."

"And you didn't try to stop him?"

"I mind my own business, Sonny. What about you?"

"Damn it! That punk *was* my business. And stop calling me Sonny." Longarm was surprised at the extent of his irritation at this fool giant in front of him.

"What's your handle, then?"

Longarm sighed and took out a very wet wallet and flashed his badge at the man. He felt faintly ridiculous doing it, but he was a little tired and more than a little frustrated. "I'm Custis Long, a deputy U.S. marshal, and that fellow you let go has tried to kill me a number of times. Now just who the hell are *you*?"

The man spat a huge wad of chewing tobacco at the ground between them. The tobacco appeared to make everything around it wither. Longarm wondered if the giant was challenging him. He had the odd feeling that the man was really Robinson Crusoe, or had stepped out of some Mountain Man epic written by Ned Buntline. Longarm would have smiled if he hadn't been so damned aggravated.

"My name's Riley," the apparition said. "Folks call me Yellowstone Riley. What do folks call you?" He smiled then, revealing a well-worn row of tobacco-stained teeth.

Longarm took a deep breath and cooled his temper. The fool giant was, after all, trying to be friendly. "Longarm."

"And you're all in a lather 'cause I let that little boy get away."

"Just tell me which way he went," Longarm said wearily.

"I'll do better than that. I'll show you."

The man went for his saddle horse and a packhorse in among the rocks. As he led them out, Longarm mounted up, considerably mollified by the giant's apparent desire to cooperate. As the man pulled up beside Longarm, he pointed due west. "When that cloudburst commenced rumbling, the little feller got on his horse and galloped toward that peak. He was a sight, he was, riding all hunched over and trying not to get wet. How come a little feller like that's got a big man like you all riled?"

"He's a nuisance. A dangerous nuisance. He's trying to kill me to please a lady." Longarm glanced at Yellowstone. "That make any sense to you?"

"Yes it does." He sent a dark stream of tobacco at the ground. "Man'll do most anything to please a lady. Not that it'll do him a mite of good." He grinned wolfishly at Longarm. "Don't worry. The little man won't get far."

"How do you know?"

"He wasn't treating his horse careful a-tall."

Longarm nodded. That made sense. Sammy Wentworth had already ruined one horse, and the mount he had taken from those two green prospectors could not have been in the best of condition. He felt a little better.

His failure to stop Longarm had frightened Sammy Wentworth. As Yellowstone Riley and the lawman tracked the fellow, this soon became obvious. He was riding flat-out, with little or no concern for his mount, and was making no effort to cover his tracks as he galloped straight west.

Unfortunately, Sammy was riding a horse that contained a bigger heart than he deserved. It was two full days later, on a bright afternoon, that the two men came upon the dead horse. There were still fresh traces of lather hanging in fine threads from the horse's mouth, and great patches of it, dried completely in the sun, still clung to its forelegs and chest. The animal looked as if it had been cruelly used, and as Longarm and Yellowstone dismounted and gazed down at the beast, both shook their heads in pity.

"Any man does that to a horse," Yellowstone muttered, "deserves to be ridden the same way."

Sammy had left the saddle on, and Longarm had to restrain himself from reaching down and loosening the cinch to remove it.

The horse was lying on a trail that led through a canyon. Longarm glanced about. Sammy Wentworth was nearby. He wasn't a man able to get far on his own, not this one. He was most likely on the rim of that canyon, waiting for another chance to bushwhack Longarm. Yellowstone saw the lawman's glance about him, and nodded.

"Yer right. He's around. I can smell the little son of a bitch. And he's most likely up there, like the last time."

"Let's get off the trail," Longarm suggested, as he turned and remounted.

Yellowstone mounted up also, and Longarm led the way into high rocks well in under the bluffs looming over the trail. Still astride his horse, Longarm turned and waited for Yellowstone to come up beside him.

"One of us should continue into the canyon," Longarm said, "staying close to the rocks and making just enough noise to keep Wentworth's interest alive. I figure that should be me. He won't be expecting anybody else, but he sure as hell should be expecting me. Now, if you could just get up there behind him, Riley..."

The big man nodded easily. "Just let me get my hands on that little feller's neck," he said fervently.

Longarm smiled. "Just be careful. This 'little feller' is trouble—all the way. He is as slippery as a sidewinder and just as dangerous."

"Just give me enough time to get up there."

Longarm nodded. Yellowstone backed his horse, then turned it and rode back up the trail. Longarm shook his head in wonder as he watched. He sure as hell was a big man.

After what he considered a long enough interval, Longarm took a deep breath, urged his horse out of the rocks, and started toward the mouth of the canyon. The river that had cut it was only a trickle in the middle of it. He found himself following a dim game trail that led down the center of the canyon. Fortunately, the trail was in shadow. Longarm followed it until he was well inside the canyon, then moved closer to the canyon wall, letting his mount pick its way through the rocks and gravel. The sharp clacking of its hoofs on the stone echoed loudly.

Longarm drifted still closer to the canyon wall, and kept himself from looking up. He did not want to alert Wentworth to the fact that he suspected anything. There was a break in the rim above him, allowing a bright splash of sunlight to bathe the entire canyon floor ahead of him. Crossing that bright patch would be dangerous if Sammy Wentworth was where Longarm expected him to be—in among a large rock outcropping that hugged the canyon's high rim like a stiff collar. A long, open shelf tilted down from the rimrocks. If Sammy Wentworth was anywhere, he was up there ... waiting.

What Longarm had to do was make him show himself, draw his fire if need be, in order to enable Yellowstone Riley to find him and make his move. All of which meant he was going to have to ride across that patch of sunlight. He kept going, nudging the claybank smoothly along, then clucking to it softly as he emerged into the blazing sun. As the shadow of the rim passed clean over him, leaving him and the horse caught entirely in the bright light, Longarm fought an impulse to glance up just once at the outcrop of rock above him—looming closer with each passing second.

But he rode steadily ahead, his right hand resting casually on his right thigh, a chill creeping steadily up his back despite the hot sun that rested on it. When the shot came, it was almost as if Longarm had seen Sammy Wentworth tucking the rifle stock into his shoulder as he squeezed the trigger. Even as the rifle's sharp crack echoed between the canyon walls, Longarm was bending suddenly over his horse, spurring it with cruel insistence into the shadows ahead of him.

Longarm heard the round spang off the rock just behind him. He glanced up. Two men were on the bluff. One of them was dressed in drab, dusty clothes, a funny-looking derby tipped rakishly on his head, sunlight gleaming off the long barrel of the rifle he held. Behind him was a giant of a man, his right hand raised over his head. A second before Longarm's plunging horse took them out of view, he saw the giant's hand come down, bringing with it the flash of sunlight on metal.

Well in under the overhanging rock, Longarm reined in, snaked his Winchester from its scabbard, and started for the canyon wall to find himself a way up to that rim.

A shout from high above halted him in his tracks. "Longarm! Here he is!"

A blood-chilling scream shattered the canyon's silence—and grew in awful intensity as Sammy Wentworth's twisting body neared the canyon floor. Glancing back, Longarm was just in time to see the body strike. The sound it made when it hit the hard surface was sickening, the scream shutting off with a fearful suddenness. Longarm did not need to go back to identify

Wentworth's body, but he was drawn to it, nevertheless. As he got closer, he saw the bloody, crushed derby hat, and pulled to a halt.

"Longarm!"

The tall lawman turned and looked up. He could not see Yellowstone. "You finished him, Riley! Come on down!"

"Leave him for the vultures—and get up here! I'm hurt. Hurt bad!"

Longarm turned quickly away from the broken body, and set off on a steady run. There was a game trail that looped around a huge boulder and climbed steeply upward. The narrow, twisting path was so steep at times that he was climbing rather than running, forced to use his hands and arms. But he kept going and soon burst out onto a smooth rock face that led on a slight incline to the rim.

He cut along the rim to the outcropping where Wentworth had stationed himself, and saw Yellowstone Riley sitting in among the rocks, his back against one of them, his beaver hat pushed back off his head, a dark stain standing out on his buckskin shirt.

"What happened?" Longarm asked as he came to a halt in front of the man, then went down on one knee beside him.

"He was a sneak, that one was! I caught him good and proper. Before you came into view, I found him skulking up here, the treacherous little assassin!"

"What *happened,* Riley?"

The man shook his head and looked away from Longarm. The scars that ran down his face from the patched eye socket seemed to become more livid as he contemplated Sammy Wentworth. "He was a meek little feller when he saw me. Let me take his rifle." The big man shook his head bitterly. "He was shivering like a branch in the wind, that he was. When I reached out to take the rifle, he stuck me with his knife. Then he kicked me a little to warm his black heart, and left me with his Green River sticking out of my ribs. Oh, he was a fine one, that he was."

Despite the seriousness of Yellowstone's wound, Longarm could not help smiling slightly at his account of what had happened. This man had simply removed the knife from his side, got up, and followed Wentworth to the rocks. What Longarm had glimpsed from below was Yellowstone giving that knife back to Sammy Wentworth.

"Where's your horse?" Longarm asked.

"Back in among them rocks over there. I've been losing blood, and I don't feel up to riding far. What you got in mind, sonny?"

"If you can make it as far as Heart Butte, we can camp there until the rest of my party arrives."

"Them dudes you're taking into the park, hey? It's a terrible thing you're doing, and that's the God's truth. This is land the way God made it. It will be a calamity to let humans stink it up. Already the place is lousy with greenhorns." He shook his head in sorrow. "It is a terrible thing to see Yellowstone Riley depending on a party of greenhorns for his safety—but I think that little sneak cut me in two. At least it feels that way every time I take a good breath. You'll have to strap me on my horse, Longarm."

Longarm stood up and nodded. "First I'll have to stop the bleeding."

"You do that, sonny, and I'll be much obliged." He winked at Longarm. "Did you hear that miserable bastard scream?"

"I did. I also heard him land."

"It was music to my ears, it was."

He leaned his head back against the rock and passed out. Longarm looked down at the giant for a moment, contemplating what it would take for him to get the man onto his horse and then tie him there. The trip to Heart Butte with this wounded man was going to take considerably longer now than he had anticipated, and this would delay the party's arrival at the park. But hell, that didn't matter.

Longarm owed Yellowstone Riley. He owed him a whole hell of a lot. Now, if the big Mountain Man would just stop calling him *Sonny* ...

Chapter 7

When Longarm rode into the camp the next day, Jim Travers greeted the wounded Yellowstone warmly. The two men had hunted together in years gone by. It was a ticklish job, getting the enormous fellow off his horse without letting him fall to the ground. During the long ride to Heart Butte, he had not uttered a single word of protest, but he had lost blood steadily, and every jolt, Longarm realized, must have caused him considerable pain. He was equally stoic now as Longarm, Travers, and Tyson eased him gently off the horse and led him, still upright, to Hilda Guernsback's tent. Hers was the biggest of the maids' tents, and it was Irene McAllister who suggested it. Hilda seemed not to mind the invasion and took immediate and skillful charge of the big man, waving the rest of them out of her tent as soon as Yellowstone had been made comfortable.

Walking to the campfire then, Longarm was trailed by the congressmen and their entourage while he gave as brief an account as he could of his meeting with Yellowstone and the death of Sammy Wentworth. That Longarm had left his mangled remains for the vultures, he did not bother to mention. When he had finished, the members of the party looked at each other in obvious relief. They had heard of this Sammy Wentworth, it seemed.

Longarm turned to Frank. "I sent a couple of prospectors to meet up with you at the camp along the

119

river. Did they get there all right? One of them was wounded by Wentworth."

Frank nodded somberly, and at once Longarm caught the look in the eyes of the congressmen and their women.

"What happened?" he asked.

"The one that was shot died," Melinda Clinton said softly.

"Despite everything Melly could do," her husband interposed grimly. "He died the same night he arrived."

"He had a terrible fever," Melinda told Longarm. "He was simply burning up. It was blood poisoning. There was just nothing I could do."

"The other fellow rode on back to Billings," Frank told Longarm. "I don't imagine he's going to do any more prospecting for a spell."

That statement of Frank's seemed to spark something in Paul Laxalte's face. At once Longarm sensed that the congressman had been building for this moment, had been waiting anxiously for Longarm to return so he could tell him something—and Longarm had a pretty good idea what Laxalte wanted to say.

The congressman cleared his throat and stepped resolutely forward. "I've been doing a lot of thinking," he announced, his voice heavy, his face florid. He had been drinking, Longarm realized, more than likely in order to build himself up to this moment. "I have been thinking that there is no reason for us to go on any farther. We have already seen what we have here—a dangerous, unfriendly wilderness. Jean was half scared to death by witless aborigines. We have been attacked by grizzly bears. We have met dying prospectors. Who knows what we will meet next? Certainly that madman who was after you could just as easily have shot one of us. I see no reason for going any farther into this wilderness. And as far as I am concerned—and I am sure my colleagues will agree with me in this—I see no earthly reason for preserving this land as a park. We would do better to keep people out of here, for their own safety."

"We are not *at* the park yet, Paul," said Big Jim.

"We're close enough," Laxalte replied bitterly.

Longarm shrugged. "I was just told to guide you gents and your ladies to the park and back. If you don't want to go there, that's all right with me."

Laxalte took a deep, satisfied breath and looked about him, a sudden smile of victory on his face. "You heard that," he told the others. "No reason at all why we can't go back right now."

"That the way all of you feel?" Longarm asked, looking about him at the congressmen, as well as at their women. He had not lied. It was all right if this was what they wanted, but he had a vague sense that going back now would be a failure of nerve, and that these people would always regret the action. "We can start back tomorrow, if that's your wish."

"That's not *my* wish," said Big Jim forcefully. "Laxalte can go back if he wants. And all the rest of you. You too, Irene. I know this has been hard on you. But I'm going on. Maybe the deputy will consent to go on with me—or Mr. Travers. I set out to see this Yellowstone Park, and I mean to see it before I die."

"You just try and go on without me," Irene snapped, her face suddenly red as she glared at her husband. "The very idea. I've gone through worse than this with you."

Big Jim looked at her and smiled, a grin as big as his stomach. "Yes you have, my dear," he told her fondly. "Yes you have."

Peter Eliot spoke up then. "I know I've caused some of the difficulties that Paul referred to," he said, his voice clear and resolute. "For that reason, I think I should state my position as forcefully as he has stated his. I am as yet undecided about the worth of setting aside this patch of wilderness as a park. You realize, there is no other country in the world that has ever done such a thing. Yet I do think that since we have come this far, we should see it through. I, for one, have great confidence in the marshal and his two aides." He touched his chin gingerly and smiled. "I have good reason to know that he is a man who can back up his words with suitable actions."

There was nervous laughter at this, and Longarm could not help but smile. Peter's wife looked up at her husband with her dark, flashing eyes, and hugged his arm. Her love for him shone in her face, and Longarm was pleased to see it. Perhaps the fellow was doing a little better now, during these long, cool nights.

"And so," Peter concluded, "if Longarm is confident he can take us to the Yellowstone Park and back, without our suffering any great harm in the process, I am willing to go on with him." Peter looked down at Mary. "What about you, Mary?" he asked.

"I am with you," she said clearly. "You know that, Peter."

"Well," David Baxter spoke up, "I don't know what to make of this Yellowstone Park. "That's why I made this trip. And if Big Jim is willing to go on, I am too." He turned to his daughter. "What about you, Olivia?"

"Do I have a choice?" she asked, laughing.

"You most certainly do. If you want to go back, we'll do so."

"I don't want to go back, but I certainly wish it were possible for women to ride astride as the men do. I understand Indian women can ride astride. I don't see why I could not wear pants and ride astride. It would be much easier. I have talked this over with Cindy Lou and Daisy. They both agree with me."

"That's another matter," Baxter said, blushing. "And I don't think this is the time for a discussion of that."

"I do," said Cindy Lou. "And Melly feels the same way."

"That's right," Melinda Clinton confirmed decisively. "I think we should be able to ride astride, but of course I realize how shocked you men are at such a thought, and I suppose it would cause too much trouble to change things at this stage. But a great deal of the difficulty many of us women are experiencing on this trip is caused by having to ride sidesaddle. And it seems to me that the ground over which we are now riding is getting to be much rougher than that which we traversed when we were just leaving Billings."

Many of the women nodded at this.

Travers looked at Longarm. "We had the devil of a storm the day before yesterday," he said. "The heavens purely opened up and there was considerable thunder. The women kept their horses under control, but I don't know yet how they managed."

Melly smiled at Travers. "That is a fine compliment indeed, Mr. Travers. I can only add that there were times when I myself had no idea how I was able to manage."

Longarm smiled at Melinda. "Thank you, Melly. Maybe we can do something about this matter later. But right now I'd like to hear from Charles Clinton. He is the only one who has not spoken up yet. Do you want to go back, Clinton?"

Charles Clinton smiled. "I don't think Melly would mind going back. This has been pretty hard on her. I think we should vote on it. I'll go with the majority."

"Can the women vote?" snapped Melly.

That took Clinton by surprise. But a look at his wife's face told him the answer. "Why . . . of course."

Melinda looked quickly around her at the other women. "Go tell Hilda we're going to vote," she said to Cindy Lou.

Cindy Lou hurried to get Hilda. There was nervous talk among the congressional party, while Longarm and Tyson conversed quietly. Travers allowed that there would be no difficulty in getting back, perhaps making the return in less time than they had taken to get this far. He seemed unconcerned about the vote, willing to go either way. Frank Tyson seemed anxious about something that Longarm could not put his finger on, but which he felt had little to do with going on to the park or turning back.

Cindy Lou returned just a little out of breath, her dark hair flying, her sharp eyes eager. "Hilda says she's not going to leave that wounded man. But she told me what her vote was."

"Shall we vote, then?" Laxalte suggested.

There was a general murmur of agreement to that.

"There's no one else who has anything further they want to say?" he prodded.

"Let's get on with it, Paul," growled Big Jim.

"All right, then. I suggest a show of hands. Will you count, Longarm?"

Longarm nodded.

"All those in favor of returning to Billings at once," Laxalte said, "raise your right hand."

Laxalte's hand shot up. He glanced at Jean. Her hand went up also. And that was it. Laxalte looked at Cindy Lou. "What about Hilda?" he asked her.

"She wanted me to vote to keep going," Cindy Lou replied.

Big Jim looked happily about him. "All those who want to go on!" he cried. "Let me see your hands!"

It was an impressive sight. When Baxter saw how overwhelming the vote was in favor of continuing on to the park, he raised his hand willingly. Longarm found himself pleased with the result of the vote—and pleased, too, at the way Big Jim had apparently recovered. He looked as hale and hearty as he had when the journey began.

"We'll move out first thing tomorrow," Longarm told them. "We should reach the park early tomorrow, before noon." He smiled at them. "It would have been a shame to have turned back when you were this close."

This news seemed to make everyone feel a lot better. The group broke up and the congressmen moved back to their tents. As soon as they were out of earshot, Jim Travers asked, "How did you know we were that close?"

"Yellowstone told me."

Travers nodded. "He knows this place like the back of his hand. Think I'll look in on him and see how he's doin'. That Hilda is a tough woman. And Yellowstone don't take kindly to women with minds of their own. Fact is, he don't take kindly to women at all."

As Jim Travers hurried off, Longarm looked at Tyson. "What do you think, Frank? Would you prefer to go back? Do you think these dudes can take it?"

"I think the women will be able to take it a damn sight easier than the men."

Longarm grinned. "Should we let them ride the way a man does?"

"You mean the way an Indian woman does? Hell, yes. But the shock would be too much for these dudes, I am afraid." He chuckled and shook his head. "I found Cindy Lou Ryan riding astride this afternoon. I was wondering why she was lagging so far back. My God, Longarm, the amount of finery they place between a woman and her body in this day and age! It is a caution. It is a wonder they can even move, let alone ride a horse."

"Yes it is," Longarm said, looking shrewdly at the deputy. "It purely is, but I don't expect the womenfolk half mind a hand now and then relieving them of all that excess baggage, isn't that right, Frank?"

To Longarm's amusement, the deputy blushed and looked quickly away. "Hell, Longarm, I was just . . ." His voice trailed off.

Longarm laughed and started for the cook tent. He was hungry and the campfire was blazing. Tim and the cook were busy, and already his stomach was grumbling.

As if to celebrate the fact that the party was going to continue on to Yellowstone, the cook pulled another ace out of his sleeve. A nearby stream had provided trout, and wild onions, resembling tiny scallions, were growing in all the meadows. The cook had stuffed the trout with the wild onion, packed the fish in clay, and rested them in the campfire. After the clay had baked hard, he had broken it open and peeled the skin and scales back. The result had been impressive. Longarm made it his business to seek Amos out after the meal and compliment him and Tim. The cook beamed his pleasure.

Anxious to get an early start the next morning, Longarm visited Hilda Guernsback's tent to check on Yellowstone Riley. He found the man fast asleep, a nearly empty bowl of succulent meat stew beside his cot, Hilda alert and on guard in a canvas chair beside the unconscious giant. If Longarm was not mistaken, there was a glow in her lean face, a light in her eyes.

She rose quickly from her chair at his entrance, and swiftly but firmly pressed him back out of the tent. Only then would she consent to speak aloud.

"What do you wish, Mr. Long?"

"Just checking to see how Yellowstone is, that's all. He seems to be sleeping. You managed to stop that bleeding, I reckon."

"Yes," she snapped. "And I cleaned his wound as well. Thoroughly. For a big man, he certainly made an awful fuss. But he ate like a famished wolf and now, as you say, he is sleeping. Is there anything else you care to know, Mr. Long?"

"Nope," said Longarm, backing up a little. "Guess that about covers it. Good night, Miss Guernsback."

"Good night."

He watched her disappear back into the tent, then

took off his hat and mopped his brow with his handkerchief. Yellowstone was in firm hands, and it didn't really matter if he took kindly to women or not. He no longer had any choice in the matter.

As he started back across the dark ground to the campfire, Olivia Baxter materialized out of the dusk and began to walk beside him. "Do you mind if I keep you company for a bit, Mr. Long?" she asked.

"My pleasure, ma'am."

"Mine too. You know, you were a real mystery to me, Mr. Long."

"How's that, ma'am?"

"Call me Olivia, please."

"If you'll call me Longarm," he countered, smiling. "Now, what's this about a mystery?"

"You always went off someplace to sleep whenever you camped with us. And you were gone for days at a time. Then we found out about that awful fellow who was after you. I am so glad he won't be bothering you anymore. Now you can stay close by, and sleep with the rest of us."

Longarm felt himself blushing, and was grateful for the darkness. It would have embarrassed him even more to have let Olivia Baxter see his surprise. If Longarm was not mistaken, and he knew he was not, this lovely, shy daughter of Congressman David Baxter was importuning him. He kept walking toward the campfire, and was mildly surprised to see that both Frank Tyson and Jim Travers were no longer sleeping alongside the campfire as they had been earlier.

The fire was still blazing merrily. He sat down beside it, leaning back against his saddle and bedroll, and took out a cheroot. Spreading the folds of her long skirt carefully, Olivia sat down next to him facing the fire, her arms tucked around her knees, her pallid features glowing in the light from the dancing flames. Longarm lit his cheroot with a flaming twig from the fire, tossed it back into the flames, then leaned back to inhale the smoke deeply, enjoying the lift Lady Nicotine gave him.

"I wish I could do that," Olivia said softly.

"You'd only get sick."

"I know."

Longarm looked at her. She was, he realized, blossoming during this trip. Earlier, she had given him the impression that she was little more than a wallflower, painfully shy. Her hair was a violent red, and her pallid complexion had been sprinkled liberally with freckles. Her best features were her high cheekbones, her strong, formidable jaw, and a surprisingly graceful neck. The freckles had faded somewhat. Her flaming red hair had darkened to a deeper shade. And she had filled out some, where it counted.

But Longarm was not going to allow a young innocent like this to seduce him. He had a great deal of respect for David Baxter, and for his justifiable passion in seeing that no harm came to his beloved daughter. Longarm had his scruples, and he carried them easily. He knew what Olivia was trying to do, and he was not going to let her do it.

Feeling a mite smug after making this resolve, he smiled paternally at Olivia and said, "How are you liking this trip, Olivia? Are you pleased we're going on to the park?"

"Oh yes! I've heard so much about it. Geysers! Steam and flames coming out of the ground. It sounds like something out of Dante."

"Dante?"

She turned to gaze into his face. "Oh, I guess you haven't heard of Dante, have you?"

Longarm smiled. " 'Through me is the way into the woeful city; through me is the way into the eternal woe; through me is the way among the lost people. Leave every hope, you who enter here!' "

She laughed. "I should have known. You have

depths that have not been plumbed. Like me." Her eyes gleamed in the firelight.

"Let's just say that a lawman sometimes has more free time than he knows what to do with. He sees a lot of empty hotel walls, and he gets tired of reading local newspapers. And after all, Dante's *Inferno* is right informative. It gives a fellow a pretty good idea about the lay of the land of his future home."

"Oh, please! Don't joke about that! You are certainly not going to hell, Longarm."

"I hope not. But then it never hurts to hedge your bets."

"I like you."

Longarm didn't know how to reply to that, so he took a deep drag on his cheroot. It gave him time to think. "I think you're pretty nice too, Olivia."

"Do you?"

"Of course."

"I am not what I seem, Longarm. Just as you are not what you seem."

"Don't reckon any of us are, at that."

"That's not true. Most people are *just* what they seem. No more. No less. But not you and I."

"We're different, huh?" Longarm smiled slightly.

"Don't mock me, Longarm!"

"I didn't mean to, Olivia."

That seemed to mollify her. Longarm took refuge in his cheroot, while the young woman stared moodily into the flames.

At length, without glancing at him, she said, "Do you know what my father is doing now?"

"Sleeping, most likely."

She glanced quickly over at him, her eyes alight. "I should hope not. Violet is a most demanding woman."

"Violet?" Longarm repeated, almost choking on the smoke he had started to inhale.

"Violet Fleur, my maid—my father's mistress."

"Oh."

"Are you shocked, Longarm?"

"It takes a great deal to shock a man nowadays."

"I am not shocked. I am pleased that my father has an outlet for his manhood. And Violet is good for him. She is good for me too. She has helped me to emerge from my shell. She has shown me what a real woman can do for a man."

"That so?"

She looked shrewdly at him, the faintest ghost of a smile dancing in her eyes. "I do believe you're blushing, Longarm."

"Maybe so."

"There's no need to. Surely you have had a woman, a man of your age."

Longarm removed the cheroot from his mouth. "Reckon I have at that, if it's any concern of yours, Olivia."

"Are you angry with me?" She seemed crestfallen, suddenly. "Do you think I am a hussy for talking to you like this? Can't a woman be honest with a man? It is all so *difficult*, Longarm! No one says what one thinks! And if one does . . . !"

Without warning, she began to weep. He reached out to comfort her, but she pulled away—angrily, he thought. Alarmed that her tears would awaken the camp, he took her by the shoulders. This time she did not shake him off. Smiling gently, he peered into her face.

"It's all right, Olivia," he told her. "There ain't no need for crying. I understand. You didn't shock me worth mention. You were just telling me what you felt, and I don't reckon there's a thing wrong with that."

When he said this, she flung her arms around his neck. Unable to disengage himself from her fierce embrace, he reluctantly enclosed her with his own arms. Immediately, she hugged him still tighter; despite himself, he felt her exciting warmth igniting him.

But he was reluctant to let this business go any further, and she could sense his unwillingness.

She pulled back and looked at him. "What's wrong, Longarm? Am I too ugly? Don't you want me?"

Longarm didn't know if Olivia was challenging him or if she genuinely wanted to know what he felt, but they were questions he found exceedingly difficult to answer directly. Certainly she was not ugly, and yes, damn it, he did feel a stirring of honest desire for her. But tarnation, that wasn't the point.

"Of course you're not ugly," he replied, smiling. "You are a very lovely young lady, but . . ."

"Then what is wrong?"

"Well, ma'am," he said, "it seems to me you ought to wait a spell until the right fellow comes along and can do this for you the right way." Longarm was perspiring, he realized. He released her and sat back, hoping she had the gumption to understand what he meant.

She looked closely at him, her eyes wide. Then she laughed, tipping her head back with delight. "You think I'm a virgin, don't you!"

"Hush, ma'am," he told her, leaning suddenly close and looking quickly around. He was certain their voices must be carrying, so quiet was the night. The tents were all dark and the campfire was dying down, but if anyone heard them and stepped out of their tent, they would be sure to draw the wrong conclusion—or worse, the correct one.

"That's it, isn't it?" Olivia insisted, leaning close, her voice soft. "You think I've never had a man before."

"You do seem to me a mite green, yes, ma'am. Not ugly. I didn't say ugly. But shy and not very . . ." He was suddenly at a loss for words.

". . . and not very experienced," she finished for him. "Is that what you were going to say?"

Longarm nodded.

She smiled and leaned close. This time her lips found his, and awkward though they were at first, there was a powerful urgency and need and . . . yes, *assurance* in the way they probed his lips. She kept moving toward him, and soon he found himself lying on his side, her lips still on his, her hand running excitedly up and down his face and then through his hair. By the time she pulled herself gently back and released his lips, he was beneath her and thoroughly aroused.

"We can't go to my tent," she whispered, "but couldn't we find a spot away from this fire?"

Longarm nodded. "We can do that, Olivia. Yes, we can. Let me get ahold of my gear and we'll be off. There should be a spot on the other side of that knoll."

"Yes! Out under the stars," she said softly. "You go ahead. I'll join you as soon as I'm ready."

The stars hung low and were incredibly bright, but Longarm saw little of them as Olivia prowled, insatiable, over his long body. She had come to his soogan with little else but her long white nightgown on, an apparition materializing over the crest of the knoll, running on silent bare feet to his embrace. But she had wriggled out of her nightgown long since, and he had found her as tight as a clenched fist. For just a moment, he had questioned her assurance that she was not a virgin. Immediately after his entry, however, all doubt vanished. Her movements were dictated as much by experience as by the youthful passion that governed her.

Now they lay in each other's arms while she nibbled on his ears and let her hand roam wantonly over his long frame. She was delighted with the extent of him, it seemed. With all of him.

"Mmm," she said, snuggling closer. "This is so nice. Much better than sleeping alone." She chuckled. "I didn't see why I should sleep alone if my father couldn't manage it. And as I said, Violet is so good for him."

"I'm glad to hear that," Longarm said. "Think maybe you should go back to your tent now? We'll be getting an early start tomorrow."

"As usual."

"That's right, Olivia. As usual."

"Well . . . if you're finished. I mean, if that's all you—"

She stopped and giggled. Her hand was closing about his erection. The size of it astonished even him. Her warmth, her snuggling, and the expertness of her stroking had brought him around again. He was more than a little astonished at Olivia's facility. "Guess I'm not finished at that, Olivia. But we better get this taken care of and get us some shut-eye."

She giggled and slipped over onto him. She peeled the soogan's flap back and sat down upon him. "You see?" she said. "We *can* ride astride! We can ride and ride and *ride!* Just like the Indian women! Are you going to let the women ride astride their horses, Longarm?"

As she asked this, she lifted herself off him in a deliberate attempt to drive him frantic. She almost succeeded. "That ain't my say, Olivia," he managed. "It ain't up to me."

Giggling like the naughty schoolgirl she was, she toyed with his moist erection with delicate up-and-down movements until she found herself unable to hold back. Longarm sighed with pleasure as she plunged down hard upon him, engulfing him completely.

Then she was riding him astride, as she put it, moving up and down with amazing vigor as she leaned forward, swinging her tiny nipples across Longarm's face.

She gasped and rode him over the hills and through

the valleys, the stars wheeling overhead until they both exploded, and then the only thing left in the night was the sound of his heavy breathing and the feel of her soft warmth. He held her in his arms, cuddled warmly and snugly against him, while the memory of their wild ride filled him with a pleasing drowsiness.

At last he stirred. "You'd better get back to your tent, Olivia."

"I know," she said. "I know."

"Olivia, we can't let any of the others . . ."

"I was thinking the same thing," Olivia said. "It wouldn't do. My father wouldn't understand. He might insist that you marry me."

A chill ran up Longarm's spine.

"But I don't think that would be such a good idea," Olivia ran on happily. "I mean, we come from different worlds, and all that. But it *was* nice, Longarm. I feel so much better now. And you *will* see what you can do about letting the women ride astride? We could do it just as prim and proper as you silly men want."

"Hell's bells, Olivia. It don't matter to me how you ladies ride, so long as you get there and back safely. You'll just have to take that up with the congressman. But I promise I won't speak out against the idea. How's that?"

"That's just fine," she said, reaching up and kissing him lightly on the lips. "You are a dear. You really are."

Olivia got to her feet swiftly. He caught a momentary glimpse of her lithe nakedness as she slipped her nightgown over her head. Then, with only a softly spoken good night, she vanished over the knoll.

Waiting a decent interval, Longarm gathered up his bedroll and returned to the campfire. He was no longer on guard against Sammy Wentworth, and in case of trouble, he thought it would be a good idea for someone in charge to be sleeping within reasonable distance of the fire.

The campfire was by this time only a bed of glowing embers. As he neared it, he was surprised to find that both the deputy and Jim Travers were sleeping soundly beside it. He almost laughed aloud when he realized the significance of their earlier absence from the campfire.

But he didn't want to disturb their contented slumber.

Chapter 8

The revolution began as soon as breakfast was finished and Tim brought the women their horses. Charles Clinton was the first to notice that the third pommel had been removed from three of the ladies' saddles, and in addition a crude but apparently sturdy groom's pad had been slung over the saddles.

"What's this, Tim?" he cried, moving swiftly closer to one of the horses to inspect the altered saddle and the pad. "What have we here?"

Tim, flushed, looked past Clinton to Olivia Baxter for help. Olivia stepped quickly forward and spoke quietly to Clinton: "There's no need to question Tim," she told the man. "I've made up my mind. I'm going to ride astride. And so are Daisy and Cindy Lou."

"Olivia!" cried her father, hurrying over. "What do you mean by this?"

"I mean," she said, "to set an example. I think those of us who want to ride astride should be allowed to do so."

Irene McAllister spoke up. "Really, Olivia, I admire your determination. But surely you realize that riding like men, astride puts you in rather . . . indelicate company. It is almost indecent."

"Almost, perhaps, but not quite. I prefer it. That's how I learned to ride, after all. Just as you did."

"Yes, but . . ."

"I don't think we should allow it," said Clinton. "Altering the saddles in this fashion might be dangerous. If you women fell off and injured yourselves, we would feel responsible. I think it is dangerous." Clinton looked at Peter Eliot. "What do you think, Peter?"

"Well, I don't know what to think." He looked at his young wife. "Mary, do you think it would be more dangerous astride? You're an excellent horsewoman."

She smiled at her husband, looked at Olivia, then shrugged. "I understand how Olivia feels, Peter. The riding is getting much rougher."

Peter turned to Longarm. "We'll let you decide, Longarm," he said. "If you think it will not harm the ladies, I suppose we'll have to give it a try. What do you think?"

Olivia looked at Longarm. She looked lovely. Her eyes were clear, her complexion glowing. And he knew what she was recalling. Longarm swallowed and looked at Frank Tyson and Jim.

"What do you boys think?"

They shuffled their feet awkwardly, and looked as if they wished Longarm would just let them out of it.

"Tell us, Jim," said Cindy Lou, her eyes fixed brightly, mischievously on the old guide. "Do you think it will hurt us to ride astride?"

Jim actually blushed and nodded his head. "Hell, no," he muttered in obvious consternation. "I've seen many an Indian woman ride astride. Don't seem to hurt them none, and they don't have all that much for a saddle, neither." He took out a red bandanna and mopped his forehead.

"And you, Frank," Daisy said. "Do you think it's possible for me to ride astride a horse without hurting myself?"

"Oh . . . sure!" Frank said. He looked desperately at Longarm. "I think maybe we ought to let the ladies give it a try—those who want to, anyway. Don't you, Longarm?"

Longarm looked back at Olivia. By now he saw the humor in the situation, and understood completely the intricate game that had been played the night before—not only with him, but with the deputy and Jim Travers. "Might as well give it a try, Olivia, if that's what you want." He chuckled. "I'm sure you'll do just fine." He smiled at her then, and winked.

She flushed crimson, turned swiftly, took the reins from Tim, and mounted at once. Longarm caught a glimpse of long black bloomers under her dress, which she quickly arranged modestly over the pommel and the rest of the saddle so that no trace of the shocking undergarment was visible. Daisy and Cindy Lou mounted almost as swiftly, Cindy Lou having a little difficulty in throwing her right leg across the saddle, due to the heavy folds of her long dress. It dawned on Longarm, then, that all three woman could not possibly be wearing corsets, or if they were, they must certainly be wearing them laced quite loosely.

Mary looked up at Peter. "I think tomorrow I should like to try it myself, Peter. Would you mind?"

"Of course not. If you think you'll be all right."

"I'll be fine."

Irene McAllister, Jean McPhee, Violet Fleur, and Melinda Clinton immediately indicated that they had no intention of riding astride. They expressed themselves in varying stages of indignation and shock, but Longarm detected a slight hint of envy in their voices as well.

Not long after, as Longarm rode on ahead of the party beside Frank Tyson and Jim, he glanced at the two men riding alongside each other beside him. "I suppose you two are now going to be championing voting rights for women."

"Sure enough," drawled Jim, scratching his beard and glancing with a merry eye at Longarm, "jest so long as the women know how to convince me."

Frank chuckled. "I notice you got back to the campfire after we did, Longarm," he said.

Longarm smiled. "Well, hell, I *left* after you did."

The three men laughed, then glanced back at the long line of riders and packhorses snaking along the ridge. The three mounted amazons were doing fine, it appeared, riding one behind the other and chatting amiably as they rode.

By midmorning, they were high in the mountains and in sight of the thickly wooded slopes far below when Longarm and his two companions pulled up. Snowbanks, at this height, were scattered throughout the valleys and ravines, and on one small plateau directly ahead of them, they saw an odd sight. A black bear was industriously raking his claws across a bright expanse of snow.

As the three men sat on their horses and watched, they were joined by Peter Eliot, Baxter, and Laxalte. At once, the men wanted to shoot the bear. But Longarm protested. They did not yet need the meat, and there were plenty of elk about. Reluctantly the men held off, and soon the entire company had caught up and was watching the antics of the huge black bear.

Whatever the bear was raking in with his claws, he was eating with great gusto.

"What *is* he eating?" asked Olivia, at length.

"Let's go see," suggested Melinda.

Longarm glanced at her. The frail, wispy blonde of a week ago seemed to have blossomed. Now, as she gazed excitedly ahead to the bear scratching away on the snowbank, her cheeks were aflame, her eyes bright. The cool, bracing air at this height seemed to have done wonders for her. "Sounds like a good idea, Melly," he told her. "I'm sure we got the time for it."

Longarm urged his horse on, the rest falling in behind. As soon as the bear became aware of the party's approach, he glanced up, stood for a moment on his hind legs, then ambled off in the usual ludicrous manner, turning his head first to one side and then to the other to watch the approaching riders. In a moment he had vanished into a thick stand of lodgepole pine beyond the snowbank.

Dismounting some distance from the snowfield, Longarm and the rest of the party left the ridge and waded across a small stream being fed by the melting snow, then climbed the slope to the snowbank. They saw that the entire snowfield was covered with grasshoppers, which had obviously become benumbed while crossing the high range at this point. At the edge of the snowbank, where it was melting, the water carried great quantities of the grasshoppers to the stream—and the waiting trout below.

It was this dark carpet of grasshoppers the black bear had been devouring.

Before mounting up again, the party stood on the ridge beside their mounts and looked beyond the ridge toward the Yellowstone Park preserve, stretching across a beautiful plateau that reached as far as the towering Absarokas beyond. Just below them, what Jim Travers called the Grand Canyon of the Yellowstone sliced its way through the sharp, pine-clad ridges, dotted with groves of glittering aspen and cottonwood.

Jim explained that they would not attempt to ford the Yellowstone at this point, but would cross the river to the west of Mammoth Hot Springs, where they would pay their respects to the park superintendent, Colonel Norris. Since this was agreeable to all parties, they set out down the far slope, keeping to the northern bank of the Yellowstone as they followed it into the park.

Soon they were riding through thick stands of timber. The going was smooth enough, and the sound of the women's occasional laughter echoed through the pines. Emerging finally onto a sloping meadow, they found the going a little more troublesome as they were forced, at times, to pick their way through tangled stands of chaparral.

It was during this portion of their ride that they startled a band of elk, which rose up before them and trotted away in a body. Again the congressmen were eager to shoot, but Longarm restrained them. It would mean stopping to dress whatever they killed, and there would be plenty of game when they camped later. Impatiently and not with good grace, they put down their rifles and contented themselves with watching the stately bucks, their heads thrown back and noses in the air, as they trotted off, true monarchs of the forest.

They passed a small pond not long after and were crossing a lush meadowland when Longarm was reminded of the tick problem. In passing through grass so tall that it brushed against his thighs, he noted a small black tick crawling up his thigh. He brushed it off swiftly and called out to Jim and the deputy, advising them to ride back along the line of riders and alert them to be on the lookout for the little buggers.

Another large pond appeared through the pines a little before noon. They descended through the grove and camped where the timber was open, on a clear patch of meadowland free of underbrush. While the deputy and the cook fished in the pond for the noon meal, Longarm took the opportunity to acquaint the party with the danger he saw in the ticks he had warned them of earlier.

"I reckon you've all heard of Rocky Mountain fever," he told the assembled party, "and want no part of it. And so far we've been lucky."

"What have those ticks got to do with the fever, Longarm?" demanded Laxalte.

Longarm turned to Jim, who was standing beside him. Jim cleared his throat nervously. "The Indians hereabouts figure the fever is carried by them ticks."

"The *Indians*! Surely you are not going to place any credence in what these aborigines believe, are you?"

Jim sent a dark stream of tobacco juice to the ground at his feet, then looked carefully at the congressman.

"Maybe you ain't, Congressman. But I sure as hell am. They been livin' here one hell of a lot longer than you or the rest of us heathen whites. They know this country—and it don't much resemble Washington D.C., and that is for goddamn sure!"

The surprising—even startling—vehemence of Jim's response to Laxalte's query took them all by surprise. It rocked the congressman back on his heels. Jean McPhee took the man's arm and said, "Please, Paul. Why not listen to what these men have to say before we challenge them? I do think they are trying to help us."

Laxalte's face went very dark; he started to respond angrily to Jean's not-so-gentle rebuke, thought better of it, and simmered down slowly.

"Go on, Longarm," said Peter. "Let's hear what you've got to say about these ticks."

"First off, they perch on twigs and grass stems until something warm-blooded brushes past. Then they get on you and bury their heads under your skin and start sucking." Longarm heard a few of the women draw in their breaths at this grisly thought, but he continued without pause, "The little fellow don't sting and you don't feel a thing. But they keep on drinking and swell up with blood and drop off when they're all finished."

"My God!" someone whispered.

" 'Course, if you see them first, you'd best get them off you before they start drinking."

"But how, Longarm?" Irene McAllister cried. Her eyes were wide, her face pale.

"That's why I'm taking the time to tell you all this. No need to get panicky if you'll just listen careful. The thing *not* to do is just grab the tick and yank her off. You do that, and you'll only squeeze the blood and tick-guts into your wound. Furthermore, the head will stay in under your skin, and even if you don't get the fever then, you will most surely wind up with a painful infection."

"So what do you suggest?" a nervous Big Jim McAllister demanded. "Will we have to *talk* the damn things off us?"

There was nervous laughter at this, but it did not seem to lessen the tension. Longarm smiled at Big Jim as he answered, "Talking might do it, Jim," he said, "but I suggest the best thing is to keep the damn things off you to begin with. Keep an eye out when you're riding through tall grass or brushing past bushes. Just don't let them get a hold on you. I brushed one off my thigh this afternoon, before I sent Jim here and the deputy back to warn you."

"But how shall we get rid of one if it's already on us?" Jean McPhee asked.

Longarm took out a cheroot. "Come to me. I'll light this cheroot and hold the burning end near the tick's rear end. The heat will make her back out, head and all."

Baxter spoke up then. "I've got plenty of cigars for any of you men—or women—who need them."

"And that's the *only* way to get rid of them?" Violet Fleur asked. She was standing beside Baxter, and was staring at Longarm boldly. "It doesn't give a woman much of a chance—unless she has a man around."

"That's about the size of it," Longarm admitted.

"Now, you don't have to worry about *that,* Vi," Baxter said, grinning at her.

For a moment it looked as if the woman were going to blush; instead, she smiled and shrugged. "It's a man's world," she said lightly.

"All right," Longarm said. "That's all I have to say."

The congressmen and their women broke up into groups and began talking. Tim was busying himself with the fire, and Longarm noted that Frank and the cook were walking back from the pond with gleaming strings of fish.

It was then that Longarm found himself wondering

about Yellowstone Riley and Hilda Guernsback. She and the Mountain Man had not attended his little lecture on the ticks and Rocky Mountain fever. He looked around and finally spotted them well away from the rest of the party, settled in a small pine grove. Longarm left Travers and walked across the meadow to the pine grove.

He found Yellowstone propped up in front of a lodgepole pine, wrapped in blankets, Hilda Guernsback hovering over him protectively. She had not even left the man to hear what Longarm had to say about the ticks.

"Hilda," Longarm told her, "why don't you go back over there so your mistress can tell you about the discussion we just had. I think it might turn out to your advantage." The big lawman spoke politely, but his tone did not encourage a refusal.

She looked hesitantly at her hulking charge propped up against the tree, then, nodding briskly to Longarm, she marched off across the field. Longarm watched her go for a few seconds, then looked at Yellowstone Riley.

"I'm weak," the man told Longarm, without his having to ask, "but if you don't cut me loose from that schoolmarm, I'm going to get a whole lot weaker! If I'd knowed what saving your fool hide was going to lead to, I'd've let that little creeper fill you full of holes!"

"Now, now," laughed Longarm, holding up his hand. "She ain't that bad, is she?"

"She's my mother come back to haunt me, that's what."

"You look a little better."

"Oh, I am. I stopped bleedin', I did. But there's more to livin' than not bleedin'."

"Was it bad riding this morning?"

"It was fearful, and you won't mind, I'm sure, that I didn't need to visit any snowbank to know what a bear was doing on it. But I'll be able to ride without my mother tomorrow—at which time I will be glad to guide you greenhorns through this park. *Through* this park, I say—and then *out* of it! Tourists! You'll scare off all the game, and before another snowfall, they'll be bringin' in trains so they can shoot from the windows."

"I don't think so, Yellowstone. These people are here to see if this here park should be kept free of settlers."

The big man frowned. "You know that for a fact, do you?"

"Some of the congressmen are not so sure that's a good idea, but the others can be convinced, I guess, if they like what they see. So far, it's hard to tell. One of them, Laxalte, tried to get the rest to turn back yesterday, but they voted to keep on to the park."

"You mean if these congressmen like the park, they'll keep it the way it is? No railroads, no settlers, no cattlemen, no prospectors?"

Longarm smiled. "Just tourists."

The man frowned thoughtfully. "I'll be riding with you tomorrow, then. Wouldn't want them congressmen to get unhappy. Me and Jim'll see to that. The sooner they see this place, the sooner they'll get back East."

He glanced past Longarm.

"Oh, oh," he said. "Here comes Hilda. I hope I look better or she'll start cluckin' and fussin'."

Longarm turned and nodded briskly to Hilda. "Riley is looking just fine, Hilda. Keep up the good work, and see that he doesn't get a chill."

She beamed. "Yes, Mr. Long. I'll see to that."

Longarm left her with Yellowstone, a smile on his face as he heard Riley protesting that he did not need another blanket . . .

Their progress for the rest of that day was slight—and very frustrating as they were forced to pick their way through a maze of windfalls. The fallen timber was well covered by the tall grasses, so that their unsuspected bulk was all the more galling when they came upon them. Since clearing them was seldom possible, they found themselves riding alongside the fallen logs, first in one direction and then in another, until it seemed that they were making no forward progress at all.

When at last they did break out onto a gentle slope, they found, to their surprise, that a rude road was following its crest, and on this road was an open wagon being driven by a sturdy team of horses. The wagon contained six women and one gaudily dressed fellow; the driver sported a long, tobacco-stained beard, yellow suspenders, and a huge paunch.

Curious, Longarm left his party, spurred after the wagon, and overtook it. As soon as he was abreast of the team, the driver reluctantly braked, cursing mightily at his four horses. The open-sided station wagon had its canvas sides rolled up, and the women and their lone male companion were all visible and seemingly very merry. They waved gaily at Longarm, while the gentleman took the cigar from his mouth and waved it at the lawman, a broad smile on his smooth-shaven face.

"What's the matter, chief?" the driver said, his foot resting on the brake lever. "Them pilgrims with you want to ride, do they?"

"Some of them, maybe."

"No room, as you can see."

"I'm Deputy U.S. Marshal Long, and I'm wondering what you are doing here."

"What I'm doing here? I got a government franchise to run tourists into this park and out again. You want to see my permit? These here tourists is from Cooke City, and we're heading for Mammoth Hot Springs. Some of these here ladies is thinkin' of takin' the cure in the baths." He craned his neck around and looked in at one of the girls. "Ain't that right, Minnie?"

"Yeah, you old reprobate. I'm goin' to take a bath, a real *hot* bath."

The driver looked at Longarm. "That answer your question, lawman?"

"What's your name?"

"Willis Toady."

"And I'm Duke Farrington," the fellow in the wagon called out. "And these here lovelies are all hardworking ladies of leisure. Ain't that right, girls?"

There were nervous shrieks of laughter. Longarm glanced at them, touching the brim of his hat to them as a gesture of respect. He noted that they were all blondes, and all of them were dressed in a loud, garish manner, with their hair, in most cases, down to their shoulders. Soiled Doves, each and every one of them, with their pimp in attendance. A needed holiday for these busy professionals was what Willis Toady was providing. Longarm saw no reason for detaining them any longer.

As he nodded to the driver and watched the wagon pull away, Jim Travers and the deputy pulled up beside him to watch, and a moment later the rest of the party was crowding around Longarm, bursting with curiosity.

"Tourists," Longarm said, in response to the volley of questions that were fired at him from all sides. "Tourists from Cooke City. They're heading for Mammoth Hot Springs. All we've got to do now is follow their wheel tracks."

Melinda spoke up: "Those girls, Marshal. They certainly were very gaily dressed for an outing this far from civilization. And I thought I saw only one man with them. How strange."

"Yes, I reckon it is peculiar," Longarm replied nervously, "but it sure ain't against any laws that I know of."

She nodded. "I don't suppose it is. But all the same, I thought it was rather odd. The way they acted, I mean. And their dress."

Longarm began to perspire at Melinda's unfortunate persistence. It was Jean McPhee who came to his rescue.

"I don't care how they were dressed," Jean announced flatly, as she pulled up beside Melinda. "I'm just glad we don't have any more windfalls to ride around. Let's just follow them."

That was a judgment everyone could agree on, it seemed, and for the rest of that afternoon they kept on the road, well behind the station wagon. Crossing on a crude bridge that spanned the Yellowstone, and proceeding almost due west, they came at last to a soft, murmurous waterfall that Jim identified as Tower Falls. Pulling up along the bank of the Tower River, the party fell silent, contemplating the falls.

Jean McPhee pulled up beside Longarm. She smiled tentatively at him, then directed her gaze at the cataract. "It . . . it looks so chastely beautiful, Longarm," she said, "hidden away away in the dim light of all these overshadowing rocks, almost as if it didn't want to be discovered by us. We could barely hear it as we rode up. I wonder how many have passed it without seeing it or visiting it."

"Quite a few, I reckon." Longarm shifted his weight, and for a moment the only sound, above that of the fall's whisper, was the creak of his saddle beneath him. "How is Laxalte getting on?"

"He's drunk, Longarm. Grossly, stupidly drunk. He has almost fallen off his horse twice. It is getting to be more than I can stand."

"We'll camp nearby, then."

"What do I smell, Longarm?"

He smiled. "Sulfur and brimstone, I imagine. Look at the ground on both sides of the river. Those wisps of clouds are coming from sulfur fumaroles. We're getting near to Colter's Hell, don't forget."

She glanced quickly up and down the shore, her eyes lighting with astonishment. "I must tell the others," she said excitedly.

As she rode back toward the others, Longarm started up, reluctant to leave the falls, but anxious to push on through what was a rugged patch of ground. Turning in his saddle, he saw Jim and the deputy riding hard to catch up. He reined in and waited for them.

Frank spoke first. "Laxalte is in a bad way, Longarm," he said. "We might better camp along the river as soon as we can find a spot. He's liable to fall off and hurt himself before much longer."

Longarm nodded. "Jean just told me. Let's keep going, then. It might do the fellow some good if he did fall off his horse—and landed on his head. Might knock some sense into him."

"Or ruin the entire expedition," Frank pointed out.

Longarm nodded soberly. Of course, Frank was right. Longarm did need to be cautious. At the same time that he thought this, he became aware that Frank Tyson had also become, almost without his knowing it, an advocate for this park—one more person eager to see it set aside, protected from exploitation. Longarm had an idea that Jim Travers shared this wish. How many in the party, besides Big Jim McAllister, felt this way, Longarm mused, as he rode on up the river.

The ground was lifting precipitously under them. The windfalls were numerous and the going was slow. But no likely camping spots presented themselves, and Longarm kept going. They were traversing the east flank of a rugged mountain by this time, giving them all a panoramic view of the surrounding country.

Abruptly, Longarm glimpsed, just head of him through the gap in the mountain formed by the river, a column of smoke—or steam—rising from the dense timberland beyond to a height of several hundred feet. Longarm's first thought was that it might be a column of smoke, that there was a fire—and then he realized what it was. He pulled up to watch the phenomenon, and soon the entire party had pulled up also to watch the puffing column of steam escaping from a vent in the mountainside.

They started up again, all silent and watchful, and soon the sound of this steaming cataract became audible, its roar echoing in the deep timberland along the river. No one seemed willing, then, to camp. Leading the way, Longarm kept on up to the peak of the mountain, leaving the river behind on their left, and just before nightfall, they found themselves on the crest.

Yellowstone Lake lay before them, the Yellowstone River issuing from it. They saw the stupendous canyon it formed, and the falls, both of them, and in all directions over the plateau, evidence of boiling springs and geysers. Colter's Hell, in truth. They dismounted and stood around in hushed groups, each picking out areas that attracted their attention, all talking excitedly. Even Laxalte seemed sobered somewhat by the experience as Jean kept at his side, supporting him patiently.

At last, near-darkness drove them on down the far side of the mountain to a level glade where they set up camp. Amos requested Longarm to see to acquiring them some fresh meat. Longarm asked Peter Eliot to go with him, aware that the man would appreciate the invitation very much. Jim and Frank took the far side of the slope, Longarm and Peter the near side.

Longarm did not expect much luck at this late hour. The sun had not yet set entirely and the sky was still bright, but the light in the thick woods was poor. As it was, they were lucky. Stepping out around a thick growth of juniper, Longarm almost blundered into a large bull elk reclining in the shade of a tree. At first he thought his eyes were betraying him, that he was looking at a dark tangle of juniper, the antlers simply bare shoots sticking up through it.

The elk convinced him differently. It came to its feet instantly, seemed to look at Longarm with haughty astonishment, then gathered itself to bound away into the woods. But by that time, Longarm had aimed and fired, a split-second before Peter. The magnificent animal fell on the spot. Scrambling the twenty feet or more that lay between them, Longarm saw that his bullet—or Peter's—had found the animal's heart, killing him instantly.

"It was your shot, I'm sure," said Longarm to Peter.

"Perhaps, Longarm. But it seems to me your shot came sooner than mine, and it was that round that dropped him."

"We won't argue about it," Longarm suggested with a smile.

Longarm opened up the bull and removed most of its viscera, then, leaving Peter by the animal, went back for packhorses.

It was late, and a leaping campfire lit the woods enclosing the campsite. Having got this far, and having seen for the first time what it had journeyed so long to find, the entire group was suffused with excitement. The fresh meat had added to the sense of celebration, and as they all watched, the cook did some celebrating of his own. He had announced that he was going to bake fresh bread and had invited all of them to see how he did it.

He dug a trench one foot in depth, at the bottom of which he and Tim placed red-hot coals. On top of the coals he placed iron mess pans containing already-raised bread dough. On top of these pans, Tim and the cook inverted slightly larger pans, and then heaped more hot ashes and coals over the covered bread pans.

The cook finished up by covering the entire trench with turf.

"Now you wait until morning," he announced to his spectators.

With that admonition ringing in their ears, the members of the exhausted party broke up and retired gratefully to their tents. Longarm found himself a spot on the rim of the campground under a pine tree, and was nearly asleep when he felt a gentle hand on his shoulder. He almost groaned aloud, but thought better of it as he turned his head and glanced up to see Jean McPhee leaning over him.

"It's been such a long time, Longarm," she whispered.

"Yes," he said.

"You have been so discreet. I don't think anyone knows . . . about us, I mean."

"How's Laxalte?"

"He's unconscious with drink," she said bitterly. "But I didn't come here to talk about him."

That was about what Longarm had figured. He took a deep breath and flung back the flap of his soogan. Jean dropped beside him eagerly. As her lips found his and her hands roamed swiftly over his long frame and found what they were seeking, Longarm sighed inwardly and gave himself up to the woman's need, astonished, as always, by the marvelous recuperative powers he seemed to possess at times like this . . .

Chapter 9

That next morning, after the trench was uncovered, Longarm and the rest of the party were astonished at the light, delicious bread that came from it. It was crisp to the touch when broken, as sweet and wholesome as any that ever came out of an oven. Together with the elk meat, which was steam-roasted in a Dutch oven, the bread capped a hearty breakfast, and seemed to augur well for the day ahead.

Laxalte changed all that.

During the breakfast, he had been obviously out of sorts, and Jean had done what she could to placate him. Unsteady on his feet before he reached the campfire, he had added generous amounts of whiskey to his coffee and grown steadily more unpleasant and belligerent throughout breakfast until at last his sullen temper could no longer be held in check. It was Frank Tyson who set him off. The deputy was moving over to his horse when Laxalte decided to leave the group at the campfire and turned directly into Frank's path. Instead of ducking to one side, he pushed deliberately into Frank, muttering something uncomplimentary under his breath as he did so.

The deputy grabbed Laxalte's arm and spun him around to face him, his lean face dark with sudden fury. "What was that you called me, Congressman?" Frank demanded.

Staggering slightly, Laxalte pulled his arm angrily

out of Frank's grasp. "You know damn well what I called you! You want me to repeat it, do you?"

"You do, and I'll flatten you."

"What's the matter, deputy? You ashamed of being a squaw man?"

Before Longarm could intercede, the deputy had swung on Laxalte. Frank's clenched fist caught the man on the side of his face, just under his left cheekbone, sending him sprawling backward. He tried to catch himself, but his boots caught on a log and he went down heavily on his back. Several members of the group exclaimed in surprise. Jean uttered a small cry.

Laxalte sat up, shaking his head blearily, a thin trickle of blood coming from the corner of his mouth. Looking up at Frank through narrowed eyes, he said, "That was a sucker punch, squaw man. You wait until I sober up."

"Hell," Frank spat. "I can't wait that long. Doesn't look to me like hell's going to freeze over for some time yet. Stand up. Congressman, and I'll knock you down again."

Longarm strode to Frank's side. "No you won't, Frank," he told the deputy. "You've done enough already."

"Damn it, Longarm, you heard what he called me."

"He's drunk, and I think you've punished him enough. Go on now, we've got to get moving."

Reluctantly, the deputy swung angrily off. As he did so, the rest of the party, hushed and shocked at the violence that had erupted so suddenly in their midst, moved off also. Longarm looked back down at the congressman. Jean was trying to get the big man back up onto his feet, but was having a difficult time of it. Longarm helped her, and as soon as the congressman was back on his two feet, he pulled himself angrily away from both of them and lurched in great, drunken strides back across the campsite toward his tent.

Jean looked unhappily at Longarm. "He's been drinking steadily. Whenever he gets like this, he doesn't really know what he's doing. I'm afraid, Longarm."

Longarm nodded and hurried after the congressman. He was not able to overtake him before the man disappeared into his tent. Frank Tyson, mounted by this time, rode up to Longarm and leaned over to speak to him.

"Leave the son of a bitch be, Longarm. Let him stew in his own juices for a while. Either that, or let me handle him. This is my fight."

"No it ain't, Frank. I'm in charge of this here circus. So ride out. We got a ways to go yet, and we've already wasted too much time."

With a shrug, Frank turned his horse. He was clapping spurs to its flanks when the congressman emerged from his tent, a rifle in his hand. Before Longarm could warn Frank, Laxalte fired at the deputy. Fortunately, Laxalte's condition was such that, even at that distance, an accurate shot was out of the question; nevertheless, an attempt had been made to shoot down a member of the party. Frank saw the situation at once and had the presence of mind to lean low over his horse's neck and spur the animal swiftly away from Laxalte's tent.

Longarm, meanwhile, was running full tilt toward the deranged congressman. As the fellow turned toward Longarm and started to bring up the rifle, Longarm flung himself through the air, catching Laxalte just below the waist. Longarm heard the man's sudden expulsion of breath as he went down. He heard the rifle fire also, and hoped to hell the shot went wild and didn't hit anyone. Even as he thought this, he clawed the gun out of Laxalte's grasp and, breathing heavily, scrambled to his feet to tower over the still-groggy congressman.

"Damn you, Longarm," the man said coldly. "I . . . I was just trying to scare that son of a bitch."

"I don't believe you, Laxalte. But let me tell you something. You do anything like that again, and you'll be sent back to Billings with Frank Tyson, and I'll have a full report on Marshal Billy Vail's desk before you get back to Washington."

"And *that* should read very nicely in the Washington papers," Jean McPhee said icily. "Really, Paul. Haven't you made enough of an ass of yourself by this time?"

Jean's searing sarcasm cut deeper even than Longarm's threat to have him sent back under guard. The man got to his feet, his face purpling with rage, then flung himself off in the direction of the corral.

With a sigh, Jean said to Longarm, "I'll strike his tent. I've done it enough, now, that I'm used to it."

"I'll help," said Longarm, handing her Laxalte's rifle.

The two did not have to work alone, however; Cindy Lou and Daisy hurried over to help. As soon as Longarm could be sure they were not going to delay the party's departure by helping out with Laxalte's tent and gear, he hurriedly left them to find his own mount. He was worried about the congressman; there was no telling now what he would do in his drunken rage. He was angry and foolish and drunk enough to ride off and get himself scalded to death in one of those hot springs they had all glimpsed beyond this mountain.

An hour later, Longarm was still trying to overtake Laxalte when he heard a rider coming up hard behind him. He pulled up and twisted about in his saddle.

It was Yellowstone.

"What the hell are you trying to do?" Longarm asked the towering Mountain Man. "Kill yourself?"

Riley shook his head grimly as he reined up beside Longarm. "Nope. I'm trying to *save* my life. Longarm, do you have any idea how much lovin' a woman like that has saved up all them years?"

Longarm laughed. "It wasn't that bad, was it?"

"At first, it wasn't. No, sir." He grinned. "But I'm a sick man, ain't I, Longarm? She fixed me up, but she didn't fix me up *that* good." He sobered. "I heard you're lookin' for that congressman what shot at Frank Tyson."

"That's about it, Riley. You sure you can handle a ride like this? He's gone off toward the lake, and it don't look like he's very careful about how he rides or where."

"Think maybe he sees snakes instead of grass?"

"Could be."

"Let's go. Like I told you before, I want these here tourists in and out of this land, and I don't want them carryin' any bad stories back with them when they go. I figure the best thing is for them to want to keep this place as a park. That means we got to keep them happy while they is here. Let's go save that donkeyhead from hisself, Longarm."

At the base of the mountain, they rode past bubbling, plopping mud springs that gave off a strongly sulfurous odor. Passing close beside a few of the springs, they found Laxalte's tracks. Longarm was right; the congressman was heading toward the lake. Continuing on, they passed a lake surrounded by a meadow, crossed a couple of small ridges, and soon came in sight of a little cloud. It was straight ahead of them. They kept going, and soon Longarm realized that this was one of the geysers he had heard about.

"That's Old Faithful," Riley told Longarm, pulling up to watch.

Longarm pulled up also, his ears ringing with the roaring fury of the geyser. The stench made him wrinkle his nose in discomfort, but he could not look away from the fountain of boiling water several feet in diameter that was shooting up to a height of more than a hundred and fifty feet. The early-morning sunlight turned the clear water into a mass of glittering crystals, and a gentle breeze wafted the vast white curtain of steam far to the right across the flat. Abruptly, it died down. The intense roaring faded, as did the loud popping sounds that had accompanied it.

Longarm glanced around at the flat. There was little vegetation. The place was pocked with craters and mounds of varying sizes, from many of which wafted plumes of steam, and from all of them, that persistent stink of sulfur. Over the entire flat hung clouds of vapor like shifting curtains of fog. Suddenly, far to the right, another, smaller geyser began to spout, while the ground underneath began its ominous rumble.

Riley grinned at Longarm. "If that congressman rode this way, he'll be certain he's done kicked the bucket and gone to hell."

Indeed, Laxalte's tracks had led past the geyser basin and on into an unbroken pine forest. Once in the pines, they lost Laxalte's sign, but kept going, nevertheless, moving as straight as was possible on the assumption that Laxalte was making no effort to lose his trackers. It seemed likely that he was interested only in riding fast and far. On the other side of the timber, they found themselves on a broad, grassy plain, with Yellowstone Lake well ahead of them beyond the plain, and looming magnificently above the lake, the Grand Tetons, the sunlight reflected brightly from their white flanks. It was an impressive sight, and Longarm found himself impelled to stop so that he could take it all in.

"Yup," said Riley. "She's sump'n', all right. Nature's handiwork, I calls it. Them Tetons is as clean and powerful as the day God put them there."

Longarm nodded, then let his gaze move over the plain. Frowning, he peered closer at a spot near the lake. He stood slightly in his stirrups. Yes. A lone horse was cropping the grass near the shore. It could be Laxalte's mount.

Longarm pointed to it. Riley followed his hand. His

one blue eye narrowed, and he nodded quickly. "Think maybe he went for a swim."

"I hope not," Longarm muttered, spurring his horse to a gallop.

Laxalte had gotten as far as the lake shore. He was sprawled facedown, his fingers dug into the soft sand. The man appeared to be unconscious. Longarm dismounted and pulled the congressman over onto his back.

The fellow's eyes flickered open. He swore softly, then tried to pull away—and lost consciousness. "Get his horse," Longarm told Yellowstone. "We'll tie him on and take him back."

Laxalte tried to take a swipe at Yellowstone as the big man lifted him over the saddle, but Yellowstone just chuckled and ignored him. He was not going to be very comfortable riding that way, but he was not going to have any say in the matter. Yellowstone and Longarm used rawhide thongs to tie the man in place on the saddle. He appeared to be snoring as they rode off.

They were on their way to Mammoth Hot Springs, where the rest of the party had agreed to meet Longarm, when a herd of cattle broke over the southern ridge on their left. A moment before, the sound of shrill whistles and the bawling of the cows had swung Longarm's head in that direction. He was startled to see the herd and the four cowpokes driving them.

Longarm pulled up as the cattle spilled over the grass toward them. It looked like a good-sized herd, close to a hundred head. "What the hell?" Longarm muttered.

"I know 'em," said Yellowstone. "The owner of the herd says he's got a permit to run his cattle on this grass."

"What's his name?"

"Stan Slocum. He's got a ranch just outside Cooke City. Them boys with him is plenty tough. Took me twenty minutes to whup Biddle, Stan's segundo."

"What was the ruckus?"

"A saloon play they tried to make on me 'cause they know I'm agin their using this country for their beef. People in Cooke City hate the government keeping all this lovely land away from them."

"Don't seem to me the government's doing such a good job keeping land away from Stan Slocum and his cows."

"Like I said, he claims he has a permit to use this here grass."

By this time the lead cattle were flowing behind them. As Longarm turned his mount so as to keep out of the herd's way, he heard a shout and wheeled to see an angry cowboy flogging his horse in an effort to overtake him. Longarm promptly pulled up to watch the cowboy and his three partners race toward him.

"The lead feller is Stan," Yellowstone said quietly. "He's all steamed up 'cause you ain't gettin' out of his herd's way fast enough."

As Stan Slocum pulled his horse to a sliding halt in front of Longarm, the lawman took a good look at the fellow. He was a smooth-shaven, hawk-faced young man with boyish eyes. The only thing wrong with the face was the stamp of meanness that covered it like dirt.

"Didn't you see me comin'?" he demanded of Longarm.

"I saw you," Longarm allowed, politely enough.

"He saw us!" Stan brayed at his sidekicks, now reining up about him. "Now ain't that just fine!" He looked back at Longarm, pointedly ignoring Yellowstone. "You got a permit for bein' on this here land?"

"Have you?"

"Damn it, mister! You ain't askin' me! I'm askin' you!" Glancing at Yellowstone, he said ominously, "And Riley knows all about that. Don't you, Riley?"

Yellowstone didn't bother to reply to Stan. Instead, he looked the other three over carefully, as did Longarm. The rider closest to Stan was obviously his second-in-command. He was chewing on a grass stem at the moment, enjoying himself, content to let his boss do the hazing. He was a paunchy fellow with enormous arms and shoulders, and if this was the fellow Yellowstone had taken twenty minutes to whip, Longarm could understand why. The third fellow was a dirty, squint-eyed sneak who hung back a ways, as if watching to see which way to jump. The fourth man was a kid no older than seventeen, a towheaded fellow with blue eyes and a clean, narrow face, who was obviously doing his best to look as disreputable as his companions.

"Well?" Stan demanded. "You got a right to be on this here land of mine? I got it leased all legal and proper from the authorities. If you and Yellowstone and that poor slob sleepin' on that horse is thinkin' of building here, you better get another thought."

"You say you have leased this land?"

"That's right. And I got a permit to prove it."

"Which means you want me to move on, then. Right?"

"Well now, ain't you smart. You kin go right to the head of the class!"

The chunky fellow had ridden close to the horse carrying Congressman Laxalte. The big man was leaning over to look more closely at Laxalte's face. "Hey!" he cried out gleefully. "This here fellow's had a snootful. Smells like a vat of moonshine! Yes he do!"

"Leave him be," Yellowstone said quietly.

The paunchy fellow just looked up at Yellowstone and grinned. Then he drew his sixgun so swiftly and effortlessly from its holster that it seemed to appear as if by sleight of hand. Yellowstone leaned back warily in his saddle. The other one laughed and then probed at Laxalte's ass with the barrel of his Colt.

"You heard what Yellowstone said," Longarm said ominously. "Holster that weapon and back off."

Stan Slocum hooted. "You heard him, Bird! He don't want you to bother his friend. Now you just better back off and be a nice boy."

Bird just grinned at Longarm and poked again at Laxalte's fleshy behind. The marshal nudged his horse alongside Bird's, and backhanded the man with such force that he went flying backward out of his saddle. His head slammed down upon Stan's thigh as he tumbled to the ground between their two horses. By the time Stan and his two remaining men had recovered from their shock at Longarm's action, Longarm had drawn his own Colt and was holding it on Stan Slocum steadily. The tall lawman's gunmetal-blue eyes glinted coldly. It was not a gaze that most men would care to confront.

Clawing himself furiously to his feet, Bird found himself standing in front of Yellowstone Riley, who had dismounted swiftly and now stood just before him, toe to toe, waiting eagerly for any indication that Bird wanted to continue the argument.

"Suppose you show me that permit you were blabbing about just now," Longarm said evenly, holding his hand out toward Stan.

"You'll pay for this, mister," Stan fumed. "I got friends."

"I am glad you got friends, Stan," Longarm drawled, smiling slightly. "You are going to need them, judging from the way you throw yourself around."

Stan looked with a sudden, feral alarm at Yellowstone. "Who the hell is this man, Riley?"

Riley smiled. "A deputy U.S. marshal, that's who. And guess who he's escorting through the park, you pig-brain. A passel of congressmen from Washington D.C., that's who. Congressmen and their ladies." Yellowstone grinned wolfishly. "You picked the wrong dog to kick this time, mister."

Sullenly, Stan pulled a tattered, well-folded paper from his pocket and handed it to Longarm, who took it and found that the permit was in the name of the Yellowstone Park Improvement Company, and gave Stan Slocum, owner of the Bar S, rights to graze his herds during the summer months on certain extensive lands adjacent to Yellowstone Lake. The man was also entitled to build single-floor dwellings for the comfort of his men. Longarm could not read the signature, but it was signed and notarized by a justice in Cooke City. Longarm handed it back to Stan.

"Okay, you've got the permit. But who authorized this company to issue permits?"

"The next park superintendent," Stan Slocum said. "And he's going to be around a long time."

Longarm smiled. "Well, maybe these congressmen who are looking through this park right now will see to it that permits like this ain't tossed about so freely from now on."

Stan looked down at his segundo, who was still standing beside his horse, his senses obviously not completely collected as yet. "Hurry the hell up there, Bird," Slocum snarled. "Get back on your horse. The stink around here is getting fearsome."

As he spoke, he hauled his horse's reins cruelly back and then spurred it off. Bird clambered into his saddle and took off after him, the quiet one and the kid strung out behind. Longarm watched them go, then glanced at Yellowstone.

"Their names," he said. "I'd like their names."

"Bird's full name is Bird Biddle. That quiet little skunk behind him is Arny Sloat. The kid's name is Benny Capper."

"That crew don't look like they got enough brains among them to blow their noses, let alone run a ranch."

"Now that," Yellowstone said, climbing aboard his horse, "is a thought. It purely is."

As the two men started up again, they heard Laxalte stir. They both turned in surprise. He had begun to sing. Cutting through the Bar S cattle, they smiled as Laxalte's voice gained strength.

To Longarm's surprise, the congressman did not have such a bad voice, at that. He shook his head and the trio continued on over the next ridge.

During the ride to Mammoth Hot Springs, Yellowstone told Longarm about the fellow who had first tried to convince the world of the existence of this high, seething plateau in the Rockies, John Colter.

The fellow had originally come this way with Lewis and Clark. Later, after his discharge from the service, he returned to the area to trap. He ranged as far as the Pacific on one occasion, and then back across the mountains to the Yellowstone Valley, and saw enough of the place to fill him with wonder—and also to make of him a man who related miracles too astonishing to be believed. As with Marco Polo so long before him, the stay-at-homes simply could not comprehend the wonders Colter described.

"Since when have you known about that fellow Marco Polo, Yellowstone?" Longarm inquired, surprised.

"Just because I dress like this, sonny, it don't mean I can't read. We got long winters up here, don't forget. I took after Bridger, I did. He was always spouting Shakespeare—though he didn't much like that son of a bitch, Richard the Third."

"My apologies, Yellowstone. Go on. I'm interested in this Colter."

In the spring of 1808, Colter and an old friend set out on another trapping expedition, but this time the lucky Colter almost ran out of luck. One morning, while Colter and his sole companion were in a canoe examining their traps, they were surprised by a large party of Blackfoot Indians. Colter's partner attempted resistance and was slain on the spot.

Colter, with more presence of mind, gave himself up,

realizing it was his only possible chance to avoid immediate death. The Indians then went into a conference to decide how best to kill the trapper, while still gaining the most personal satisfaction from the dead. Colter was questioned by one of the braves concerning his fleetness of foot. Immediately Colter assumed a piteous expression and lamented the fact that he could not run worth a damn. He began hobbling about painfully, and at once the heathens' faces lit. They would make the poor bastard run for his life.

Accordingly, he was stripped naked and led by the chief of the war party to a point three or four hundred yards in advance of the waiting Blackfeet. The Indian told Colter to save himself if he could, and Colter didn't wait for any more palaver. He took off, and the Indians saw right away that there was nothing at all wrong with the Mountain Man's feet. Furious, they took after him in a body, their howls filling the wilderness.

Colter ran like the wind, however, and his exertions were so prodigious that blood began streaming from his mouth and his nostrils, forming great crimson ribbons of blood down his naked torso. Prickly pear and the rough ground lacerated his naked feet. As Colter ran, he saw six miles ahead of him, a level plain, beyond which was a fringe of cottonwood on the banks of a river. Short of that six miles lay not a shadow of a chance of concealment. It was six miles, then, or nothing.

As he raced across the plain toward that beckoning fringe of cottonwood, desperation gave him wings. Gradually the Indians fell back, and when Colter finally dared a glance back, he saw that only a small number of the Blackfeet were still after him. This sight encouraged him mightily, and he put on a fresh burst of speed.

But there was one Indian who was almost too much even for the desperate Colter. Steadily, relentlessly, he shortened the distance between himself and the racing trapper. At last the brave was within a spear's throw of his fleeing quarry. Colter glanced back and saw the Indian readying his lance. He did not wait for the Indian to hurl it. Suddenly whirling about, he confronted the Indian. Astounded at this sudden move, and obviously unnerved by Colter's bloody appearance, the savage faltered for just a moment, and in trying to save himself and hurl the spear at the same moment, he stumbled forward, breaking the spear as he fell to the ground.

Colter fell upon the Indian, snatched up the broken spear, and plunged its barb deep into the fellow's back, pinning him to the earth. Then he resumed his flight, reached the river beyond the cottonwoods, and dove in, swimming toward a raft of driftwood caught against the headland of a small island in the river. He dove under this raft and found a spot where he could keep his head above water while still being hidden by the raft. Under the raft, barely able to keep his face out of the water, he waited in suspense as the Blackfeet combed the banks of the river, then explored the island thoroughly, not omitting the raft. More than one Blackfoot brave padded across the tangle of wooden logs and vines, driving Colter's face below the surface each time.

At last the Indians abandoned their search, and when evening came, Colter swam several miles downriver before daring to clamber onto shore. For seven days he wandered, naked and unarmed, over sharp rocks, past cacti and the prickly pear, scorched by the heat of the sun and chilled by the frost of the night, finding his sole subsistence in whatever roots he could dig from the ground—until at last he reached Manuel Lisa's Missouri Fur Company trading post on the Big Horn River.

After still another year in the wilderness, Colter got into his canoe and swept down the river. He made three thousand miles in thirty days, reaching St. Louis after an absence of six years.

"What happened to him after that?" Longarm asked, shaking his head in wonderment at Yellowstone's vivid account.

"He went around telling folks what he'd seen hereabouts, and people commenced looking at him funny, so he went back to St. Louis, got married, and kept his mouth shut ever after. Poor feller died broke." Yellowstone shook his head at the pity of the tale, and went on, "Can't say I blame folks much for not believing old Colter's story—don't know as I'd have believed it myself, but now, you and me, we're riding across it."

And so they were. The region through which they were now riding had a desolate, hellish aspect, and the stench had a great deal to do with that feeling, Longarm realized. Bubbling, fuming springs were everywhere. Off to Longarm's right was one hole about ten feet in diameter, out of which noisily bubbled large, irregular globs of mud. It reminded Longarm of boiling soap. Some of the other hot springs were hurling mud to heights of five or six feet, and along the side of a small ridge to Longarm's left, hot steam was issuing from holes in the ground with a deafening, shrill scream. Longarm glanced back at Laxalte. The man was peering uncomprehendingly about him at the satanic landscape.

Longarm smiled and turned back around. Good. This trip just might convince him that he should stay away from the stuff. It might, but Longarm would not want to bet on it.

They kept to a path through the springs, with Yellowstone in the lead now, since he apparently knew the area well. Longarm could hear water bubbling underground some distance from the trail, and the sound of the horses' hoofs over the ground gave Longarm the impression that they were thumping over a hollow vessel of immense size. On all sides of him, needles of snowy white limestone jutted upward, some of them as tall as six feet.

Beyond the field of mud springs, they came to a crater filled with boiling water. It looked to be about three hundred feet in diameter, and from this pool streamed an effluent that contained three distinct colors, white on the west side, in the middle pale red, and on the east side a light sky blue. The water in the crater itself was a deep indigo blue and was boiling fiercely, the whole looking like some oversized cauldron, the edges of which were polished to a white sheen.

Circling slowly around this natural wonder, Yellowstone led Longarm into a patch of timber and called back over his shoulder, "We should be at Mammoth Hot Springs before nightfall."

At that, Laxalte cried, "Let me down from here! Untie me, damn it! I'm sober! Cold sober, damn it! If you men are bent on punishing me, you've done it! Now let me down!"

Longarm looked at Yellowstone. The Mountain Man shrugged and pulled up. Longarm nodded. Laxalte was probably right. After what he had just seen, he just might be cold sober.

The two men dismounted and untied the weary congressman.

Chapter 10

It was a sober, even repentant, congressman who rode into camp late that night with Longarm and Yellowstone. The camp was on a meadow overlooking Mammoth Hot Springs, and the sharp, acrid tang of sulfur hung heavy in the air. Jean McPhee came running to greet Laxalte; and Hilda Guernsback was standing somewhat angrily beside Yellowstone's horse as the big man eased himself wearily and painfully out of his saddle. Longarm, dismounting at the same time, saw Riley begin to protest as Hilda started to lead him off toward her tent, then give it up and go willingly with the woman.

Jim and Frank were standing beside Longarm, watching Yellowstone being led off. Jim shook his head. "Never thought I'd see the day," he said. "Yellowstone Riley on a leash."

"He hasn't been hogtied yet," commented Frank. "I give him a fifty-fifty chance."

"Any excitement, Jim," Longarm asked, "while we were off chasing that lush?"

Travers scratched his beard and looked up at Longarm with a gleam in his eyes. "Sure was," he replied, chuckling. "Them instructions you gave us for getting rid of ticks worked out just fine. Dave Baxter had a fine time with that cigar of his. Women were getting them ticks up into the darnedest places."

"They get 'em all out?"

"Seems to me they did," said Frank, grinning. "Baxter gave us both lighted cigars, and we all went to work with a will before we settled down to eat."

"Never saw so many ankles and shanks in my life," Jim confessed happily. "I figure I owe some of them females a few dollars, at least."

The three men chuckled a bit at that, and then sobered as Jim looked at Longarm and asked, "How we goin' to handle this here Laxalte, Longarm?"

"I think, for his own good, he should go on back to Billings and dry out," Frank said.

"He wouldn't dry out in Billings," Longarm pointed out. "Besides, I have a better idea. Come with me."

Longarm then led the two men over to Laxalte's tent. He stopped before the entrance and called out, "Miss McPhee, it's Longarm. Can we come in?"

Jean ducked her head out of the entrance, a frown on her face. "Yes, what is it? Paul's resting."

"Just as well, I guess. Can I speak to you?"

She left the tent and came to a halt in front of Longarm. Looking unhappily up at him, she brushed a stray lock of her ruddy hair off her forehead. She regarded him with surprisingly icy eyes. "Paul told me how you tied him over his saddle and led him over hell and beyond. That wasn't very thoughtful, Longarm."

"I don't expect it was, ma'am. I didn't mean it to be."

Jean took a deep breath and straightened, her eyes now cold and almost defiant. It occurred to Longarm in that instant just how lovely this tall, green-eyed secretary of Congressman Laxalte's was—and he found himself almost envying the man. "What is it you want, then?" she asked shortly.

"I want you to bring out every bottle of whiskey Laxalte has, along with any other alcoholic beverage the man might have on hand for variety. Brandy, wine, anything."

Her eyes narrowed. "Everything?"

"You heard me. And I don't want you to hide one single bottle."

"You don't."

"No, I don't."

"I think Paul will have something to say about that."

"No, I don't think he will."

"We'll see about that." She turned to go back into the tent, obviously to awaken Paul Laxalte and tell him what Longarm planned.

"Miss McPhee?"

The girl paused and looked back at Longarm, her face white, defiant.

"Do you have some reason why you *want* Paul drunk most of the time?"

"That's a rotten thing to say, Longarm!"

"Just trying to figure you out, is all."

"Well, don't try!"

She vanished into the tent. Longarm, with raised eyebrows, looked around at Jim and Frank. Behind the two men a small crowd was gathering, but staying well back. Baxter was with Olivia and Violet, puffing happily on his cigar, and Peter Eliot was standing with Big Jim and Clinton. When Longarm caught Melinda Clinton's eye, she smiled encouragingly.

A moment later, a groggy Paul Laxalte emerged from the tent. When he saw the three men and, behind them, the crowd of onlookers, his face darkened. Behind him, Jean stepped from the tent and came to a halt beside Laxalte.

"What's this Jean tells me, Long?" Laxalte demanded.

"I'm confiscating your firewater, Congressman," Longarm replied. "For your own safety and to protect the peace of mind of the rest of this party."

"You can't do that. Do you know to whom you are speaking? I am a member of the Congress of the United States of America!"

"You're not in Washington, D.C. now, Congressman. You're on federal land, and I'm a federal officer, sworn to keep the peace. I figure you're doing all you can to disturb it. You'll do as I say."

"Now, see *here* . . . !"

Melinda Clinton's clear voice cut Laxalte off at that moment: "Paul, why don't you begin to *act* like a member of congress? We all know what sorrow weighs you down, but if you will look to your left, you will see someone who is offering you not only love and companionship, but loyalty as well. Give Longarm your liquor. Surely you can see how little good it is doing you."

The simple good sense of Melinda's words stopped Laxalte short. He started to say something in response, then glanced at Jean and frowned. Looking swiftly back at Longarm, he said, "All right, damn you. Go ahead. Take the stuff. All of it. I don't care. I don't need it. You'll see. All of you will." He swung around then and ducked back into the tent.

Jean took a deep, unhappy breath and followed him in. A moment later she emerged with an armful of bottles and handed them to Longarm, Jim, and Frank. Twice more she returned to the tent for bottles. The last bottle she handed Longarm contained champagne, and she gave it to the tall lawman reluctantly.

As Longarm took the bottle from her, he looked deep into her icy eyes. "Is this all there is?"

"Will you take my word for it, or do you insist on searching the tent and all our effects?"

"I'll take your word, Miss McPhee."

"That's all there is, every bottle, every drop. Now would you please leave us, all of you?"

Peter Eliot and David Baxter helped Longarm to dispose of the firewater, emptying each bottle regretfully into a quiescent crater close to the edge of the simmering plain below the camp. The moon was up by this time, and the light it shed over the bubbling, hissing flat gave it the aspect of some strange, volcanic moonscape. On the far side of the springs, the headquarters building that had been constructed by Norris stood on a pedestal-like outcropping of rock. It was a two-story affair, and was the first substantial building Longarm had seen in the park, though Jim Travers had told him that a hotel had just been built in the Lower Geyser Basin by a man called Marshall.

"You say Norris is not there?" Longarm asked Frank as they returned to the camp.

"I rode over when we arrived. The fellow in charge told me that Norris is off somewhere, either exploring or building a road. He wasn't much help."

Longarm turned to Jim. "Well, then, where do we go from here?"

"From here I reckon we should head for the Lower Geyser Basin and maybe let some of the ladies rest up in the hotel." He smiled. "Some of them who was riding astride are a little sore now, it seems. From there we could go to the Upper Geyser Basin and then on to Yellowstone Lake. That ought to give our visitors a pretty good idea of the place."

Longarm nodded. "All right, then. We'll pull out tomorrow."

"Not early, Longarm," said Peter Eliot, who had been listening to the conversation as he walked back to the camp with them. "I think we'd like to explore this fabulous basin below the camp before we leave. Would that be all right?"

"Fine," Longarm said. "And maybe you'd like to go with me on a hunting trip again sometime tomorrow. We must have finished up that elk already."

"I'd be delighted," Eliot said, beaming.

The cook emerged from his tent and approached Longarm as the lawman came to a halt in front of the campfire. "I got some venison stew simmering inside," he told Longarm. "And some coffee."

"Thank you, Amos," Longarm said, aware suddenly

of just how famished he was. "I think maybe Yellowstone would appreciate something to eat, as well."

Amos grinned. "Oh, that Miss Guernsback already came for his food. She's takin' good care of Yellowstone Riley."

Longarm smiled. He should have realized Hilda would have tended to Yellowstone long before this. He shook his head and followed the cook into his tent. He was exhausted. He hoped that this night he would have no visitors in his sleeping bag, and to insure that, he decided he would sleep close by the fire, right alongside Tim and the cook.

To his surprise, he found, later that night, that he was sleeping alone by the fire. With a shrug, he rolled over to place his backside a bit closer to the glowing coals, and slept.

It was a little after the noon meal when the rest of the party, with Travers and Tyson in charge, started for the hotel in the Lower Geyser Basin, leaving Peter Eliot and Longarm free to lift into the Gallatins in search of elk.

They rode across several swift-running streams with no deer or elk sign, but they kept on, and late that afternoon, they crossed trail after trail of bands of deer heading for the cedar ridges on the south side of the ridge they were following. Turning after the most promising sign, they rode with caution into the cedars and came upon a small band of elk strung out along an opening in the cottonwoods. In reaching for his rifle, however, Eliot caused his horse to shy suddenly.

In an instant, the small herd had vanished beyond the cottonwoods, and Peter Eliot was a very contrite man. Longarm said nothing. He knew there would be plenty in this upland. Sure enough, a half-hour later they came upon more sign. They camped near cedar ridges in a river bottom, and moved into the cedars. It wasn't long before a small herd came to drink.

Longarm allowed Eliot to make the kill. On Longarm's advice, Eliot shot the smallest male elk in the herd, since they would be carrying it a long distance before sundown.

The two men had just finished tying the elk over the pommel of Peter's saddle, when distant shouts broke the stillness. Longarm turned in the direction from which the cries were coming. The shouting grew louder. Leaving the cedar ridge and stepping out onto a small grassy sward, Longarm and Peter caught sight of a single man running alongside the river toward them. Peter's shot must have alerted this fellow to their presence in the area.

When the man saw them, he veered directly toward them and stopped shouting. But he did not slow down. The closer he got, the more unkempt he looked. He had obviously not shaved in weeks, and his hair hung in dirty, greasy strands about his collar; yet the fellow was dressed in what had once been fine trousers and was wearing a well-tailored jacket that was now, unfortunately, worn through at one elbow.

Longarm and Peter left the grassy knoll and went to meet the fellow. He stopped in front of them, puffing like a steam engine, his jowly face florid, perspiration tracing a grimy path across his forehead and cheekbones. He squinted unhappily at them and tipped his head a little, as if he had trouble making them out, even though Longarm and Peter were within a few feet of him.

"Lost my glasses!" the man burst out. "Can't see so good!"

"What's all the shouting?" Longarm asked.

"Indians! That's what! Indians! They attacked our camp last night and robbed us. Took everything! Our tools, our food, our weapons. We're helpless in this wilderness now, and it's all because of them savages! You got to help us!"

"Hold it. Just hold it a minute. Let's eat this here

apple one bite at a time. Who are you? What are you doing here?"

"I'm Carl Dinwiddie, and my partners and I are prospecting for gold."

"How many are you, and what are their names?"

"There's three of us. Lucas Salter and Milt Feeber are the others. We're camped down the stream. When we heard your shot, they sent me after you."

"They hurt?"

"Lucas is, and Milton don't feel so good. They're still mighty scared about what happened last night!"

"I can imagine," said Peter. "What a terrible experience it must have been for you." He looked at Longarm. "Hadn't we better warn the rest of our party?"

"Now just hold it a minute," said Longarm. "I ain't so sure it was Indians who cleaned out these here pilgrims. Seems to me prospectors are mighty easy pickings in this park." Longarm looked back at the nearly blind prospector. "What makes you so sure it was Indians, Dinwiddie?"

"Their feathers! We saw their feathers! And their faces were painted! They were Indians, all right. Their cries were bloodcurdling."

"I can imagine," said Longarm. "We'll go get our mounts and check this out. We don't want to start an Indian war on the say-so of three prospectors, one of them half blind."

"I can see very well at a distance!" the man huffed.

"Just wait here."

The prospector's camp was a sorry sight, reminding Longarm of those other prospectors' camp just outside the park. Everything was litter. Sleeping bags were still unrolled, cooking utensils were thrown about uncleaned, flies buzzed about half-emptied cans and the droppings of the men themselves. If it was Indians that had attacked them, undoubtedly it was the stench that had brought them.

Dinwiddie was mounted up behind Longarm when they came in view of the camp. The lawman was anxious for the man to drop off; it was obvious Dinwiddie had not bathed since starting out on this quest for riches. Longarm pulled up just outside the perimeter of the camp and turned to Dinwiddie.

"You can get off now," he told him.

"Oh, sure."

As the man slipped off the horse, Longarm dismounted also. Peter, pulling alongside, the elk still across his saddle, folded his arms over his saddle horn and shook his head.

Longarm glanced up at him. "What's the matter, Peter?"

"Some mess, I'd say."

"And you'd be right."

"I can just imagine how it would look if we opened the park up completely, or if someone were to discover gold here—or just get the rumor going." Again he shook his head.

Peter dismounted and the two men followed Dinwiddie into the camp. The one Dinwiddie had said was hurt was sitting on the ground with his back to a rock. He was holding a dirty rag against his side. The rag was black with old blood. Flies were buzzing insistently around the wound, and the man's thin, spindly face was screwed into a perpetual, prunish look of dismay.

"You got to help me, mister!" he said, looking up at Longarm.

"Who's this?" Longarm asked Dinwiddie.

"Lucas Salter."

Longarm looked at the third member of the expedition. He was the one that Dinwiddie had said didn't feel so good. He too was sitting on the ground, his arms wrapped around his stomach, his body bent forward. He was groaning softly. "And this one?" Longarm asked Dinwiddie.

"Milton Feeber. He's been sick for days now. He's got the runs."

Longarm nodded. That explained the stench. Milton Feeber looked as if he had been somewhat overweight when he began the trip. But he had lost weight, and his skin looked loose on him. He glanced up at Longarm and groaned, looking like a fish under water, gulping at a mosquito.

"The Indians didn't do that," Longarm told Dinwiddie. "That was bad water and eating out of dirty pans, and cooking out of them too. Describe the Indians."

"I already did. They had feathers and they made terrible howls. And they danced around us."

"One of them grabbed my scalp," said Lucas Salter. He looked like he was going to cry.

"You stay here with them," Longarm told Eliot, "while I check for tracks."

It did not take Longarm any time at all to find the tracks of three horses and three men—the horses all shod, the men booted. The tracks came from the south and halted just behind the crest of a hill overlooking the prospectors' camp. Longarm saw where the men had stood around planning their attack, and then followed the tracks—in single file, appropriately enough—as they descended on the sleeping men. The tracks they had left in departing were just as clear. Since they followed the river's shore, Longarm did not think he would experience any difficulty in following the trail.

He rode back to the prospectors. Peter was keeping his distance, Longarm noticed. The congressman was evidently appalled at the condition of the men and their camp.

"I saw tracks," he told Peter. "Get these men on their horses and help them get to that hotel or whatever at the Lower Geyser Basin. Tell Deputy Tyson I'm going after the 'Indians' that attacked them."

Peter turned to the prospectors. "Do you men have horses?"

Dinwiddie nodded unhappily. "They broke from us yesterday afternoon. They're off down the river. I can see them grazing. But they're a ways off." He looked appealingly at Longarm.

"Go after them, the three of you. And get them and mount up, or this man will leave you," Longarm commanded, his voice scathing.

"Longarm!" Peter cried, astonished at the lawman's harsh tone.

Longarm looked at him. "You heard me, Peter. I need you to get Tyson for me. I might need help. Is that clear?"

Peter nodded, then looked at the three woebegone prospectors. "Get after those horses," he said.

The man with the runs looked up bleakly. "Me too?"

"You too!" Longarm barked, "or there won't be anything left of your ass when I get through kicking it. Now git!"

A moment later, on the crest above the camp, Longarm looked back to see the three prospectors chasing their horses frantically. Shaking his head at the incompetence he saw displayed, he looked back at Peter Eliot and waved. Then he pulled his mount around and started after the white bastards who had robbed and terrorized these hapless men.

The next day he was still on their trail, deep in the Absarokas. The men had made no effort to conceal their tracks, but they had traveled fast, and Longarm had almost lost them the night before. The sun was roasting the back of his neck when he came across the skinned carcass of a bear. Two vultures were digging at it, and their hideous faces and maniacal eyes turned insolently toward Longarm as he rode up to inspect the bloody remnants of what had evidently been a large black bear.

They were bear hunters, then—out for bear grease and hides. And of course, they saw no harm in that. Anyone who would defend a bear must be loco.

Longarm saw the smoke from their fire while he was still about half a mile from their camp. Topping a ridge at last, he saw that the bear hunters had constructed a rude log cabin with a sod roof, more than likely with one of those permits from the Yellowstone Park Improvement Company, and it was from a crooked stovepipe sticking out of a window that the woodsmoke issued. The area around the log cabin was littered with cans and broken and discarded tools and harness, while out of the ground on all sides protruded the stumps of trees, looking like the earth's wisdom teeth working their way out of very sore gums. He saw the irregular patch that was the skin of the bear they had just killed stretched on a willow frame alongside the entrance to the cabin.

He heard the three men dimly. They were inside the cabin and were evidently getting very drunk, perhaps on whiskey they stole from those prospectors. Longarm rode across the ridge and down the slope to the cabin. The voices of the men inside the place got steadily louder as he drew closer. Longarm slipped off his mount just in front of the cabin, drew his Winchester out of its boot, and cat-footed it to the door. There was no lock on it, and the hinges were pieces of leather nailed to the doorjamb. He yanked it open and strode in, levering a fresh cartridge into his rifle's chamber as he did so.

The place was stuffy, and it stank. Smoke from the oil lamps hung close under the low ceiling. In the dimness, Longarm saw two very surprised men sitting at a table, with a fresh, gleaming bottle of whiskey planted on the planks in front of them.

Longarm had been trailing *three* men. Where was the third?

A shadow filled the open doorway behind him, and before he could turn, he felt the nudge of a double-barreled shotgun in the small of his back. He tried to brace himself a split-second before the third man shoved viciously with the shotgun, sending him slamming forward into the table. His Winchester flew from his grasp and clattered across the floor. The two other bear hunters were on their feet by this time. The moment Longarm struck the table and sprawled across the top of it, they reached down and yanked him smartly back and around, slamming him hard against the rough log wall of the cabin. The back of his head struck the wall sharply. Lights exploded deep within his skull. His knees turned to rubber, and he felt his back scraping against the wall as he started to slide down it. Before he reached the floor, one of the hunters kicked him expertly in the side, just under the kidney. It sent Longarm sprawling on his back. His hat went rolling oddly on its rim and disappeared under the table.

Through lidded eyes, his head aching smartly, he watched the three men standing over him. The looks on their faces gave Longarm the impression they had just taken him off a spit and were preparing to season him for the big meal of the day. One of them—a short, powerfully built fellow as bald as a cue ball—was actually licking his chops as he leaned his head close and smiled down at Longarm. The fellow with the shotgun spoke up then.

"Now what in hell we got here, boys? He ain't friendly a-tall, is he? Comin' in here like that an' invitin' hisself to a drink without even knockin'!"

His companions thought that was hilarious and could hardly contain their mirth, so they moved closer and began kicking at Longarm. Longarm turned away from their boots, and was reaching under his coat for his Colt, when the fellow with the shotgun chuckled and booted his hand away, then reached under the jacket and removed the Colt from its holster.

"That's a nice one," he exulted, examining the weapon. "A double-action!"

He kicked Longarm viciously in an excess of good feeling.

The three of them pulled away then to look down at Longarm. Their mirth subsided gradually, and for that Longarm was grateful. He felt as if he'd just finished falling down a mineshaft.

"Who are you, mister?" the one with the shotgun asked.

"Who the hell are *you*?" Longarm managed angrily.

The tall fellow leaned his shotgun against the wall and sighted on Longarm with the Colt. He flicked the end of the barrel with his finger, noting that Longarm had filed off the front sight. He was a long, lanky fellow with sandy hair. His face was dirty and carelessly shaved, his wide mouth loose, his hazel eyes malevolent.

"My name is Will," he said, showing Longarm his yellow, broken teeth in a sudden smile. "Will Tramp."

"Pleased to meet you," Longarm managed. "I'm Custis Long."

"Introduce yourselves, gents," Will told his companions. "We should let this fellow know who it is that's goin' to skin him alive!"

Giggling and wiping his running nose, a small, round fellow with hectically flushed cheeks stepped forward. With a careless swipe of his hand, he brushed his dark thatch of hair back off his forehead. Longarm saw the bright, tiny, moving bodies of lice moving hastily back, seeking the warmth and protection of the man's head of hair. "I'm Sandy Patton," this worthy announced, smiling broadly and nudging his partner. His teeth were black stumps. For a moment, as he opened his mouth, he looked like a panting dog.

184

The bald fellow beside him was of medium height, dressed all in furs, and smelled like an overripe bear. "Name's No-Hair Beebe, Long, and it shore is a pleasure meetin' up with you. Goddamn!"

As No-Hair said this, he stepped forward and kicked Longarm in the butt. It lifted him and sent him rolling under the table. Longarm felt his head striking pieces of greasy, fly-encrusted meat. The three used the space under their table as a garbage dump, obviously. He twisted his face away from the stinking pieces of rotting food, causing the three hunters to double over with laughter. He had seldom run into three men so easily amused.

Reaching up to grab the table, Longarm pulled himself to a sitting position. "You three don't look like Indians, and that's a fact."

The three exchanged glances, then burst into a roar, slapping their thighs. "Them prospectors done sent you after us!" Will Tramp declared, beside himself. "What is you, mister—a lawman?"

"That's it, Will. You hit the nail on the head, and I guess you three are under arrest for robbery."

"Oh my goodness gracious! You hear that, No-Hair?"

"I'm all upset. Yes I am. Let's drag the son of a bitch outside and stretch him alongside the last bearskin we set out." As No-Hair spoke, he took out a mean-looking blade that had a cruel upward curve at its tip, a skinner's knife that looked as if it had seen plenty of service. "Go get 'im, Will."

Will Tramp eagerly strode toward Longarm, and bent down to grab him by his hair and yank him upright. Longarm got his feet under himself in a hurry. Tucking his shoulder down, he drove it into Will's midsection, lifting the man off his feet and slamming him back against No-Hair. Will still clutched Longarm's Colt in his right hand, and he clung to it grimly, so that even as he was slipping sideways after striking

No-Hair, he squeezed off a quick shot. The round buzzed past Longarm's right earlobe as the lawman brought his knee up under Will's chin. The fellow's head snapped back with sickening force against the wall. He let the revolver fall from his hand, and Longarm bent to retrieve it, only to find himself struck from behind with such fury that he went hurtling against the table, overturning it.

It was Sandy Patton who had flung his arms around him and driven him clumsily away from Will. As Longarm and the table upended, Sandy himself went flying over the top of Longarm. He landed on his side and scrambled to his feet in time for Longarm to club him on the side of the head with a clenched fist. As Patton staggered back, Longarm was afraid he might have broken his hand. But now was no time to check that out.

A mewling cry of fury behind him alerted him to the fact that No-Hair was closing in on him. He ducked swiftly, almost double, then turned. No-Hair, rushing at Longarm with his skinning knife extended, ran heavily against his crouching figure and went sailing over the lawman. Before Longarm could turn, he heard a scream. Glancing back, he saw that No-Hair had plunged his hunting knife haft-deep into Sandy Patton's gut, just below his belt. Sandy was backing up with the blade's handle protruding from his belly, his filthy hands grappling with his bloody entrails.

"Oh, *shit!*" No-Hair said, watching his companion sit down suddenly on the floor with his back to the wall, and begin to cry.

"Damn you!" cried Will from behind Longarm.

Longarm turned and saw Will, conscious now, reaching for his shotgun. The overturned table was between them. Longarm started to clamber over it as Will Tramp caught up the shotgun and swung it around. Longarm clawed his derringer out of his right vest pocket and fired, almost in one continuous motion, discharging both barrels. Each round found its mark. One slug obliterated Will's left eye, the other printed a neat hole under the right one. As Will slipped sideways to the floor, he dropped the shotgun, his remaining eye still open and staring at Longarm in what appeared to be stunned surprise.

That left No-Hair. Looking back, Longarm saw that Beebe, his knife still lost in Sandy Patton's gut, had snatched up an ax from the floor's litter of equipment and was advancing menacingly, the ax held high. Longarm flung himself over the table, snatched the shotgun up off the floor, and fired at No-Hair. The ax was already slicing through the air. Ducking aside as he fired, Longarm felt the blade shiver into the wall beside him, then looked back at No-Hair.

Longarm couldn't find him—not his head, at any rate. The headless torso swayed grotesquely, then slipped out of sight as it slumped to the floor on the other side of the table, a dark fountain of arterial blood pulsing from the spot where the head should have been. Both barrels must have caught the man squarely in the neck, and at less than two feet, the charges had decapitated No-Hair as surely—if not as neatly—as the blade of a guillotine. Scrambling to his full height, Longarm looked beyond No-Hair Beebe's torso at Sandy Patton.

The fat rogue was still sitting with his back against the wall, his face slack, his dirty hands still clutching his mess of gray entrails, Beebe's shiny bald head resting beside him where it had finally come to a halt. But Sandy Patton was not concerned about No-Hair's condition. His wide eyes were staring straight ahead of him, unblinking, at nothing at all.

Acrid smoke dug at Longarm's eyes. He glanced to his left and saw that one of the two coal-oil lamps had set a portion of the cabin's wall on fire. The other lamp had crashed to the floor when the table went over, and had been snuffed out. Longarm snatched up the fallen lamp's base, lit the wick from the flames, and flung the base at Sandy. With a heavy *whomp*! fire splashed like blood up the wall, igniting Sandy's clothes in the same instant.

Longarm picked his hat, his Colt, and his rifle up off the floor, and fled the cabin. A moment later, astride his horse on the crest overlooking the cabin, he took one last look back at the blazing structure—and shuddered. He had been foolish, walking into that nest of sidewinders that carelessly. And he had been lucky. He shrugged and nudged his horse off the ridge. As he always reminded himself at times like this, he'd much rather be lucky than smart.

Chapter 11

Before Longarm rejoined the party at the Marshall hotel the next day, he was met by Deputy Tyson and Yellowstone Riley. Descending a mountain slope on his way to a fork that gave a clear view of the plateau below, Longarm saw the two horsemen riding rapidly in his direction. He dismounted to await their coming.

"You find those Indians?" Frank inquired quickly, as he and Yellowstone dismounted.

Longarm looked at Yellowstone. "You ever hear of some bear hunters named Will Tramp, Sandy Patton, and No-Hair Beebe?"

Yellowstone scratched idly at the two scars below his patched eye, and grinned. "I figured they might have something to do with that hoo-rah." He shook his head. "A mean threesome, they are—just about as unpleasant as a grizzly with a toothache. They put some feathers on, did they?"

"That's what they did. I didn't recover much of what they stole. Fact is, I didn't bother to hang around after I finished with them. The stench was something fearful. The stench and the slaughter."

"Slaughter?" Frank said, frowning.

"The three of them are dead. They offered resistance, so I was forced to shoot them, and they went up in flames along with their cabin. How are those prospectors?"

The deputy chuckled. "They've got the whole camp stirred up, they have, with their tale of being attacked in the dead of night by the fierce aborigines. You can imagine how Clinton and Laxalte are taking that news."

"And the women?"

Frank shrugged. "Seems to me Melly Clinton and Olivia Baxter are keeping the rest of the ladies calm." He grinned at Longarm. "They seem to think you can handle anything. They're camped by the hotel now, waiting for your report. Eliot came riding in with the prospectors, all anxious that I should go after you, so here I am."

"I tagged along," said Yellowstone, "to get away from Hilda. I hope you don't mind. She's bound and determined she's goin' to throw a halter over my head and ride me into old age." He smacked his lips and grinned suddenly. "I must admit, though, she ain't lacking in enthusiasm for the bed, and it seems to have done wonders for my wind."

Longarm laughed, then looked back at Frank. "I told Peter to get you just so I could give him a good reason for leaving me and getting those prospectors to the hotel. I didn't want him tagging along and getting his butt shot off. Somehow, the way I look at it, we got to make sure this passel of big shots makes it back to Washington with all their teeth and enthusiasm intact."

"Which means we might have problems," said Yellowstone.

"Oh?"

"You tell him, Frank," said Yellowstone.

"Peter Eliot ran across something on his way back with those prospectors, something to do with those cattlemen you and Yellowstone met bringing Laxalte back. You remember them, don't you?" he added with a sly grin.

"I remember. What about them?"

"Well, Peter didn't know what he saw exactly, if you take my meaning. He just found himself overlooking a couple of log shacks and some rope corrals. Those cattlemen were busy branding, they were."

"With a running iron?"

"Peter didn't say that. I don't guess he knows what a running iron is. But from the way he explained it to me, that's what they were using, all right."

Longarm thought that over. Why not? If they were just cowboys herding cattle on the off-limits range, they wouldn't have been so touchy. Poaching on U.S. grass isn't all that terrible a crime in these parts. On the other hand, stealing other cattlemen's beef is a hanging offense. Longarm considered the matter carefully now. They were pretty far from the railroad, and there was still quite a bit of open range to the east. If Stan Slocum's Bar S was little more than an outlaw hideout, then all Stan and his boys had to do was drive his stolen cattle into this parkland, rebrand them, give the brands time to heal, then drive the cattle on back to the Bar S in the fall. Neat. Very neat.

And that explained Stan Slocum's attitude and that of his men.

"Did this Slocum or any of his boys see Peter?"

"Peter said he thought one of them did, but he couldn't be sure," Frank replied.

"If he was seen, why didn't they chase him?"

"Peter said it was close to dusk when he spotted them. Soon after he rode away with the prospectors, he was in deep timber and it was dark. I figure that if they were seen by any of Slocum's men, it would be hard for them to know who it was looking down on them, and maybe impossible for them to follow Peter that late."

"Until Slocum finds out who that was—if Peter *was* seen—he's going to be a very nervous rustler," Longarm said, chewing worriedly at a corner of his mustache.

"And a mite dangerous," Yellowstone commented. "Let's get on back to them congressmen and their ladies," said Longarm nervously. "I don't like this a-tall."

Longarm mounted up swiftly and led the two men toward the fork at a fast gallop. He wanted to reach the party before sundown this day. He needed to talk to Peter Eliot. He felt like a wagonmaster debating mentally as to whether or not he should circle the wagons. Only it wasn't Indians he was worried about. It was white men, with a damn sight more ingenuity in the way they raised hell.

It was all those centuries of civilization, Longarm realized, that gave men like Slocum such a talent.

They arrived at the Lower Basin camp, which was perched on a long, grassy knoll a quarter-mile from the hotel, just before nightfall, and found the members of the party gathered around the blazing campfire, engaged in a debate so acrimonious that no one seemed to notice their approach until they were within a few yards. Longarm quickly dismounted.

"What's the excitement?" he asked Jim Travers, who seemed quite relieved to see him. His face was ruddy in the firelight, his expression one of resigned exasperation.

"Whores," the man replied laconically.

Longarm smiled. "How's that?" He was not sure he had heard correctly.

Olivia came forward quickly. "You heard what he said, Mr. Long! Whores. And that is just what they are. Over there! Look!"

She pointed to a collection of tents on the grounds of the hotel, which was a two-story log affair. At first glance, the hotel appeared to be more porch and peaks than a hostelry, but the important thing, obviously, was the activity on the grounds. Longarm had seen such tents before, of course, but in trail towns and mining camps. He was startled to see such an establishment here, in this federally protected park. The strange thing was, he did not know for sure if such business was or was not allowed.

Charles Clinton strode forward, Melinda at his side. The tall, handsome man radiated indignation. "What do you plan to do about those . . . harlots, Longarm?"

"Not so sure there's anything I should do. Don't seem to me they're hurting anyone, are they? I do recommend, however, that we all get a good night's sleep and ignore the activity in those tents."

"That's just it, Longarm!" snapped Big Jim. "Listen a moment, and you'll see why we damn well *can't* ignore it."

The men and woman who were crowded around Longarm immediately quieted. And right on schedule, as if the silence of those around Longarm were its cue, there was the sound of a bottle breaking, followed by a woman's high-pitched laughter. A loud roar of masculine laughter followed that, and a moment later, what sounded like two bottles breaking filled the night.

Laxalte moved closer to Longarm. "Seems to me, Longarm, you made it pretty clear that I was breaking the peace around here." He smiled sardonically. "And I daresay you were right. Well, then. What about that nonsense over there?"

Longarm smiled at Laxalte. The congressman had a point. "All right," he said wearily. Then he looked around for the cook. He saw Amos standing in front of the cook tent. "Feed Yellowstone and Frank, will you? We been riding all day. I'll be right back."

"You don't have to go alone," said Yellowstone.

"That's right," Tyson offered. "I'm not that tired. I'll go with you."

"It's just a passel of soiled doves and their pimp, Frank," Longarm said wearily. "I can handle it."

There was still enough light for Longarm to take in the awesome spectacle of the Lower Geyser Basin, and as he trudged across the gleaming white geyserite rock that covered the surface of the basin, he could not help wondering how the members of the congressional party could let themselves be distracted so easily from such a stupendous natural phenomenon.

Everywhere he looked, steam was venting from fissures and hung in the air just above the basin, occasionally obscuring the hotel ahead of him. The sound of the escaping steam and the sudden rush of geysers filled the air. Under his feet the ground rumbled continuously, ominously. As Longarm picked his way over the hellish landscape, his boots broke through the crust every now and then, warming the soles of his feet alarmingly. He walked carefully, at times veering well around bubbling springs and pools of water that were seething from the subterranean heat beneath them.

He was almost to the hotel when a geyser to his left suddenly erupted. The eruption was fierce and noisy, but lasted for only a few minutes. Longarm glanced at it and kept going toward the hotel.

Reaching the high ground on which the hotel stood, he started for the tents and was immediately seen by the man Longarm had felt for certain was the pimp in charge. Duke Farrington was smoking a cigar and was resplendent in a checkered vest, bowler hat, and fawn-colored pants. A diamond stickpin gleamed in his cravat. A most prosperous pimp, obviously.

"Ah, it is Marshal Custis Long! Pleased to see you again, Marshal."

"Thought you were going to Mammoth Hot Springs."

"Business was poorly there," he said, grinning. "It's much better here, near the hotel."

"This is what you would call a working tour, I reckon."

The pimp appreciated that. He laughed and nodded.

Longarm continued, "I came to tell you to get out.

And soon. You're making too much noise—or were, a few minutes ago. I heard bottles breaking."

"Forgive us, Marshal. I promise. We will be quiet. I shall see to it. Wouldn't want to wound the delicate sensibilities of your high-toned guests. Of course, any one of them is welcome to come over anytime. Drinks will be on the house."

Just then, one of the prospectors, the one who was supposed to have had a terrible case of the runs, emerged bleary-eyed from a tent with a blond dove on his arm. He seemed to be in excellent shape, though he was still a stranger to a razor. When he saw Longarm, he turned abruptly about and, still hanging on to the girl, went back inside the tent.

Longarm looked at the pimp. "Break one more bottle, and I'll have reason to send you packing. And keep the noise down. It'll be full dark soon, and the members of my party aim to get some sleep."

At that moment, the driver of the station wagon that had brought the women into the park, accompanied by another, paunchy fellow—well dressed, his thinning black hair greased back flat on his balding pate—hurried from another tent and headed for the hotel. It was clear that Longarm's presence was making itself felt.

"Who was that with your driver?" Longarm asked.

"Phoggs, the manager of the hotel."

"I see."

"What's the matter with you, Marshal? Don't you know that men are only human, and have appetites like any other normal creature?" He smiled again. "How can you begrudge any man the warmth and comfort of a woman's presence? And what makes those politicians into such high-minded snobs? Politicians are always my best customers—day *and* night."

"Their wives, and in one case a daughter, are with them."

"Oh."

Two yelping cowboys suddenly erupted from a distant tent. They were laughing uproariously and almost sprawled on their faces, so precipitously did they make their exit. Behind them in the tent's entrance, a woman appeared, her crimson robe open carelessly, and swore at them. She was blonde, like all the others that Farrington had brought into the park. Longarm was certain he did not know her—yet there was something about her that troubled him.

He walked toward her, peering closely at her in the poor light, but when she saw him coming, she disappeared inside the tent. A plump girl appeared in the tent's entrance, and as Longarm stopped before her, this other girl said, "Maud don't entertain lawmen. That's her policy."

"She's right," said Farrington, as he followed Longarm to the whore's tent. "Maud just doesn't take to lawmen."

Longarm glanced over at the two cowboys. They were familiar. Bird Biddle and Arny Sloat. They stood watching Longarm, weaving slightly.

"Any more Bar S riders in there?" Longarm asked mildly.

"What the hell's it to you?" Bird said, belching loudly.

Sloat giggled appreciatively.

"Get on back to your boss, both of you," Longarm said, not because he had any right to tell either of them what to do, but simply because he suddenly felt mean enough to want to provoke them. Surprisingly, they shrugged, and without further hostility, turned and lurched toward the hotel in search of their mounts.

Longarm looked at Farrington. "I think maybe I'd like it better if you and this here tent city of yours would just fold up and move out, first thing in the morning."

"Move out?"

"All the way to Cooke City. That clear?"

"You know you have no right to make me leave here."

"It don't matter to me if I do or not. I just told you what I'd like—and I'd like this carnival out of here. You want to give me some trouble on this, Farrington, and I'll be glad to oblige."

The man smiled easily and raised his right hand, palm out. "I'm a peaceable man, and moving on is what I and my ladies of leisure do best. We just came out for the scenery, anyway, and we have seen plenty of that. Good night, Marshal Long."

Longarm nodded, left the man, and picked his way wearily back across the steaming crust of the basin. As he walked through the noisome night, with the geysers and fumaroles around him filling the darkness with sound, he became aware of a deep uneasiness; so deep was it that he could not isolate its cause. Then he remembered how important it was that he find out from Peter Eliot the location of the Bar S outfit. Abruptly, the tantalizing smell of stew coming from the cook tent wiped all other concerns from his mind, and he knew only that he was famished.

The camp was quiet. Longarm, his stomach full, was sitting crosslegged by the fire, finishing a cheroot and sipping at the bottle of Maryland rye from his saddlebag, trying to discover the reason for his earlier uneasiness. Frank Tyson and Jim Travers were snoring quietly in their sleeping bags on the far side of the campfire. There was no sound now from the tents near the hotel, and a little while ago, Yellowstone had wandered not too reluctantly toward Hilda Guernsback's tent and been invited in. Her inspection of Yellowstone's wound had apparently not lasted long. The lantern in her tent had winked out rather quickly.

Tim appeared out of the night. "Mr. Long," the boy said. "It's Miss Olivia. She says to come quick!"

Longarm smiled and rose slowly to his feet. "Thanks, Tim. I'll go check."

"She was real scared, Mr. Long!"

Longarm took another drag on his cheroot and nodded to the young man. "I'll see to it, Tim. You go on back to them horses and get some shut-eye."

Tim turned and vanished into the darkness. Longarm corked the bottle of rye, replaced it in his saddlebag, and started for Olivia's tent. He knew which one it was, since there was a lamp still lit inside, and he had heard Tim coming from that direction. There was a slight tingle of anticipation running up his back as he neared Olivia's tent. She had been afraid that Longarm would think her unattractive. It had been a baseless fear. Longarm had found her delightful. As he reached her tent, he flicked the stump of his cheroot into the darkness, took a deep breath, lifted the tent flap, and ducked inside.

"What's wrong, Olivia? Tim was a mite alarmed."

She was lying face down on her cot, wearing only a long chemise with pink ribbons threaded through ruffles in the sleeves, about the neck, and along the hem. Her violent red hair and green eyes were in startling, dramatic contrast to her milk-white complexion. No, to Longarm's way of thinking, Olivia Baxter was not at all ugly.

"I think . . . there's a tick on me, Longarm," she said softly, her eyes wide in genuine fear and horror. "On my back, under the chemise! But I can't reach back there, and I'm afraid I'll do what you said we mustn't do—break it off with its head inside."

"Lie still," Longarm commanded, and lifted the chemise so that he could see her back.

Yes. A gleaming, swelling little bugger had fastened itself to Olivia between her shoulder blades. A perfect spot for a night's repast.

"Stay quiet," Longarm said, backing swiftly out of the tent. He turned, peered into the darkness where he had thrown his still-lit cheroot, and saw it glowing on the ground not far away. He hurried over, picked it up, and headed back toward the tent.

Before he reached the tent, he pulled up. He was not sure, but he thought he heard something out on the basin that did not belong. He listened carefully, but heard only a loud popping and the hiss of a small geyser spewing scalding water into the night. Impatient to get back to Olivia, Longarm hurried into the tent.

She was still lying on her stomach, her face pale with the tension. It was not pleasant for Olivia to imagine that tiny creature burrowing into her flesh, its insatiable jaws feeding on her life's blood. Longarm sat carefully on the cot beside her, and again lifted the chemise with his left hand. With his right, he brought the lighted tip of his cheroot near the bloated tick's rear end, and waited.

"Hold steady, Olivia," Longarm said softly.

She said not a word, and did not move an inch. Longarm held the lit end of the cheroot still closer to the swollen tick. And then he saw movement. It was beginning to back out of Olivia's skin. Longarm kept the cheroot's glowing tip near the tick's backside, and with a quick movement, the female tick removed her head. With a swipe of his left hand, Longarm snatched up the little beastie and dropped it onto the ground by Olivia's cot, then stomped it into the ground.

Olivia twisted around, making no effort to conceal her long, bare limbs. "Is . . . is he gone?"

"He's a she, Olivia," Longarm told her with a smile. "All biting ticks are female. And yes, she's gone, dead. Let me look at your back now, to make sure she didn't leave anything." He put the stub of his cheroot on the small table alongside the cot.

"All right." Olivia rolled back onto her stomach.

Longarm lifted her chemise well over her buttocks and up to her shoulder, and inspected closely the small hole left by the tick. The area was slightly discolored, but the incision left by the freeloader was a neat one.

Longarm bent close and kissed her back just above the tiny mark. "Just keep it clean," he told her, "and you should be all right. She's gone, all of her."

Olivia rolled over onto her back, her chemise still drawn well up under her. With a smile, she flung her arms about his neck and drew him down onto her. "Thank you," she murmured, kissing him softly, tenderly, on his lips. "Now there's one more place I'd like for you to examine, if you would, please."

He drew back and looked down at her, a smile on his face. "Another tick, is it?"

"I'm not sure," she said impishly. "It doesn't feel the same. It's rather like an itch—an itch I can't seem to scratch."

He smiled and kissed her on the lips, allowing his hand to rest on one inner thigh. "About here, is it?"

"Yes," she whispered, pulling his head down and blowing softly into his ear. "That's close, but you're not there yet."

Longarm kissed her long, graceful neck and moved his hand farther up her thigh.

"Yes . . . oh yes, Longarm. That's the spot . . . Mmm . . . !"

Laughing gently, he pulled back. "I'm still dressed," he told her. "I think maybe we better get organized."

"Yes, Longarm. But hurry! And get the lamp, as well."

He reached for the lamp, and was turning down the wick when he heard something outside the tent that alerted him. He blew out the lamp with a quick movement, drew his Colt, and stepped out of the tent, ignoring Olivia's soft query.

Now he knew what he had heard that didn't belong: the clink of spurs against geyserite rock out in the basin. Only this time, the spurs had sounded outside Olivia's tent. An oath exploded out of the darkness in front of him. Longarm heard the click of a hammer being cocked. Even as he flung himself down, a sixgun thundered and fire lanced the gloom. Lying flat on the grass, Longarm fired at the gun's flash, then squeezed off two more shots, keeping each one low. He was rewarded with a sudden howl of pain.

Scrambling to his feet, he bolted toward the groaning sound and nearly tripped headlong over someone on his hands and knees who was trying to crawl back to the basin. In his confusion, he pulled back, and as he did so, a second man struck him on the head from behind, clubbing him to the turf. Longarm refused to lose consciousness. Rolling swiftly away from this second assailant, he kept his gun in play and fired upward at the shadowy figure looming over him.

Both shots went wild, but they were effective in discouraging the fellow, who turned and bolted out onto the basin. On his feet in an instant, Longarm found that the blow had momentarily weakened him. He sagged back down onto one knee and closed his eyes for a second in order to get his bearings. He could hear the fellow's spurs chinking as he raced out onto the basin. Glancing to his right, Longarm caught a glimpse of the man he had wounded, still crawling toward the pines bordering the small meadow. The fellow was moving much slower now, and was silent. Longarm did not expect any more trouble from that quarter. It was the other one he wanted.

Feeling somewhat steadier on his feet now, Longarm—ignoring the outcry coming from the camp behand him—moved swiftly, carefully out onto the geyser basin. The moon was high and cast a ghostly sheen over the pebbled surface of the basin, turning it a bright, milky white. The various pools and craters were outlined clearly in the moonlight—as was the figure of the man he was after.

He saw the man turn and fire. A piece of the rocky ground at Longarm's feet exploded into fragments.

Longarm kept going, intent only on closing the gap. He thought he recognized the fellow now. He had the slouch of Biddle, and the big belly, as well. And that made sense. The two cowboys had been incensed at having Longarm order them from the tents, and had not gone peacefully, after all.

Bird Biddle had disappeared behind one or the other of the curious, cone-like rock formations that dotted the basin. They made excellent cover, he realized, as he crouched and looked quickly around. Steam was rising continually about him. Every once in a while, there would be a soft rumble and another geyser would erupt, some sending ghostly plumes ten to fifteen feet into the chill night air. Drifting clouds of steam occasionally obscured the rock formations, which was one reason why Bird Biddle had been able to slip out of sight.

Looking down at his feet, Longarm saw that one of his boots had broken through the thin crust. It was his right boot, and that explained why his right foot was beginning to warm up. Longarm moved cautiously on over the fragile crust. He had the image in his mind of a seething caldron of hellfire just beneath him, with this crust of geyserite rock the only barrier between him and its fiery maw.

A sudden explosion of escaping steam riveted his attention off to his right. At the same moment, Longarm heard a scream so filled with pain and terror that he straightened to his full six feet four in astonishment. He recognized Biddle's voice and ran as cautiously as he could manage over the surface of the basin toward a low cone of rock from which a furious, shrilling geyser of hot steam and water was pumping. It was from this rock formation that Biddle's scream was coming.

He knew what had happened before he got to the geyser. The geyser had been in a quiescent state when Bird Biddle had clambered into it to await Longarm's coming. But instead of Biddle catching Longarm unawares, the suddenly active geyser had found Biddle.

Longarm had to stop before he reached the rock formation from which the geyser was pulsing. He stood, shading his face from the drifting spray, and peered into the geyser's seething bowels. He could barely see Biddle's dark form huddled in among the rocks at the base of the geyser. The man was no longer screaming. He was moaning loudly, desolately, the screeching tumult of the geyser effectively drowning out most of his torment.

Suddenly the geyser's shriek died. The pulsing plumes of steam fell back. A moment more, and the geyser was almost perfectly still. As the night wind carried the last vestiges of steam away, the moonlight revealed in stark fashion the reddened, scalded body of Bird Biddle. Longarm clambered carefully over the still trembling rocks, pulled himself up onto the rough, still-hot rocks that formed the geyser's base, and looked down at Biddle. Wisps of steam were still escaping from his clothing, but it was his face that shocked Longarm.

This close, with the moonlight shining directly onto it, Longarm found that he was looking into the raw, cooked remains of what had a moment before been a human face. Biddle's eyes were still open, what remained of them. His eyebrows were gone, his skin puckered and blistering, a high, scratching sound coming from his torn, blistered mouth. Longarm realized the man was trying to speak. He leaned close to the destroyed face and saw the man's neck, already blistering.

"That you . . . ?" Bird managed. "That you . . . Longarm?"

"It's me."

"You son of a bitch . . . almost got you. Would've, too . . ."

"Take it easy, now. We'll get you out out of here."

"No!"

"What do you mean?"

". . . son of a bitch! Kill me . . ."

"That's not likely, Bird."

"Damn you!" The fellow still had his sixgun in his hand. Though strips of raw flesh now hung from his wrist and hand, Longarm saw the man raise the revolver. He intended to goad Longarm into killing him. With a quick swipe, Longarm snatched the gun.

At once, Bird fell to whimpering. "You . . . got to . . . I'm scalded. Please . . . !"

Longarm straightened. Biddle would not survive this scalding. He was in terrible pain. Longarm considered a moment longer, then leaned forward and placed Bird's sixgun back in his right hand. Then he guided its muzzle back toward its owner.

"Do it yourself, Biddle, if you've a mind to. I'm going back to the camp now, to see about your partner."

"I can't do it . . ." the man whimpered.

"You will if you have to," Longarm said, lowering himself gently onto the ground. He looked back at the huddled figure. "Goodbye, Biddle."

Longarm started to walk away. He glanced back and saw Biddle slowly raising the gun to his face. Before he turned back around, Longarm saw the barrel of Bird's sixgun disappear into the man's mouth.

A moment later, as he moved cautiously back across the gleaming white geyserite rock, he heard the muffled crash of Bird Biddle's gun.

Chapter 12

Bird's sidekick, Arny Sloat, had taken two rounds, one in his thigh, the other in his shoulder. He was alternately weeping piteously and swearing a blue streak, despite the presence of the women crowding around. All Longarm could get out of him was his and Bird's fury at Longarm and the others in his party for attempting to control his or any other citizen of Cooke City's right to use the park. Wildly, at times incoherently, he swore that his boss, Slocum, would make amends for his injury, that no deputy U.S. marshal could come in here and tell them what to do on their land.

While the cook dosed him with whiskey and probed for the two bullets, Sloat's tirade became louder, if not more intelligible. Longarm noted the reaction of Laxalte and Clinton to Sloat's intemperate outbursts. Both men had serious doubts themselves about the wisdom of setting aside the Yellowstone Park as a preserve for all the people. And that put them squarely in Arny Sloat's corner. It was obvious to Longarm that neither man enjoyed that prospect. It was extremely unpleasant for them to hear their arguments espoused in such a fashion by a drunken slob who had just come a cropper while attempting to murder a federal officer.

Early the next morning, Longarm watched as the station wagon carrying Farrington and his ladies of leisure pulled out onto the rutted road that led northwest to

Cooke City. The wagon had two extra, nonpaying passengers: the body of Bird Biddle and the very unhappy, wounded Arny Sloat. Farrington had protested, but not too successfully, and one of the blondes had assured Longarm that though there wasn't a hospital in Cooke City, there was a doctor who was sober most of the time. To add to Farrington's distress, Longarm had made him a deputy, charged with the responsibility of seeing to it that the town marshal kept Sloat under lock and key until Longarm arrived later in the week to prefer charges. One of the blondes stuck her head out and waved to Longarm. He waved back, as another blonde pulled the first one angrily back inside the wagon.

Peter Eliot was astride his mount beside Longarm. He chuckled when he saw the way the woman had been hauled back inside the wagon. "Looks like most of those ladies don't think much of you."

"It ain't me they don't think much of, Peter. It's the law that bothers them. That Cooke City must be a nest of very unhappy people—and all of them unhappy at the federal government."

"Because of the park?"

"You heard Sloat last night. Yes, the park—and the fact that they can't exploit it. Now, tell me all you can about Stan Slocum's spread. I think I'd better ride up there while the rest of you go on to the Upper Geyser Basin."

"Ride up there? What for, Longarm?"

"From what you told Frank, I think those boys are rustling cattle. And that's another reason for them to act a mite unfriendly."

"It's west of here, beyond that ridge," Peter said, pointing to one of the pine-studded ridges that encircled the basin. "There's a pass up there, and if you keep on through it and head for the tallest of the peaks just beyond, you'll have to cross a small valley. That's where they've built a couple of log cabins, at the head of the valley."

"How long a ride, would you say?"

"Shouldn't take you more than half a day. I'm coming with you, Longarm."

"No. It might get a little hot up there, and you've got a new bride and you're a member of congress. You might say you're too expensive to throw away on a two-bit rustler, and that's a fact."

"I resent that, Longarm."

Longarm guided his horse carefully around the rim of the geyser basin, clucking to it softly, considering how best to answer Eliot. "You shouldn't resent it, Peter. I guess you legislate and pass bills back there in Washington. Right?"

"And sit in many boring committees, Longarm. You have no idea. It was my family's idea that I go into politics."

"Well, you're in politics, and that's your job. Right?"

"I would have to say yes, Longarm."

"And my job is tracking down no-accounts like Stan Slocum. And I wish you would let me do it without any interference—just as I let you legislate and sit in committees without interfering with you." Longarm smiled at Eliot. "You see what I'm driving at, Congressman?"

The man sighed and returned Longarm's smile. "I see, Marshal."

Yellowstone Riley pulled up quickly and looked back at Longarm. The Mountain Man had been right, evidently, as a rifle cracked from somewhere on the ridge and a bullet ricocheted off a boulder right alongside Longarm. He slid from his mount, dragging his Winchester out of its scabbard, and raced for the timber, with Yellowstone right alongside.

As the two men flung themselves down behind a clump of juniper and craned their necks to look up at the ridge's crest, Yellowstone said, "I told you I saw something."

"They were up there waiting," Longarm commented dryly.

"Looks that way, sure enough," said Yellowstone, "and we don't know how many."

"There's one way to find out."

Yellowstone sighed. "I was hopin' you wouldn't say that."

Longarm chuckled and darted around the juniper and into the pines, with Yellowstone on his tail. The ground lifted sharply under them as they scrambled up the steep slope, and more than once the slippery pine needles caused them to lose their footing and slide back a few feet, but they kept going, hauling themselves up with the aid of the narrow lodgepole trunks. They were within sight of the ridge when a shot from directly above them sliced off a piece of a pine tree to Longarm's right.

Both men flattened themselves and looked up the slope. Through the trees they could see the blue sky, but nothing else. No movement.

"They heard us coming," Yellowstone muttered, lifting his eyepatch slowly and peering up the slope with both eyes.

"You can see out of that other eye?" Longarm asked, astonished.

"Nope. It's just a habit. Whenever I'm in a tight spot, I always hope the damn thing will come back on." He turned his head and grinned at Longarm. "Know what I mean?"

"I guess maybe I do."

Yellowstone chuckled and began to pick the pine needles out of his whiskers with one hand while he kept his Hawken trained on the ridge with the other. "Let me go up there and see what I can find."

"Go ahead. I'll be right behind you, covering you."

"You do that, sonny."

Longarm was about to demand that Yellowstone stop calling him *sonny*, then shrugged and thought better of it as the huge trapper pulled himself stealthily up the slope toward the ridge. Longarm followed after him, his eyes shifting anxiously as he looked for some sign of the rifleman who had fired on them a moment before.

He saw no one. Not a hat, no movement, no glint from a rifle barrel. Nothing. He kept on just behind Yellowstone, and in a few minutes they were on the rocky spine that topped the ridge, the pines below them. Yellowstone got slowly to his feet, his huge frame lifting as he peered around him, his long beard blowing sluggishly in the high, cold wind that swept off the snowfields above them. Longarm also got to his feet and looked around.

Then he saw the casings. He knelt and picked them up and smelled them. They had only recently been fired. And there were only two of them. Yellowstone found the rifleman's tracks then.

"Just one man," he said, "and he's headin' acrost the ridge. Looks like he might be goin' down the other side."

Yellowstone crossed the rocky, boulder-strewn ridge, his eye on the rifleman's sign, Longarm right behind him. Suddenly Riley stopped. Longarm saw him try to bring up his Hawken, but a shot from below the ridge echoed sharply and the big man bucked convulsively. He staggered back a step, then brought his Hawken up and fired. Longarm ducked low and raced to Yellowstone's side. Riley was holding his stomach. His face was as gray as his beard.

"I'm gutshot," he rasped. "But I think I got the son of a bitch. He was down there on a ledge, just waiting for me."

"I'll make sure," Longarm told him, a desolate fury building inside him. Yellowstone's wound was mortal, he had no doubt.

Keeping as low as he could, Longarm inched his way on his stomach down the far side of the ridge. He used every possible cover—boulders, junipers, bushes—and kept moving ever lower on the slope. He had gone about forty yards in this fashion when he heard a rock bounce on another rock, then precipitate a small avalanche as it continued to roll on down the slope. The rock had been dislodged just below Longarm from behind a boulder that sat heavily on a narrow ledge—most likely the same ledge Yellowstone had mentioned.

Keeping the boulder between him and the ledge, Longarm continued on down the slope. When he reached to within four or five feet of the top of the boulder, he left the slope in a crouching leap, landed as lightly as he could on the top of the rock, then peered over it onto the ledge. The rifleman had heard Longarm, and was at that moment raising his rifle, but Longarm's was already pointing down at the man. Longarm squeezed off a quick shot, and as the fellow buckled, the lawman sent another round into him just to be sure, the rage he had felt when he saw Yellowstone clutching at his gut suddenly bursting from him. He levered a third round into the rifle's chamber and was about to pump still another bullet into the bushwhacker until he saw that he was aiming at the young kid he had seen with Stan Slocum, Benny Capper.

Longarm swore and looked quickly around, a galvanizing alarm alerting him. He saw nothing, but jumped quickly down from the boulder and crouched beside the fallen Capper. The shot came just as he landed. A second rifle shot whined off the boulder behind him. Peering around the dead rifleman, Longarm saw what must have been Stan Slocum. The man was on the mountainside that faced the slope where Longarm was crouched. Between them was a drop of hundreds of feet to a narrow canyon far below; the stream that cut it was only a thin blue trickle from this height.

The distance was too great for Longarm's Winchester. Slocum had a long gun that looked as if it might be a Sharps. He was resting the barrel on a forked branch he had driven into the ground. The man was making no effort to conceal himself as he sighed along the long barrel. Longarm kept his head down as Slocum got off his third shot. This time the bullet kicked up pine needles and rock shards just in front of Longarm's face. Longarm took a deep breath, grabbed the dead Capper, and pulled him over so that he was resting in front of him. The next round from the Sharps slapped sickeningly into the young boy's corpse. Longarm winced at the sound, but kept his head down.

Then he glanced skyward. There was a lot of daylight left, too damn much. He kept himself low, his body hugging the cool limestone ledge, as another round from Stan Slocum's rifle burrowed into Benny Capper's body.

There was a sudden, unexpected shot from the ridge behind Longarm. Yellowstone! The Mountain Man had brought his Hawken into it!

Longarm looked across the gorge at the dim figure of Stan Slocum. Yellowstone fired a second time. A puff of dirt erupted at Slocum's feet as the man leaped sideways to take cover behind a rock, his Sharps abandoned on the slope, the improvised support on which its barrel had rested in pieces. A third shot from Yellowstone pinged off the rock face behind which Slocum was crouching. Slocum waited a moment, then darted into a patch of timber.

Longarm gained his feet and raced back off the ledge. In a moment he had pulled himself back up the slope to the crest of the ridge, where he found Yellowstone—his back resting against a pine—slowly, laboriously reloading the Hawken. His head was bent over the breech. As Longarm dropped beside him, the man's big hands stopped fumbling with the rifle and his head sank forward over the stock. As he rolled onto his side, his one eye flickered open, and he smiled slightly at Longarm.

"The son of a bitch almost got you, sonny," he managed. "Used that kid, he did. Used him to draw us down that slope." He smiled then, proudly. "But my first shot hit that Sharps of his."

"It was a fine shot, Yellowstone."

"Bury the Hawken with me."

"There's no sense talking like that."

"Hell, sonny, I'm dead, and you know it. I don't want to go around without half my gut, and I left most of it climbing back up here. You tell Hilda Guernsback that if I'd met her before this, I would've shot a deal less bear and trapped a thousand less beaver—willingly. You tell her that, sonny?"

"I'll tell her."

"Bury me up here. I like this spot. It's as good as any. Ain't no gold to dig way up here, and it's where I seen many an eagle fly." Yellowstone grabbed Longarm's arm, his fingers like steel cables as they tightened on him. "I'm just sorry it was that pure no-account, Slocum, what done me. I met a few bear in my time should've taken me with them. And I would've gone with them proudly. Brave fellers, all of them."

"I'll see to Slocum," Longarm told the Mountain Man quietly.

"Now, I know that, sonny. But I don't want you to get in no trouble over me. You hear?"

Longarm nodded.

Yellowstone turned his head and gazed out over the gorge, then up past the massive flank of the mountain wall, toward the sky. The snowfields gleamed in the late-afternoon sun. The breeze continued strong—and chill. The big man shuddered. Longarm looked closely at Yellowstone, and saw his single eye staring sightlessly at the blue sky.

Longarm closed Yellowstone's eye. Then he got to his feet, bent and took up the fallen Hawken, and with its massive barrel he began to dig a trench behind the pine tree. It was a long and tedious process, and when he had dragged the Mountain Man's powerful frame into the trench, he placed the Hawken alongside him, filled the hole with soil and pine needles, then went in search of stones and boulders large enough to discourage the wolves. Satisfied at last, he took off his hat and stood with head bowed for a while, thinking that there were too few men like Yellowstone Riley left in the world. Most, like Yellowstone, had been driven back into the earth from which they seemed to have come.

The snowfields above him were flushed pink when he turned his back on Yellowstone's grave and moved back down the slope to his horse.

Longarm cut down the main street of Cooke City. Of the dozen or so false-front stores that lined both sides of the street, a depressing number were out of business. The imposing brick hotel at the other end of town looked as if it had closed off its third floor. The shades in each window were drawn and had faded considerably in the sun.

It was a town in trouble, Longarm realized, and the park was undoubtedly an ideal whipping boy, useful when it came to explaining why things were going to hell. Longarm rode on past two of the town's saloons, aware of the hardcases on the porches watching him. He kept going until he reached the hotel. It was called the St. James. Dismounting stiffly, he tied up his horse at the hitch rail and went inside.

A tall beanpole of a man got up from a swivel chair behind the desk and approached the counter. He was dressed in a dusty black suit. He smoothed his thinning black hair needlessly with a long-fingered hand as Longarm stopped at the desk.

"A room for the night, sir?" the clerk asked.

Longarm nodded. "And maybe you can tell me where I might find the town marshal."

"Try the Lucky Lady. If he's not passed out, he'll be playing poker." The clerk did not speak with bitterness or irony. It was just a simple statement of fact. "Will you sign here, sir?" the clerk asked, handing Longarm a pen.

Longarm signed the register. The clerk swung the register around. His eyebrows went up a notch as he head what Longarm had signed: *Custis Long, deputy U.S. marshal.* "Is this . . . official business, Marshal?" the clerk asked.

"That's right. Official business. Get a boy to look after my horse, will you?"

"Of course, sir."

Longarm dropped a silver dollar on the desk and left the hotel.

After burying Yellowstone, Longarm had found Stan Slocum's hidden ranch. The cattle were all gone, as was Slocum. Longarm waited for a couple of days in the hills surrounding the ranch, in hopes that Slocum would return to the place. When he didn't, Longarm returned to the congressional party and told Jim Travers and Frank Tyson that as soon as they had shown the party Yellowstone Lake, they should return to Billings, where Longarm would meet them.

Longarm rode out for Cooke City then, without saying goodbye to anyone. They hardly noticed, so enthralled were they by the park's spectacular wonders. As Longarm rode out, he was pleased to see Jean McPhee and Laxalte riding side by side, laughing, with the congressman looking considerably better than when he had first approached Longarm outside Billings. Indeed, Longarm could not help noticing, they *all* looked a lot healthier as a result of this trip into the high country.

Now, four days later, he had arrived in Cooke City, and was making no effort at all to conceal his identity. He figured that if Stan Slocum was here, the knowledge that Longarm was too would either draw the man out or cause him to panic and leave the place. Either way, Slocum would have to show himself.

The first saloon he entered was the Lucky Lady. Longarm asked the bartender if the town marshal was in the place, and was told he was next door. Longarm thanked the barkeep and went next door. This place was called the High Lonesome.

He didn't have to ask the barkeep where the town marshal was this time. He saw the man, sporting a bright badge over his left shirt pocket, sitting at a poker table, his beefy face red, his eyes gleaming as he studied the cards in his hand.

"You the town marshal?" Longarm asked the man.

"Nope. I just wear this badge to keep the mosquitoes off."

The three other players enjoyed that. They smiled happily up at Longarm. Longarm smiled. "That was very funny. And I reckon that question was a mite stupid, at that. Could I speak to you for a minute, Marshal?"

"Sure. Soon's I finish cleaning out these citizens. Sit down. It won't take long."

"Think I'll go have a beer and wait over there at that table. Maybe you could join me when you finish up here."

"That's a good idea. Why don't you do that?" The town marshal smiled slyly at the other players. He was a fleshy fellow with brows so beetling that his eyes were almost out of sight. He had a round cupid's bow of a mouth, and a flaming red nose. His skin was pasty from too much beer and too much poker.

Longarm walked up to the bar, ordered a beer, and

took it over to the table he had pointed out to the marshal. He sipped it slowly, enjoying its cool tang. He had swallowed a lot of dust these past four days, and the cold beer was just what he needed at this juncture. The poker game continued. Longarm bought a second glass of beer. The marshal watched him purchase this second glass and followed him with his eyes as Longarm sat back down at the table. Longarm raised the stein in a salute to the marshal. The marshal said something to the other players and they burst into laughter. Longarm smiled and sipped his beer.

The poker game continued. Longarm waited patiently. The laughter at the table increased in frequency and volume. Longarm finished his fourth glass of beer and, thoroughly refreshed, walked over to the poker table.

"Do you think maybe you could have that talk with me now, Marshal?" Longarm asked politely.

The marshal glanced up at Longarm. "Later. This is getting to be a very interesting game. Very interesting."

Longarm kicked the legs of the marshal's chair out from under him. The marshal went flying, his arms windmilling, his cards scattering like confetti through the air. He came down on the floor awkwardly, the back of his head taking almost the full brunt of his collision with the unyielding surface. The three other players jumped back from the table, overturning their chairs in the process. The saloon's patrons, what few there were at this time of the day, went ominously silent as they watched the groggy town marshal lift his head from the floor and blink dazedly up at Longarm.

"Could we have that chat now, Marshal?" Longarm inquired politely.

"Why, you . . . !" The fat man clawed his sixgun out of his holster.

Longarm kicked the gun out of his hand, reached down, hauled the marshal to his feet, and slapped him, hard. Then he backhanded him. "Now you listen to me, you poor excuse for a lawman. I came in here to talk to you about a man I am looking for—and I want your help. His name is Stan Slocum. *Have you seen him around?*"

Stunned, defeated completely, the marshal nodded. "He's been in here lately, but I don't know where he is now. He usually hangs out with Farrington at the Nugget."

Longarm flung the man to the floor and looked around at the others. One of them blurted, "Stan has a case on one of Duke's girls."

"Which one?"

"The new one."

Longarm looked down at the marshal. "What's your name?"

"Trueblood."

"Well, now, Marshal Trueblood, suppose you lead the way over to the Nugget."

Getting sullenly to his feet, the marshal asked, "Who the hell are you, anyway?"

Longarm smiled. "I'm Deputy U.S. Marshal Custis Long, at your service."

One of the bar's patrons turned and darted out of the saloon. Longarm could hear his rapid footsteps disappearing down the street—toward the Nugget, Longarm had no doubt.

"Hell," replied Trueblood. "Why didn't you say you was a lawman? I wouldn't've kept you waitin' if I'd'a known that."

"Seems to me any citizen is entitled to prompt attention, Marshal. Shall we get moving now?"

The man nodded wearily. Someone handed him his sixgun. Trueblood dropped it into his holster and led the way out of the saloon. As Longarm followed him, he felt the crush of spectators moving out after them. The march down the street was all Longarm had hoped it would be. Soon an enormous crowd of onlookers had formed on both sides of the street, flowing along the boardwalks, talking excitedly among themselves. Cowboys swiftly untied their horses and rode them away from the hitch rails and into the alleys. Buggies and wagons were moved into sidestreets.

The Nugget was a corner saloon with two stories over it, and a bright yellow sign. When Longarm saw it, he remembered all the golden-haired beauties Farrington had brought to the wilderness with him. Just outside the batwings, Marshal Trueblood paused and turned to look up at Longarm.

"You want me to go in first?"

"No. I want you to go in with me, Marshal. Stan Slocum is wanted for attempted murder and cattle rustling. I thought you might like to get the credit for nailing such a notorious outlaw. It should really make your name in this neck of the woods, wouldn't you say?"

The man swallowed and looked around him. He was on a stage, he realized—but it was a performance he would rather not give. Farrington stepped through the batwings and came to a halt on the boardwalk in front of Longarm and the marshal. He was dressed as resplendently as before. This time his cravat was a deep maroon. He smiled at Longarm.

"What now, Longarm? Must I move on once again? I must remind you, this is not Yellowstone Park and I own this saloon."

"It's not you I'm after. It's Stan Slocum."

"Indeed. All of Cooke City is aware of your purpose in coming here. You are very good at advertising." He smiled around at the crowd, obviously pleased with himself.

"Just want to make sure no one in this town mistakes what I'm about and why. And since I'm still deputizing you, Farrington, I hereby order you to go back in there and bring Slocum out."

The man's face went gray. "You want Slocum, you'll

have to go in there after him yourself. The federal government is not paying *me* to get my head blown off."

"He's in there, then."

"All right. He's in there. I didn't say he wasn't."

Longarm turned to Trueblood. "All right, Marshal. Let's go."

"Now . . . now just hold it right here. I . . . don't see no warrant. Slocum's well liked around here, Long. What proof you got he's a rustler, or that he attempted to murder someone?"

Longarm smiled. "Come in with me, Marshal, and we'll find that out. I just want to talk to Slocum, that's all. No harm in that, is there?"

Trueblood swallowed. "No," he managed, "but Stan might not understand that's all you want. He might start blasting."

There was a loud murmur from the crowd at that, and cries of anticipation. Gunplay was in the offing, and there was not a citizen of Cooke City who was not champing at the bit to see the action commence.

"Stay here, then," Longarm said. "I'll go in to talk to Slocum myself."

The town marshal smiled, obviously relieved. Longarm looked around him at the men in the crowd. His eyes fastened on one, then another big fellow. Longarm nodded to both men.

"Would either of you gentlemen care to accompany me into the Golden Nugget? This is official business. You'd be helping the law."

Both men took a nervous step backward into the crowd.

"I thought not." Longarm then glanced back at the town marshal. "It looks like I don't have much choice in the matter."

"You could ride out!" someone in back of the crowd yelled. "Leave Stan Slocum be. We don't take to federal officers in this town!"

Longarm smiled. He had known from the beginning that he would be about as welcome as an ulcerated tooth in Cooke City, so that when it came to the showdown, he'd need solid proof that he hadn't been anxious to start any powder-burning contest, and that all he'd wanted was a chance to palaver with Slocum. He knew now that he had made that plain.

With a curt nod to the marshal and an ironic glance at the silent townsfolk, Longarm brushed past Duke Farrington and shouldered his way into the Golden Nugget. The Duke's golden girls were huddled against the far wall, waiting. He stepped to one side of the swinging doors as the barkeep drifted slowly down the length of the bar.

"You girls better get out of here," Longarm announced quietly, "unless you want to hang around and watch the action."

They wanted nothing of the kind. With a squealing surge, they ran bouncing across the saloon and out through the door. Their arrival on the street, dressed as they were for saloon work, brought a cheer from the waiting crowd. Longarm glanced at the barkeep. "Why don't you leave, as well?"

The man nodded quickly, ducked around the end of the bar, and hurried from the place. Longarm saw a stairway beyond the end of the bar—leading upstairs to the girls' cribs, more than likely. Since Slocum was nowhere in sight, Longarm started for the stairs.

Halfway up the stairs, he heard a shout from above. It was Slocum. "You better not come up here, Longarm! This whole town's behind me."

"That's right, Slocum. Way behind. Thing is, all I aim to do is to question you about your ranching style. They know that. Put down your gun and come out with me. I promise I'll keep everything all legal and proper."

Longarm heard the man swear angrily, followed by the sound of running footsteps. Longarm darted up the stairway then, and reached the landing just in time to see Slocum duck into a small room to his right. As Slocum vanished, his right hand flashed up and his sixgun blazed. The slug buried itself in the wall beside Longarm.

The tall federal man reached the doorway in two strides. Ducking low, he shoved open the door. A shot from the corner of the room whispered over his head. Longarm saw the figure of Slocum crouched on the other side of the bed. The lawman threw two quick shots at the desperado and dove for the bed, ramming it back against the wall, pinning Slocum between it and the wall.

Reaching over the bed, Longarm hauled Slocum out from behind it with one hand, and with his sixgun, slashed down at the gun in Slocum's right hand. The man dropped his gun onto the bed, howling in anguish. Longarm flung Slocum across the bed and against the wall. Slocum's head struck the flocked wallpaper with a crunch, and the man sank limply to the floor.

Then Longarm sat down on the bed and waited.

He didn't have long to wait. Soft footsteps sounded in the hallway. A board creaked. A moment later a blonde, heavily rouged woman appeared in the doorway, an enormous Navy Colt in her slim hand. At sight of Longarm, she sucked in her breath and halted. Longarm smiled wearily.

"Come in, Rose—or Theresa, or whatever you're calling yourself up here. Come right on in."

"Damn you!" Theresa cried. With a trembling hand, she aimed the Colt. "How did you know it was me?"

"That blonde wig and all that rouge can hide a lot of things, Theresa. But they don't have much effect on the pure venom in your eyes. Besides, Slocum and his men and Farrington kept calling me Longarm. That's a handle they shouldn't have known. I knew you were around, Theresa. I could smell you."

"Where's that fool Wentworth? I was supposed to meet him here."

"He's dead. Give me that cannon, Theresa."

She smiled. It had the chill of death in it. "Sure, Longarm. I'll give it to you. As her hand tightened and her arm steadied, Longarm flung himself off the bed and brought his sixgun around in a vicious arc, catching the Navy Colt and driving it down and away just as it thundered.

The detonation caused the room's walls to resonate like drumheads. Longarm saw Slocum's slack body buck as the round pounded into his chest. Incredibly, Theresa Mirelda managed to hang onto the Colt as she fell to her knees. With both hands, she raised the Colt a second time. Longarm kicked it viciously out of her hands. Screaming with fury, Theresa flung herself off the floor and up at Longarm, her bloodied fingers closing about his throat.

The force of her lunge drove Longarm momentarily back upon the bed. He grappled with her sharp fingers, prying them off as quickly as he could. But he was still on his back, and as she drew away, he felt her fingers close about the derringer in his vest pocket. He snatched at it as she withdrew it. With a shriek of triumph, she moved back on the bed, lifting the deadly little weapon. Longarm's Ingersoll watch dangled incongruously from its chain, still clipped to the stubby pistol's butt, as the derringer's twin bores stared coldly into his eyes.

"Now! You bastard! I knew all about that little gun!"

But she hadn't cocked it. Longarm tried to snatch it from her. The two grappled on the bed, rolling over and over. The lawman heard the click as the weapon's hammer locked back, and a second later there was a muffled explosion. Theresa Mirelda looked up at Longarm with a startled cry. The rouge on her face had smeared, and her blonde wig had been torn off in the struggle. Her eyes clouded, and she tried to say something to him, but her supply of venom was gone. Her head rolled limply to one side, the red slash of her mouth hanging open.

Longarm shuddered and pushed himself off the bed. Then he glanced down at Slocum. He saw where the slug from the Navy Colt had punched a hole in his shirt. Under him, a dark pool of blood was growing. Longarm bent to see if the outlaw was still breathing. As he did so, Slocum opened his eyes and looked up at Longarm.

"You killed me. You shot me in cold blood," the man gasped.

"It wasn't me, Slocum. It was Theresa did it, when I tried to knock the gun out of her hand."

"Theresa?"

"I guess you called her Maud, didn't you?"

He nodded. "Jesus, Longarm. She was good, you know? A real revelation. Had all the other girls working for Duke jealous. But all she wanted was for me —for *someone*—to kill you." He coughed painfully, and when he finished the spasm, his eyes were closed. In a barely audible voice, he said, "She . . . was really something . . . a real heller . . ." His voice faded away. Longarm leaned closer, then placed his hand on the man's chest. It was as still as the ground he would soon be under.

Straightening up, Longarm holstered his Colt and dropped his watch and derringer into his vest pockets. His hat was on the floor. He picked it up, brushed it off, and without looking back at the two bodies, he left the room. On the way down the stairs, he paused halfway and reached out to steady himself with the bannister for a moment or two.

Then he continued on down the stairs and out of the saloon.

Chapter 13

Sitting on the porch of the Custer Hotel in Billings two weeks later, Longarm watched the congressmen, their women, and their ladies' maids begin to leave the hotel on their way to the steamboat waiting to take them down the Yellowstone to the Missouri—and civilization.

A few days earlier, he had watched from this same porch as all of them had ridden into Billings and up to the hotel, Longarm having prevailed upon the hotel manager to increase his accommodations enough to allow the entire party to stay at the hotel until the steamboat's arrival. They had ridden up with ruddy cheeks, smiles on their faces, and Olivia, Cindy Lou, and Daisy still riding astride. Jean McPhee and Paul Laxalte seemed to have grown warmly closer, while the look on Mary Eliot's face assured Longarm that Peter Eliot had discovered, during those nippy Yellowstone nights, how to satisfy his new bride. It had added a spring to his stride as well, Longarm noticed.

Later that night, in the hotel dining room, Charles Clinton and Big Jim McAllister had joined Longarm and Deputy Tyson at dinner. During the course of it, both men made it plain to Longarm that they would do all in their power to keep the Yellowstone Park a federal preserve. Clinton intimated that Peter Eliot would support them in this, back in Washington. They were not so sure about Laxalte, however.

"It's my wife who's convinced me," said Charles

Clinton, his voice hushed. "I never saw such a change in a woman. She glows, Longarm. Positively glows! You have no idea what it's done for our marriage!"

"I'm glad," Longarm said. "It was a pleasure having Melly along."

"To think I almost forbade her to come." Clinton shook his head in wonder.

"I feel a lot better myself," said Big Jim, "but I'm not going to push it. This has been a wonderful experience for me. I've never felt better than I have these past few weeks, despite that heart attack. It's taught me something about the outdoors, Longarm. It would be a shame if this experience were not held open to every citizen of this country."

"I agree," said Longarm.

The talk had turned general then, with the two men expressing their genuine regrets at the death of Yellowstone Riley and their pleasure at having known and ridden with Jim Travers. The old guide had impressed them with his efficiency and his knowledge of the Yellowstone country. The men had a parting drink and left the table late, leaving Longarm with a feeling that he had indeed accomplished something worthwhile. All unpleasantness had been forgotten as the larger significance of the park had become manifest to these men.

Now Longarm sat back on his wooden chair, watching Big Jim and his wife hurry from the hotel, their baggage being lugged after them by two straining bellhops. As soon as Longarm saw Big Jim and his wife climb into the waiting carriage, he got up from his chair and strode into the hotel.

Hilda Guernsback was waiting for him in a secluded corner of the lobby. Longarm had managed to get word to her that he would like to speak with her privately before she left, and she had been able to return his message and tell him where she would be. As he approached, he took off his hat.

Hilda was sitting on a small sofa. Longarm sat down across from her on a velvet-covered chair, feeling extremely awkward. He cleared his throat.

"You wanted to speak with me, Mr. Long?" the prim Miss Guernsback prompted.

"Yes I did."

"Well, then?"

"It's difficult to know how to start up, ma'am."

"Let me help you. Mr. Riley had something he wanted you to tell me. Is that correct, Mr. Long?"

"Yes it is," Longarm replied, somewhat surprised at Hilda's coolness.

"Well, then. Tell me what he said."

"He said, as near as I can recall, Miss Guernsback, that I should tell you that if he had met you before this, he would have shot a deal less bear and trapped less beaver—willingly."

"Is that what he said, Mr. Long?" She seemed only mildly interested. "How nice of him. I think that was a lovely sentiment, don't you?"

"Yes, I reckon I do, at that."

Hilda got up, her long face showing no emotion. "Thank you, Mr. Long. It was good of you to tell me this."

As she walked past Longarm, her narrow frame straight and her shoulders back, Longarm saw a tear form in each eye and roll unashamedly down her pinched cheeks.

A moment later, Paul Laxalte and Jean McPhee accosted Longarm. Laxalte fairly wrung Longarm's hand.

"I'm sober, Longarm!" the man cried. "Cold sober—and I love it."

"So do I," said Jean, smiling warmly.

"I want you to be the first to know," Laxalte said happily. "Jean and I are going to get married as soon as we get back to Washington. And I owe it all to you, Longarm."

"To me?"

"For that ride, trussed up across the back of my horse. It was a most uncomfortable journey, I can assure you—but it took that, and your decision to wipe out my supply of liquor, to shock me back into this world—into this bright, fresh world, this magnificent country."

"I am very pleased, Mr. Laxalte."

"Paul! Call me Paul."

Laxalte stuck out his hand again, and again Longarm shook hands with the congressman. He didn't need to ask, to know how Congressman Laxalte now viewed Yellowstone Park. He smiled his goodbye to Jean, and she smiled back—warmly, but distantly. A real cool customer she was—and an adventure in bed. Longarm did not wonder at Laxalte's enthusiasm, or her decision to marry him. She was obviously no longer complaining about his condition.

"I hope you will both be very happy," Longarm told them.

They thanked him again, and hurried happily out of the hotel. Longarm watched Jean's tall figure go with a sigh in his heart, then shrugged and proceeded to the desk. The clerk had two messages for him. One was a telegram from Vail. The other was a sealed note.

Longarm opened the telegram and read:

TO DEPUTY U S MARSHAL LONG BILLINGS MONTANA STOP THERESA MIRELDA ESCAPED FROM CUSTODY STOP SOME EVIDENCE SHE HAS GONE TO MONTANA STOP KEEP YOUR BACKSIDE COVERED STOP VAIL

Longarm looked at the desk clerk. "When did this telegram arrive?"

The man blushed. "It was delivered to the hotel close to a month ago. We did not know where you were, so we held it. The night clerk found it last night." The clerk was perspiring. "Was it . . . was it important, Marshal?"

"No it wasn't. That is, not anymore."

The clerk seemed relieved.

Longarm opened the sealed envelope and read it swiftly, pleased.

Longarm—

I'm upstairs in your room. Hurry! We don't have much time!

Olivia

As Longarm closed the door and turned to gaze upon Olivia, he saw that she was unblemished from head to foot.

"You see?" she said, smiling wickedly. "There's not a tick on me. Nothing at all, as a matter of fact."

He smiled, went to the window, and drew the curtains. "How did you get away from your father?" he asked, sitting down upon the edge of the bed.

"I suggested that he and Violet might like to take a sightseeing trip this afternoon, and then tomorrow we could—"

"You're not going with the rest on the steamboat?"

Olivia smiled. "No," she said. "We aren't. Father likes it up here. Very much. And Violet does too. And so do I. We'll stay an extra week. Will that hamper your plans any, Longarm?"

He stood up and removed his vest. "It'll change them," he said. "But it won't hamper them. I'll send my chief a telegram. It will explain everything."

"Really?" Her eyebrows went up a notch.

"No. Not really. But it will do the trick." He leaned close to Olivia. It was difficult to believe that this was the same wispy, frail woman who had first set out with them to visit Colter's Hell. He leaned forward and kissed her gently, his hand resting on her thigh.

That was about where he had left off the last time.

SPECIAL PREVIEW

Here are the opening scenes
from

LONGARM IN THE FOUR CORNERS

nineteenth novel in the bold
LONGARM series from Jove

Chapter 1

On a cold gray Denver morning, a sheep saved Longarm's life. The sheep didn't know the tall deputy marshal personally, and wasn't trying to be a hero. Along with seven other sheep and a Mexican herder, it was mowing the State House lawn that Monday morning.

The Colorado State House stood atop Capital Hill. The grassy grounds dropped west toward the Civic Center in a series of terraced slopes. The kids of Denver liked to roll down them when they got "shot," playing Cowboys and Indians on the way home from school. Their mothers didn't like it much. The small herd of sheep, which the state kept on the grounds to keep the grass trimmed, tended to defecate all over the lawn, and a kid who's rolled in sheepshit smells just awful.

Longarm had no intention of rolling in the grass as he ambled up Sherman Avenue where it ran north along the ridge of Capitol Hill. He'd had a bath before parting with a wistful widow who lived in a brownstone just a block from the State House. His tobacco-brown tweed suit needed spot cleaning and pressing, but his shirt and underwear were almost fresh, and he'd shaved with the razor that had belonged to the widow's late husband before he left for work. He was cold sober and on time, for a change. His boss, Marshal Billy Vail, wouldn't get to chew him out this morning, and the widow had said she'd have steak and potatoes waiting for him when he got off duty that evening. So all was right with the world as he came to where Sherman Avenue dead-ended against the side steps of the State House and he turned to his left to cut across the grounds.

A sign painted on the third State House step announced that it was exactly one mile above sea level. Longarm was well over six feet tall, so the cheroot he was smoking was more than a mile high. He rounded the granite corner of the building and made a beeline for the downhill corner at Colfax and Broadway. He had plenty of time to make it to the federal courthouse down on the flats of the South Platte, but he wasn't a man for wasted motions. Whether trailing a suspect, romancing a female, or getting to the office, he liked the direct approach.

The grass was damp as he walked on it. He saw the sheep grazing along the edge of the first dropoff, but they were not in his string-straight diagonal route, so he didn't swerve. He got to the end of the flat-topped terrace and started down the bank at an angle, digging in the heels of his cavalry stovepipes. And then he swore, as he stepped in sheepshit and all hell broke loose at once.

As Longarm landed on his rump and started sliding down the slick grass, he heard what sounded like a shot, and something hummed like an angry hornet through the space his shoulder blades had just occupied! He forgot his dignity as he rolled down the terrace better than most schoolboys, drawing his Colt .44 double-action along the way. A second bullet thumped into the thick trunk of a nearby cottonwood tree. Longarm scrambled behind it on his hands and knees, as a third round tore a divot of sod from where his ass had just been.

Longarm rose behind the tree, gun in hand, as he tried to read the lay of the ambush. Off to his right, the sheep and their Mexican herder seemed to be headed in the general direction of Pike's Peak, far to the south. He had this corner of the grounds all to himself as well as the handy tree someone had been good enough to plant for shade a while back.

Longarm risked a look-see around the south side of the trunk. The State House stared back blankly. There was nobody on the steps or in the entrance. A pair of bronze cannon the Colorado Volunteers had hauled home from the War were pointing his way from either side of the entrance. He didn't think they were what had been firing at him. The shots had sounded like a deer rifle.

As if to verify his notion, a bullet slammed into the tree near his head and he flinched back. He stood there quietly as he studied the situation. He was pinned down smack in the middle of a city. The sniper couldn't get at him if he just stayed put, and by now a thousand people would have heard the shots. Some of them had to be Denver police patrolmen. His smartest move would be just to stay put and wait for the help that was surely on its way.

He glanced to his left, toward Colfax Avenue. The storefronts running up the hill facing the grounds were too far to run for. A woman in a black dress was moving up the sidewalk over there, toting a furled umbrella. Longarm wondered if yelling at her to take cover would save her life or draw the sniper's attention to her. She was within the bastard's range already. Apparently the shooter had it in for him personally. That was good to know; for a minute he'd thought he might be dealing with a maniac. It seemed the invisible enemy was only out to kill federal lawmen this morning.

The woman stopped near another shade tree, and called out to Longarm. He swore softly as he recognized who she was—Madam Ruth Jacobs, the owner of the biggest whorehouse in Denver. She called his name again as she pointed with her umbrella at something he couldn't see. Then the portly madam leaped with surprising grace behind her own tree as a bullet spanged off the sandstone sidewalk near her and ricocheted through the plate glass window of a dress shop she'd been standing in front of. Longarm swung around the far side of his tree and, knowing where to look this time, spotted the faint blue haze of gunsmoke above a clump of shrubbery near the corner of the State House. It was a distant shot, but he had five rounds in his gun, so he pumped them all into the bushes as fast as he could and ducked back to reload.

Madam Jacobs broke cover to head his way, yelling, "Hot damn, you *got* the son of a bitch!"

Since she was still breathing, he figured she was likely right. So he slid the last reload into the cylinder and stepped out in the open to join her, his gun still trained up slope at the shrubbery. He saw what looked like a wilted pink carnation sticking out from behind the base of the brush. It was a human hand. It wasn't doing anything important, so he ambled up the slope toward it as the madam tagged along on his left. She was panting as they topped the rise. She said, "I had a better view of him from across the way. What's this all about, Longarm?"

"Don't know," he replied. "But I thank you anyway, Madam Ruth. What brings you out so early? You on a call?"

"Don't be nasty, dear. You know I never work the cribs myself. I was shopping for a hat, if you must know. But now that we've met, and you owe me, there's something else I've been meaning to take to the law."

"Later. Let's eat this here apple one bite at a time. I'll be proud to hear your tale of woe after I find out who just tried to bushwhack me, and why."

They walked over to the bushes, and Longarm stepped around them for a better view. A man dressed as a cowhand lay facedown in the sheep-turd mulch, his hands still reaching for the .30-30 he'd dropped. Longarm kicked the rifle clear and rolled the body over with his boot. The sniper had taken a .44 round in the head, and his face was covered with blood and dried manure. But Longarm recognized him.

A uniformed guard from inside the State House came down the steps, his own gun out. Longarm called, "It's all right, I'm a deputy U.S. marshal, so don't shoot me."

Longarm was putting his gun back in its cross-draw holster, when a uniformed patrolman ran up from the far side of Colfax, his gun in one hand and his billy in the other. He slowed down as he recognized the tall lawman.

He joined the group around the cadaver as Longarm explained, "His name was Walter Forbes. He just escaped from Leavenworth. We've got a flier on him down at my office, if you want me to prove it."

The copper said, "You don't have to, Longarm. We got the flier too. What in thunder do you reckon made him come back to Colorado so soon? Wasn't he arrested for holding up a bank here in Denver?"

Longarm nodded. "He was. I was the arresting officer. Old Walter never had much sense, when he was alive."

"Do you reckon he was here to gun you, Longarm?"

"Can't say. At his trial, he swore he'd come back to gun the judge and jury too. Naturally, nobody thought he meant it, but like I said, he was pretty stupid. I don't see how he could have expected me to pass this way this morning. My digs are over on the far side of Cherry Creek. He must have been skulking here, waiting for a shot at politicians in general. He saw an opportunity and took it. That's how I'm reporting it, since Walter ain't in condition to explain his actions much."

"I sure wish you'd come down to the station house with me, Longarm," the patrolman said. "I mean, I'm supposed to bring folks in to jaw with the captain when there's a shooting on my beat."

"I'll drop by after I report to work. I've been begging my boss to get one of them new telephone things, but the accounting office is still sore at us about ordering typewriters. Old Billy Vail is sort of behind the times, and he raises holy Ned when I come in late."

"Well, as long as I can say you're coming in. There ought to be a Black Mariah along any minute to carry this old boy to the city morgue. I disremember if that wanted flier mentioned a reward for his recapture."

"It did. You know us federals can't file for rewards. Of course, if I have to take the credit for him when I fill out all those fool papers, *you* won't be able to claim it either."

The policeman looked thoughtful and said, "Well, I know you're a busy gent, Longarm. What if I was to do you a favor and say this rascal was shot resisting arrest by the Denver P.D.?"

"I'd say it was neighborly of you. I do hate paperwork."

The guard from the State House caught on and said, "Now, just a damn minute! *I* was in on the capture of this here desperado too! You know I came busting out as soon as I heard the shots!"

Longarm shot him a sardonic look. Then he said, "Well, you boys work it out between you. I've got to be on my way."

As he walked away with Madam Jacobs in tow, the woman said, "Damn it, Longarm, that guard stayed inside, likely wetting his britches, till he saw it was safe to come out."

"I know. But the copper didn't do much either. Don't tell me *you* want the reward."

She snorted. "Of course not. It's bad for business if word gets about that a lady in my line of work turns folks in to the law. I've got enough on my plate this morning. You said we could talk about it later. Well, it's later, damn it."

Longarm started to tell her he was going to be late to work. Then he decided he owed her for saving his hide, so what the hell.

He took her elbow and steered her toward a tea shop near the corner of Colfax and Broadway. They went in and took a booth. The waitress who took their order gave them a fishy sidelong glance, but she didn't say anything. Longarm sighed. He knew his already-tarnished reputation would be further blackened, but that was the price one paid for the company of famous women.

Madam Jacobs waited until the girl brought their tea before she took what appeared to be a coin from her handbag and placed it on the table between them.

She said, "It's counterfeit! Ain't counterfeiting a federal crime?" Longarm picked up the brass coin. It was blank on one side. The stamped inscription on the other side read: *SILVER DOLLAR HOTEL, DENVER, COLO. Good for one good screw. Madam Ruth Jacobs, Prop.*

He tried not to smile as he handed it back to her and asked, "Are you saying someone's been stamping out their own tokens, Madam Ruth?"

"That's exactly what I'm saying! You know how I do business. The customers buy these tokens from the professor, down in the parlor, before they go upstairs. My girls honor them, like it says. At the end of their shift they bring down all the tokens they've collected, and we settle up. The house gets half, the girls get half, and everybody's happy."

"I've seen these before," Longarm said with a nod. "It saves having real cash up in the cribs if some customer decides to rob a naked lady all alone and helpless. What about tips for extra services rendered?"

"They tip with extra tokens, of course. I have a house rule against money going in some flighty gal's stocking. If they can't spend what they get before they cash their tokens, they won't be tempted to make private deals behind my back."

"That sounds reasonable. How much would I have to pay for one of these tokens, Madam Ruth?"

"They're a dollar each, or six for five dollars. Of course, if *you* came by, any night but Saturday, I'd give you a handful for free."

Longarm grinned. "That's neighborly of you, Madam Ruth. But I'll pass on your kind offer."

"I know. You're one of them romantic types. Have you ever considered how much trouble you could save by just buying it, like everyone else?"

"Many's the time, ma'am. Especially when I've been having a run of poor luck. But let's get back to this counterfeiting. How do you know someone's stamping out his own tokens? No offense, but your coinage is sort of primitive. Anyone with some scrap brass and a set of letter stamps could probably whack a few dozen of these things out in one evening."

The outraged madam said, "I can *count,* damn it. I've got two dozen girls working my cribs, and even Smooth Bore Billie seldom turns in mor'n sixty at daybreak. Allowing for a busy roundup night and more ambition than most of the girls have, I ordered a hundred tokens for each girl. That's less than twenty-five hundred of the damned things. But the last time I tallied up, we had over three thousand in the box!"

He sipped his tea thoughtfully and said, "Well, I'd say you have a problem. I don't see how they've cheated you out of five or six hundred free rides, though." He smiled crookedly and opined, "It makes me sort of tired just thinking about it. I'll have to study on it."

She said angrily, "I went to the Denver P.D., and they just laughed and told me counterfeiting was a federal offense. I pay the precinct captain hard-earned cash to stay in business, and he says he can't do a thing about it!"

She ignored her own teacup as she waited for Longarm to say something. Finally she asked, "Well? Are you going to investigate the crime or not?"

He said, "Madam Ruth, the counterfeiting of a whorehouse token ain't a federal offense. Lucky for you, running a whorehouse ain't either. There's just no way I'd be able to arrest the gent who's been making his own tokens. And if I could, no jury would ever convict him. They might *laugh* like hell, but they wouldn't even consider such a charge."

The woman looked like she was about to cry. "I might have known. Oh, I tell you, it's mortal hard for an honest woman to make her way in a man's world! What am I to do? The girls have to be paid hard cash for the tokens they turn in. One of them suggested we put in a turnstile the customers could drop real money in, but how would that look?"

"Sort of unromantic," said Longarm, reaching in his coat for a pad and pencil. As he started to write, Madam Jacobs asked, "What are you doing? You have no right to report any of this if you don't mean to help!"

He said, "I never waste time reporting things to the police that they already know about. I'm giving you the name of a gent I know who works over at the U.S. Mint. But don't you go calling on him there! Catch him on his way home. I happen to know they don't pay him all that much to engrave for Uncle Sam. He likes gals, too. You offer him that deal about free trips upstairs, and he might give you a good price."

The woman brightened and said, "Oh, that's marvelous! You think a man who works at making real money for the government would know how to catch these counterfeiters, right?"

"Not hardly. I keep telling you that you're being victimized, probably by dumb kids or some old goat with time on his hands and a home workshop. Do you know that the Treasury Department doesn't even waste time *looking* for coiners who counterfeit *real* silver coins? You've got to start making ten-dollar gold pieces before they start taking you seriously."

"You're joshing me! Everyone knows counterfeiting is a deadly crime!"

"Yep. It's a lot of *work*, too. I doubt if there's a high school in the land that hasn't had some wise kid or two with the idea you could cut out a lot of middlemen by making your own money. You only need some plaster of paris and a pot of melted solder to turn out a fair imitation of a quarter or a fifty-cent piece. Of course, they sort of *clunk*, like lead, and turn black in a few days. So you have to spend a lot of time making sure you don't hand them to any shopkeeper with a sharp eye and a glass counter."

"I've had a few slugs handed to me in my day. But I still don't understand why Uncle Sam's not interested."

"The magic word is *time*, ma'am. If we went chasing after every snot-nosed kitchen-table coiner, we'd never have time to catch real crooks. You see, Treasury knows that coiners tend to reform, all by themselves, long before they put enough counterfeit coins in circulation to matter."

He saw that she didn't understand, so he elaborated, "Say you work real hard with that plaster and solder pot. You have to pay something for the pot metal. Then you have to figure what you'd have made mowing lawns in the time it takes you to cast the slugs, get up your nerve, and cash them. You can't put slugs in a bank. You have to *buy* something with them to get real change. The merchant's less likely to wonder, if what you buy is almost worth the coin you hand him. So now you're toting around all sorts of junk, and you have to hide it or take it home before you dare go into another store. You can't go back twice to the same shop, so now you're walking all over town, and if you have the brains of a gnat, you'll soon see it's less trouble to just *work*, at any old job. Most coiners quit before they've passed a hundred dollars worth of queer."

"All right," she sighed. "What's this gent at the mint going to do for me, if it's not catching the rascals making these tokens?"

"He'll make you a set of decent dies, of course. If your tokens weren't so easy to fake, they wouldn't be. Ask this friend of mine if he can put a nice-looking gal and some fancy leaves and such on the new tokens. If they're sort of racy, gents may start collecting them to show their friends from back East, and your girls won't have to do a thing for the occasional collector's purchases."

Madam Jacobs almost howled with glee as she saw the sense in his plan. She said, "It's so simple, once you study on it! No rascal is about to make a token as good as one made by a real engraver for the U.S. Mint!"

She reached across to put a hand on Longarm's sleeve as she added, "Why don't you come back to the Silver Dollar with me and let me thank you properly? I may not be as pretty as Terrible Tillie or Red Stockings, but you can't beat experience and a loving heart."

He smiled wistfully at her. "I'd sure like to, ma'am. But I'm already late for work."

"What about tonight, handsome?"

"That'd be even better, but I've an appointment with another lady."

"It figures. I'll bet she's some gussied-up amateur who makes love in the dark. You romantic gents make me sick. You know damned well that nobody does it half as good as a professional."

He shrugged and said, "You're likely right, ma'am. It must be the fool books I was reading when I discovered why boys and girls were built different. I'll take a rain check on your kind offer, and now, if you'll excuse me, I've got to get to the office before Billy Vail gelds me for being late and leaves me in no shape for any gal at all."

Marshal Billy Vail didn't chew Longarm out when he ambled in half an hour late, so Longarm knew his boss had something important on his mind. He took a seat in the red morocco chair across the desk from the pudgy chief marshal and said, "I sure hope you don't mean to send me out of town, Billy. I could tell you why, but there's some things a gentleman don't discuss."

Vail shot him a disgusted look from beneath his bushy eyebrows and said, "I know about the widow woman you've been sneaking off to on Uncle Sam's time, damn it."

Then he handed a wanted flier across the desk and said, "Read it and weep."

Longarm frowned down at the paper. It bore the heading of Queen Victoria's Foreign Office, and it had been sent from New South Wales, Australia.

"Billy, you've sent me into Mexico and you've sent me to Canada, but this is ridiculous."

"We're not after anybody in Australia, damn it. Read the M.O. You don't have to study on the names and descriptions. The Australian constabulary has that particular outlaw pinned down somewhere in the desert down there. They sent the flier as a courtesy. Ain't modern science a caution?"

Longarm scanned the fine print before he nodded and handed the paper back. "I read about Australia's armor-plated bandit in the papers. So what? Are you saying we've got *American* owlhoots acting so ridiculous?"

Vail said, "I'm not sure. I want you to go down to the Four Corners and find out."

Longarm cocked an eyebrow at his superior. "You sure are talking ugly, considering I have a good excuse for coming in late just now."

"I know it's a bitch of an assignment, old son, but you know the Four Corners."

"That's what I just said. There's nothing *down* there, Billy! The only reason the borders of Colorado, Utah, Arizona, and New Mexico all meet the way they do is that the survey parties were in a hurry to be anywhere else! It's all rimrock desert too mean even for Apache, if Apache had any sense. But they don't, so if you don't fall into a canyon or die of thirst, some damned Apache's sure to tie you down on an anthill. I'll be damned if I know why *ants* want to live down there, but they do. Big red bulldog ants, mean enough to spook a grizzly."

Vail nodded. "Like I said, you know the area. Somebody down in the Four Corners has been holding up stages with U.S. mail aboard."

"Aw, come on, I thought we were sending most mail by rail, these days."

"You thought wrong. There ain't any rails across the Four Corners country. There's this outfit that's bought up some old Butterfield stagecoaches and wrangled a government contract from the post office. But the mail ain't been getting through. Some son of a bitch road agent keeps holding up the stages down there. Washington wants him to stop."

"That sounds reasonable. But why us? We're Justice. Ain't robbing the U.S. Mails a matter for the postal inspectors?"

"It is. They've sent half a dozen men in. Not one has come out. The army's sent some patrols into the canyonlands down there, but you know the army. All they got was lost. I understand it's pretty rugged country."

Longarm reached into his pocket for a cheroot. "I admire understated humor. The Indians call that big slab of Navajo sandstone 'the Pumpkin.' The rock is sort of orange and sliced all to hell with canyons, caves, sinkholes, and such. They call it 'crawling through the Pumpkin' when they have to work through the mess. The Indians don't hunt much there. They only enter the Pumpkin when enemies are chasing them. One man could dodge an army down there in that Swiss-cheese rock."

"One man has. This gent who's been robbing the stages picks spots where the wagon trace runs through or near those canyons. He hits them late in the evening. By the time they can report another robbery, it's pitch dark and he's crawled into your Pumpkin. You're right about the country being mostly solid rock. No posse's found more than a stale horse turd here and there. Iron Shirt leaves no tracks."

Longarm carefully concealed his interest by examining the cigar in his hand as he repeated, "Iron Shirt?"

"That's what the Indians call him. No white man's had a good look and lived to give him a better name. The army talked to some reasonable Hopi. They said they'd heard about the robberies, but that they hadn't been in on them. They said they thought it was Iron Shirt, back from the grave. You know who the original Iron Shirt was, don't you?"

"Some sort of Indian haunt, wasn't he?" Longarm said as he struck a sulfur match on his bootsole.

Vail wiped his florid face with a handkerchief before he shook his bald head wearily and said, "That's the trouble with working with a man young enough to be my son. You weren't out here before the War, were you?"

Longarm touched the flaming match to the tip of his cheroot as he replied, "Nope. I was in West-by-God Virginia, learning to cut my teeth, while you and Kit Carson were all alone out here."

"As a matter of fact, if you want to be so snotty about it, I *did* ride with Carson when we civilized the Navajo not far from where you'll be headed. When we weren't shooting at Indians, we jawed some with them. That's why *I* know who Iron Shirt was and *you* don't."

"Well, hell, Billy, are you going to keep me in suspense, or do you aim to fill me in on the tale?"

"You're right about it being a spooky Indian legend," Vail said. "Frankly, we don't know if they just made the whole thing up or if there's some truth behind the old story. If it really happened, it happened long ago, back when the Pueblos rose and run the Spaniards out of the Southwest for a generation or so."

"I know the time you're talking about. Must have been in the sixteen hundreds. Get to Iron Shirt."

"He was a Spanish Conquistador, most likely. Nobody can say whether he deserted Coronado's column when they found the Grand Canyon looking for gold, or if he was just a soldier garrisoned on the frontier, later. The Spaniards wore steel breastplates long after most of us had given up the notion. Anyhow, there he was, wandering alone in the canyonlands, all gussied up in boiler plate. He rode into some Indian pueblo, and the Indians, naturally, tried to kill him. They bounced arrows off his armor till he got tired of it and shot somebody to gain their undivided attention. Then they all fell down and started praying to him. They figured if they couldn't put an arrow in him, he must be somebody important."

Longarm glanced at the wanted flier on the green blotter between them as he blew out a cloud of smoke and said, "A thing like that could look like magic to some Pueblos who hadn't gone to college. What did this lost Spaniard do then, pick out the best house in the village and send out for wine, women, and song?"

"You know it. He made himself their chief. I don't rekcon they liked it much, at first. But once he showed his own bunch he was boss, Iron Shirt led them against enemy bands, and the legend says they grew sort of fond of him. You understand this was before any Dene tribes like the Navajo or Apache had ever seen a gun.

What with his breastplate, helmet, and musket, old Iron Shirt must have been a caution to mess with. He married up with some Pueblo squaws and started raising his own National Guard. He seems to have been content to rule his private little kingdom in the canyons until he just got old and died."

Longarm held up a hand. "Wait a minute. If Iron Shirt died, I'm right. He's an Indian haunt!"

Vail said, "Yes and no. Before he died, he passed on his armor and some tactical tips to a grown son. The half-breed went on being Iron Shirt. From the length of the legend, Kit Carson figured the armor was handed down at least as far as a grandson before things went sour."

"What happened? Did the Indians figure out they were only dealing with a human being with an old rusty breastplate?"

"Something like that. The last Iron Shirt turned ornery. He acted like a tyrant."

"What did they do, catch him taking a bath without his tin suit?"

"Nobody knows. Me and Kit heard several versions. Some say a brave young buck figured out there was no backplate to his iron shirt and put an arrow in him. Others said the elders talked it over and just decided to leave. You know how tribes like the Havasupai just sort of fade away like smoke when folks are mean to them? Anyway, that's all there is to the legend. We never pinned it down to one pueblo or even a tribe. Both the Navajo and the Hopi claim Iron Shirt as their own. It all happened long ago, in the Grandfather Time."

"But the Hopi say he's back, and robbing stagecoaches. You reckon there's anything to it, Billy? Some jasper down in the Four Corners might have found Iron Shirt's grave. It's so dry down near Mesa Verde that iron don't rust, and bodies just turn to mummies."

Vail opened a drawer and took out a blue cardboard

box as he said, "It don't matter if some road agent found the old suit of armor, or just heard the story and whipped up his own. Nobody can say for sure that he's wearing a bulletproof shirt, like that fellow in Australia. But it might explain a few funny things. Here, take these and reload your pistol. Your saddle gun takes the same rounds, so load that with them too."

As Longarm picked up the box of ammunition and tried to read the German printed on it, Vail said, "Did you ever meet Hank Redrum, used to ride shotgun for Wells Fargo?"

Longarm replied, "Don't know him. Heard of him. It's sort of cute how the name he picked for himself spells *murder,* backwards."

"Yeah, Hank Redrum put a lot of road agents in the ground in his day. He won a shooting match against Bill Cody one time, too."

"Well, old Buffalo Bill's a lot of noise at times, but he does shoot pretty. If Redrum shoots better, he'd be a mean cuss to tangle with."

"That's what the Four Corners Stage Company figured. After the first couple of robberies, they hired Hank Redrum to ride shotgun for them."

"Did he meet up with this mysterious road agent?"

"He did. He lost. He's buried near the headwaters of the San Juan. The driver who survived and carried Hank's body out says they came around a turn to see this shadowy cuss standing on a rock by the trail. He yelled at them to throw down the box and drive on. Hank Redrum was packing a Henry .44-40, and as the driver braked, Hank fired six or seven shots into the outlaw from less than a hundred feet. The outlaw fired just twice, and that was the end of Hank. The driver said it was downright spooky the way the road agent said that if they were all through funning, they could just throw down the box and be on their way."

Longarm opened the box, saying, "Hank might have

been getting rusty. What in the hell is a *Panzerkugel mit Eisenstecknadel*? It sounds sort of indecent."

Vail smiled at the way his deputy's tongue tangled itself up in the unfamiliar words. "They're armor-piercing bullets, made over in Germany by Mauser. Nobody wears armor anymore, but Bismarck is worried by the gun shields the French have started mounting on their artillery since the last time they tangled. I can't read the instructions either, but it's my understanding that those bullets will go through quarter-inch steel plate."

Longarm whistled softly. "It wouldn't matter much if Iron Shirt was real or not, if somebody started throwing these things at him! But the whole notion still sounds mighty wild. I find it easier to believe that Hank Redrum missed than to swallow a tale of old Spanish armor, or road agents all the way from Australia."

Vail told him, "You load your guns with those German bullets anyway. If I'm wrong and he's just wearing ordinary duds when you catch up with him, it won't matter either way. I understand those Mauser rounds just keep going, no matter what they hit."

Longarm nodded, shrugged, and began to reload his Colt as he observed, "Finding him won't be easy. There's a hell of a lot of country down that way."

Vail said, "I know. How many other deputies will you be taking with you?"

Longarm looked blank. "Others? I generally work best alone, Billy, you know that."

"Didn't you just allow you were likely to have a hard time cutting the outlaw's trail?"

"Sure, but the army's already tried sweeping through in numbers. I don't aim to just go down to the Four Corners and run around in circles. I aim to poke about and ask a few questions. You'd never know it, just passing through, but there *are* folks living in the canyonlands. I'll be damned if I know why, but there they are. Aside from Apache, Hopi, Navajo, and such, there are settlements and ranches tucked here and there in the canyons. This owlhoot who's been holding up the mails can't be living off the country. A Paiute would starve on the rimrocks between canyons. Wherever you find water down there, you'll find someone has it staked out."

Vail leaned forward across his desktop. "In other words, between robberies, the outlaw we're after has to hole up with folks. Do you reckon we might have a Clay County situation down there, with the locals thinking Iron Shirt is some sort of Robin Hood, like the James boys?"

Longarm said, "Don't know. I haven't asked yet. You said some postal inspectors vanished down there on the same job. Do you have some places they were last seen pinpointed on the map?"

Vail reached in another drawer and produced a government survey map. As he handed it over, he said, You'll notice a lot of this is pure blank. They have the Indian reservations outlined neat as anything. I don't know how the Indians feel about it. The lines run straight as string over mesa, canyon, and butte. The army says Indians don't always show up where the map says they're supposed to be these days."

Longarm unfolded the map and studied it for a moment before he refolded it. "You're right. It ain't worth much. I hardly know the area, but some of what I know was missed by the survey boys. Like I said, they must have been in a hurry to finish. I didn't see any marks pinpointing the last known whereabouts of anybody."

Vail looked a trifle uncomfortable. "Longarm, the post office just doesn't *know* what happened to their men. When you ride in there, you either never come out again, or you get a runaround from the locals. Save for that one tip from the Hopi, nobody down there seems to have heard about the stages being robbed. Why do you reckon folks turn so surly after they've been living in the Four Corners for a while?"

Longarm smiled crookedly. "You've got it backwards, Billy. Living up a canyon don't make you surly. You have to *start out* surly to *want* to live up a canyon. It ain't hard to figure out what makes the Indians moody. Most of the tribes we pushed that far into nowhere before we decided to give it to them were sort of ornery to start with. I can tell you why the army got a little cooperation from the Hopi. The Hopi were there first. Uncle Sam's crowded in Ute, Apache, and of course, the Hopis' old enemies, the Navajo. The Hopi have always been peaceful gents, if they're left alone. But even they must be mad as hell at us right now. It's hard country to live in, even spread out."

"What about the whites down there?"

"Oh, if you expect white folks to live among hostiles, you've got to expect *them* to be ornery too. As I recollect, there's some splintered-off Mormons in some of the canyons. When Brigham Young died, and the Saints started acting like other folks in Salt Lake City, a mess of unreconstructed Mormons loaded up their wagons and lit out for wilder parts, where they could do their whatevers in peace. Remember that wild bunch I tangled with out on the Utah salt flats a while back?"

"Yeah, speaking of impossible yarns. I know about crazy Mormons. What else have we got down there?"

"There's some Mexicans. Most of the *peones* up in the canyonlands are just plain folks who lost their lands along the Gila to some Anglo with a bigger gun or a slicker lawyer. Some of them might be Penitentes. The church don't approve of their version of Christianity all that much, so the Penitentes avoid other Mexicans."

Vail grimaced. "Those are the crazy Mexicans who whip each other bloody and nail each other up on crosses, right?"

"Yeah, it's a peculiar hobby of theirs. Aside from Mormons and Mexicans, I remember a few cattle outfits run by Anglos. It's as hard a country on a cow as it is on anyone else. So the ranchers are either dirt-poor fringe operators, or else they don't have a proper bill of sale on a few cows."

Vail insisted, "You've got to take at least two other deputies, if only to cover your ass around those hardcases. Can't you see the whole bunch must be in on the robberies?"

Longarm shook his head and said, "I don't see that at all, Billy. I agree, our mysterious road agent must be hiding among, or at least fooling, *one* of the bunches I just mentioned. It's impossible for him to be friends with everyone down there. Next to hating *us,* there's nothing most of the canyon dwellers hate worse than one another."

Vail frowned and said, "Hmm. I do see how it would be hard to be friends with Hopi and Navajo at the same time. Mexican farm folks don't cotton much to Anglo cowboys, now that I study on it."

"There you go, Billy. I'll just mosey down and see if I can make friends with one bunch or the other. I'll do it better riding in alone and polite."

"Maybe. What if the first bunch you approach are the friends of the outlaw you're after?"

"I'll wind up dead, most likely. That's why I don't mean to leave for the Four Corners today. I have to console a lonesome widow woman ahead of time, in case I don't come back."

Vail frowned menacingly. "Have you forgotten who's the boss here, old son?"

"Nope. If you order me to leave this very minute, I'll just nod and say I'm going," Longarm replied equably.

Mollified, Vail grinned and answered, "Sure you would. Then you'd head right for a certain brownstone I've heard about and shack up for a week."

Longarm chuckled. "I see you're learning why I like to work alone. Can I get started on my paperwork and travel vouchers now? If I'm finished by noon, you can say I'm on my way, and she sure cooks a mean lunch."

★★★★★
JOHN JAKES'

KENT FAMILY CHRONICLES

Stirring tales of epic adventure and soaring romance which tell the story of the proud, passionate men and women who built our nation.

☐ 05686-3	THE BASTARD (#1)	$2.75
☐ 05711-8	THE REBELS (#2)	$2.75
☐ 05712-6	THE SEEKERS (#3)	$2.75
☐ 05684-7	THE FURIES (#4)	$2.75
☐ 05685-5	THE TITANS (#5)	$2.75
☐ 05713-4	THE WARRIORS (#6)	$2.75
☐ 05714-2	THE LAWLESS (#7)	$2.75
☐ 05432-1	THE AMERICANS (#8)	$2.95

Available at your local bookstore or return this form to:

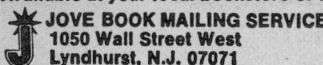
JOVE BOOK MAILING SERVICE
1050 Wall Street West
Lyndhurst, N.J. 07071

Please send me the titles indicated above. I am enclosing $_____ (price indicated plus 50¢ for postage and handling for the first book and 25¢ for each additional book). Send check or money order—no cash or C.O.D.'s please.

NAME_____

ADDRESS_____

CITY_____STATE/ZIP_____

Allow three weeks for delivery.

SK17

REX STOUT

MORE BESTSELLING PAPERBACKS BY ONE OF YOUR FAVORITE AUTHORS...

Adventures of Nero Wolfe

☐ 05085-7	BLACK ORCHIDS	$1.75
☐ 05119-5	NOT QUITE DEAD ENOUGH	$1.75
☐ 04865-8	OVER MY DEAD BODY	$1.75
☐ 05117-9	THE RED BOX	$1.75
☐ 05118-7	SOME BURIED CAESAR	$1.75
☐ 04866-6	TOO MANY COOKS	$1.75

Other Mysteries

☐ 05277-9	DOUBLE FOR DEATH	$1.75
☐ 05280-9	RED THREADS	$1.75
☐ 05281-7	THE SOUND OF MURDER	$1.75

Available at your local bookstore or return this form to:

JOVE BOOK MAILING SERVICE
1050 Wall Street West
Lyndhurst, N.J. 07071

Please send me the titles indicated above. I am enclosing $_____ (price indicated plus 50¢ for postage and handling for the first book and 25¢ for each additional book). Send check or money order—no cash or C.O.D.'s please.

NAME_____

ADDRESS_____

CITY_____STATE/ZIP_____

Allow three weeks for delivery.   SK-18